Women's Autobiography

Women's Autobiography

War and Trauma

Victoria Stewart

First published 2003 by
PALGRAVE MACMILLAN
Houndmills, Basingstoke, Hampshire RG21 6XS and
175 Fifth Avenue, New York, N.Y. 10010
Companies and representatives throughout the world

PALGRAVE MACMILLAN is the global academic imprint of the Palgrave Macmillan division of St. Martin's Press, LLC and of Palgrave Macmillan Ltd. Macmillan® is a registered trademark in the United States, United Kingdom and other countries. Palgrave is a registered trademark in the European Union and other countries.

ISBN 1–4039–0306–9 hardback

This book is printed suitable for recycling and made from fully managed and sustained forest sources.

A catalogue record for this book is available from the British Library.

Library of Congress Cataloging-in-Publication Data
Stewart, Victoria.
    Women's autobiography : war and trauma / Victoria Stewart.
        p. cm.
    Includes bibliographical references and index.
    ISBN 1–4039–0306–9
        1. Autobiography—Women authors. 2. Women authors—Biography—History and criticism. 3. World War, 1914–1918—Literature and the war. 4. World War, 1939–1945—Literature and the war. 5. World War, 1914–1918—Personal narratives—History and criticism. 6. World War, 1939–1945—Personal narratives—History and criticism. 7. Holocaust, Jewish (1939–1945)—Personal narratives—History and criticism. 8. Holocaust, Jewish (1939–1945), in literature. I. Title.

CT25.S75 2003
809'.93358—dc21   2003050965

10 9 8 7 6 5 4 3 2 1
12 11 10 09 08 07 06 05 04 03

Printed and bound in Great Britain by
Antony Rowe Ltd, Chippenham and Eastbourne

Contents

Acknowledgements

Quotations from Vera Brittain's *Testament of Youth* (1933) are included with the permission of Mark Bostridge and Rebecca Williams, her literary executors. Quotations from Charlotte Delbo's *Auschwitz and After*, copyright © Yale University are included with the permission of the publisher, Yale University Press. Quotations from *The Diary of a Young Girl: The Definitive Edition* by Anne Frank, Otto H. Frank & Mirjam Pressler, editors, translated by Susan Massotty (Viking 1997), copyright © The Anne-Frank Fonds, Basle, Switzerland, 1991, English translation copyright © 1995 by Doubleday, a division of Random House, Inc. are used by permission of Doubleday, a division of Random House Inc. Extracts from manuscript A8 of the Monks House Papers are included with the permission of the Society of Authors, the Literary Representative of the Estate of Virginia Woolf. Earlier versions of Chapter 3 and Chapter 4 appeared in *Paragraph* 24.1 (2001) and *Between the Psyche and the Polis: Refiguring History in Literature and Theory*, eds Michael Rossington and Anne Whitehead (Ashgate 2001).

I would like to thank all those who gave help, advice and support while I was writing this book, particularly: Vicky Dunne, Scott Fraser, Kate Fullbrook, William Greenslade, Robin Jarvis and Maroula Joannou. The Faculty of Humanities Research Committee, UWE Bristol, provided financial support and some much appreciated research leave. Particular thanks to Nicola King for giving invaluable comments towards the end; and to Nick Freeman for taking my mind off it all.

Introduction: Trauma and the Autobiographical

This book explores how a number of women writers, who became caught up in different ways in the First and Second World Wars, explored the personal and historical impact of these events in autobiographical writings. I consider the ways in which these writers negotiated subject positions for themselves in the light of circumstances which were often either psychologically or physically threatening. I do not set out to produce quantitative or qualitative comparisons between degrees of distress or suffering; in selecting writers from different historical and national contexts I intend to show how their responses were shaped by these local specificities, but the vocabulary of contemporary psychoanalytic theory can also assist in elucidating the narrative structures they employ. Before moving on to describe the current theoretical debates which I have found useful in exploring these texts it will be worth briefly outlining how the literature of the two world wars, and specifically women's literature, has been approached in recent criticism.

Approaching the First World War

As Claire Tylee has pointed out, one of the most influential studies of the literature and culture of the First World War is still Paul Fussell's *The Great War and Modern Memory* (1975) which attempts to assess the impact of the 'myth' of the First World War on post-war literature and culture. Fussell's study, which focuses on British literary portrayals of the Western Front, argues that the Great War introduced an ironic mode into British culture, and provided a 'paradigm [which] proves adequate to any succeeding confrontation' (Fussell, p. 86). As Tylee notes, however, Fussell's argument has a number of blind spots. Fussell treats 'time, memory and the past as if entirely separate from the political and economic developments of any concrete society', thus enabling him to 'move indiscriminately between the British experience on the Western Front, and contemporary American novels, with no explanation at all of why or how the myths of modern Europe should be inherited by the New World' (Tylee, p. 6). The lack of consideration of women's responses to the war is not so surprising given that Fussell chooses to focus on the experience of trench warfare, but as Tylee's own study shows, reducing the war to what happened to men on the Western Front skews the extent to which other types of experience, and therefore other 'mythologies', might have entered British culture.

Thus works such as Tylee's can act not so much as a corrective than as a necessary complement to work such as Fussell's.[1] Focusing on women writers' experiences is not intended as a way of denying that it was almost exclusively men who fought and died. Rather this type of work requires a broader and more far-reaching definition of what constitutes war experience. To give another example: in the first edition of his *Heroes' Twilight: A Study of the Literature of the Great War* (1965), Bernard Bergonzi included no writing by women in his chapter on post-war autobiographies and memoirs.[2] In the third edition, at the end of the chapter, after considering writings by and about the infantrymen, artillerymen and privates on the Western Front, Germans, and airmen, Bergonzi adds some scanty and rather scathing remarks about Vera Brittain's *Testament of Youth* (1933). The point here is not that Brittain's autobiography does not bear comparison with works by Robert Graves or Edmund Blunden, rather that the relationship between their texts and hers is more complex than Bergonzi allows. Brittain is either the token woman or the honourary man here, and neither of these is a completely satisfactory assessment of her work. Brittain's writing will be the subject of my first chapter. Although *Testament of Youth* has become a 'canonical' text of the First World War, its status has been challenged, by Tylee among others.[3] I intend to revisit this text and the critical debate around it, as well as considering some of Brittain's other, less frequently discussed, autobiographical and fictional writings, which, I shall argue, can add to our understanding of her strategies for dealing with the impact of the First World War on her life.

An important point here will be the extent to which 'Brittain's war' refuses to be contained within the designated temporal boundary of 1914–18. This of course is true, to varying degrees, of all those writers discussed by Fussell, Bergonzi and Tylee. *Testament of Youth* was published in 1933, and Brittain herself notes that the late 1920s saw a rash of war related writings coming into print, including Edmund Blunden's *Undertones of War* (1928), Richard Aldington's *Death of a Hero* (1929) and Robert Graves's *Goodbye to All That* (1929). Two points arising from this are relevant here. It will be necessary to consider not only the practical reasons for such a delay but the effects this is likely to have had on the writing that was eventually produced. Questions to do with the nature of autobiography, particularly as perceived by the individual writers, can usefully be considered in conjunction with ideas about history and memory. The other point is related to Fussell's description of the effects of the war on British culture: where do the boundaries of the First and Second World Wars lie, not only in terms of historical causes, but also in relation to the question of who counts as a 'combatant' or indeed a 'victim'? Debates about the nature and indeed extent of trauma tackle a similar issue of boundaries: again, my intention is to explore a range of experiences which resulted from these combats, not to quantify suffering. The second writer to be considered here, Virginia Woolf, is, like Brittain, a canonical writer, and not just within the subgenre of 'war writing'. Woolf's fictional representations of the First World War in *Jacob's Room* (1922), *Mrs Dalloway* (1925) and *To the Lighthouse* (1927) have been given renewed consideration in the light of a reassessment of Woolf which views her not as a remote and impersonal avatar of modernism but as a writer with an understanding of contemporary social and political issues, especially war.[4] However, I will be positioning Woolf as a writer whose career spanned not only the aftermath of the First World War and the outbreak of the Second, but, in addition, a third conflict, the Spanish Civil War, which also had personal resonance for her. Woolf never published an autobiography on the lines of *Testament of Youth*; my discussion of her work will range over autobiographical sketches which were not published in her lifetime as well as other texts, including for example *Roger Fry* and *Three Guineas*, in which her interest in life-writing and her struggle to encompass war in her writing, are to the forefront.

Approaching the Second World War

As I have noted, the debates about women's writing and the First World War have consisted of a process of retrieval which has not simply meant supplementing the existing 'male canon' but instead has led to a fuller understanding of what the war meant to particular individuals and social groups whose experiences had not previously been examined in detail. Studies such as Gill Plain's *Women's Fiction of the Second World War: Gender, Power and Resistance* (1996) or Jenny Hartley's *Millions Like Us: British Women's Fiction of the Second World War* (1997) have performed a similar function in relation to British women's writing of the Second World War. However, in approaching the Second World War, I have taken the decision not to focus on the British experience alone, but instead to consider a selection of autobiographical writings that arose from the Holocaust. The Holocaust has been the starting point for a number of considerations, by both historians and literary scholars, of debates about memory, survival and representation. As my exploration of recent work on trauma and testimony will show, the Holocaust is viewed as the limit case for discussions of the ethics and aesthetics of testimony. It is not uncommon for studies of Holocaust writing to foreground what is perceived to be the 'unrepresentability' of this set of events, whilst also asserting the importance of attempts to overcome this apparent impossibility.[5] Again, I am not intending to argue that (for example) because these events were worse than those of the First World War, these accounts should be read more attentively, although it is notable that in both cases writers have had recourse to autobiography. It is also important to acknowledge, as Tim Cole has pointed out, that, like the First World War, the Second World War, and the Holocaust in particular, have been subject to mythologization: 'The myth of the "Holocaust" may have drawn on the historical Holocaust, but it now exists apart from that historical event' (p. 4). Cole discusses Anne Frank's diary from this point of view, and the ways in which other writers either challenge or incorporate such culturally embedded myths will also be considered here.

However, although a critic such as Jenny Hartley can group together women's 'Home Front' writings in a way which usefully illuminates the strategies which women had for coping with their changed circumstances, applying the discourses of feminism or gender studies to the Holocaust is problematic for a number of reasons. Dalia Ofer and Lenore J. Weitzman point out, for example, that 'if women coped better in the ghettos or men coped better in the camps, we could end up blaming those who did not cope as well for their own suffering rather than blaming the inhuman policies of the Nazis' (p. 15). Focusing on the particular humiliations to which women were prone could be seen as masking the fact that they were suffering not only from sexism but, over and above that, from racism and other prejudices. Anna Hardman has also suggested, with reference to the work of Myrna Goldenberg, that 'to reduce the diversity of women's experience of the Holocaust to its impact on their sexuality', tends to 'homogenize women's experiences' (p. 58). It can also lead to the use of broad categories, such as 'motherly' or 'sisterly' behaviour, and this type of generalization, as Sara R. Horowitz notes, 'ignores important differences in cultural background, social class, age, economic standing, level of education, religious observances and political orientation' which also contributed 'to the way victims responded to their circumstances' (p. 370). For example, Charlotte Delbo, whose work I will be examining here, does on occasion express feelings of solidarity or support towards her fellow prisoners in ways which could broadly be described as 'maternal', but as Lawrence Langer points out, such moments are never unalloyed and rarely sustainable ('Gendered Suffering?', pp. 351–3). Indeed, the overwhelming impression communicated by her memoirs is 'the negation of human solidarity' (Hardman, p. 59). That Delbo was a political prisoner and not Jewish is another factor not directly attributable to gender which influences her self-definition. Therefore whilst acknowledging that some types of experience are unique to women by reason of biology, my main concern here will be on how issues to do with gender and femininity emerge at the level of representation.

Delbo's work was first placed under critical scrutiny by Cynthia Haft and has become more widely known since Lawrence Langer made it the focus of the opening chapter of *Holocaust Testimonies: Ruins of Memory* (1991). Another female writer whose work is undoubtedly a canonical example of 'Holocaust writing' is Anne Frank, whose *Diary of a Young Girl* will also be discussed here. Frank's text raises interesting issues to do with genre. Although a diary might not seem to fit the most basic definition of autobiography, that it be retrospective, Frank's is in fact a less 'spontaneous' text than some critics suggest.

However, another issue will also be relevant both in relation to the diary and, in a different way, to the texts I will consider in the final chapter. As in the case of the First World War, issues of scope and the boundaries of experience are relevant. In Frank's case, it is paradoxical that the iconic text of the Holocaust is in many respects not 'about' the Holocaust at all, and there are textual as well as contextual reasons why this treatment of the Holocaust might nevertheless have achieved such renown. With regard to Eva Hoffman, Lisa Appignanesi and Anne Karpf, the daughters of Holocaust survivors whose work will be the subject of my final chapter, the relationship to the Holocaust is characterized by a distance of a different kind. In this case the issue of how the Holocaust and its aftermath might impact on the children of survivors is important. Further, if telling one's own story necessitates the exploration of family history, the boundaries between autobiography and biography may also be questioned. Before going on to discuss some recent definitions of autobiography, however, I wish to focus on trauma, a concept which, together with the related notions of witnessing, testimony and mourning, has important ramifications for theorizations of both memory and life-writing.

Theories of trauma

> Trauma is not modern. You don't need a theory of trauma to "experience" trauma. (Geoffrey Hartman, quoted in Caruth, 'An Interview with Geoffrey Hartman', p. 640)

> [H]istory is precisely the way we are implicated in each other's traumas. (Cathy Caruth, *Unclaimed*, p. 24)

A recent upsurge of interest in trauma across the humanities has led to the consideration of texts as diverse as Holocaust testimony, accounts of childhood sexual abuse and feature films.[6] Traumatic narratives proliferate to the extent that the notion of a 'post-traumatic culture' has come into currency.[7] In examining particular, historically located and delimited experiences, I will not be attempting to identify some more 'authentic' trauma beneath this current pro-liferation, not least because such notions of origin are themselves contested in narratives of trauma. Rather I will be considering how trauma and related concepts such as mourning can help elucidate the diverse autobiographical strategies employed by the selected writers in their descriptions of war, loss, exile and imprisonment. The quotation above from Cathy Caruth encapsulates many of the key concerns of the present study: what type of relationship does an individual traumatic experience have to history? (On closer inspection, not only does Caruth's use of the word 'history' here need clarifying: 'precisely' and 'we' are also thrown into question.) The issue of how personal experiences can be shared, also implied by Caruth, is further complicated, especially because, as Geoffrey Hartman's cautious quotation marks indicate, the notion of traumatic 'experience' is in itself a problematic one. Tracing how the clinical formulation of trauma found in Freud has been reconfigured in contemporary theorizations will show the difficulties in reaching a consensus about this term.

Although my interest here is in the traumatic impact of war, and although Freud's thinking about trauma was influenced by his observation of the effects of war as manifested in shell shock, it will be helpful to outline briefly his attitude to trauma prior to the publication of *Beyond the Pleasure Principle* (1920). Having developed a theory of traumatic neurosis based on the 'seduction theory', the presumption that repressed sexual traumas of early childhood were a key precipitating factor, Freud (infamously) rethought this aetiology and, after 1897, began to stress instead the role of repressed sexual *fantasy*. The so-called 'memory wars' of the 1980s, a backlash against Freud whose most vociferous combatants included Jeffrey Masson, himself a former psychoanalyst, foregrounded Freud's apparent dismissal of claims by his patients that they had been sexually abused.[8] The fact that many of Freud's early patients were women was a factor which complicated matters, not merely because they seemed to have been victims of a sexist denial of the reality of their abuse, but also because hysteria, the primary form of traumatic neurosis under discussion at this point, was thus gendered female. As I will show in my discussion of memory, the question of the role which fantasy may play in traumatic narratives is still problematic. Susannah Radstone has argued that 'it is incorrect to suggest that Freud's [...] abandonment of the "seduction theory" [...] substituted fantasy for the memory of traumatic events. Rather, in Freud's later writings on trauma, fantasy and memory come to be conceived of not as binary opposites, but as complexly related terms' (Radstone, 'Screening Trauma', p. 86). However, although this might provide a more flexible idea of how memory works, 'fantasy' is often viewed as dangerous when truth claims are at stake.

Freud's discussion of trauma in *Beyond the Pleasure Principle*, which makes explicit reference to the treatment of shell-shocked soldiers in the aftermath of the First World War, is important in its development of an idea of trauma that rethinks the role of sexuality. In the earlier model, a repressed sexual incident (or fantasy) from childhood, not fully comprehended when it occurred, is revealed as the underlying cause or trigger for a current neurotic or hysterical episode. In war neurosis, tension arises between the desire for self-preservation and the drive to aggression, both of which, Ruth Leys points out, are 'libidinally charged' (*Trauma*, p. 22).[9] The coinage 'shell shock' can be seen as an attempt to distinguish this disorder from hysteria, and Juliet Mitchell has suggested that 'the need for men not to be feminine spelt the demise of the hysteria diagnosis' (p. 128). More specifically, in relation to one of the common means of treating such disorders, Janice Haaken notes that 'Hypnosis [...] had to be carried out in a manner that allowed a "feminine" release of emotion' whilst its associations with 'eroticized seduction' (p. 142) were simultaneously defused.[10] The shell shock diagnosis is also descended from a different type of traumatic incident, which Freud mentions briefly in the opening of *Beyond the Pleasure Principle* and elaborates later in *Moses and Monotheism* (1937). This is the railway accident, the cause of a type of mechanical or 'commotional' trauma which, as Laura Marcus has noted 'comes to stand for traumas brought about by modernity and its new technologies, the forces of civilisation and industrialisation' ('Oedipus Express', p. 178).[11] However, Freud supplements further the historically located example of shell shock with the description of the *fort-da* game, which displays similar mechanisms, and is also about adapting to changed circumstances, albeit of a radically different origin. The shell-shocked soldier replays terrible events in his nightmares, in order to master occurrences for which he was not prepared when they first befell him. This helps to solve the problem of why these bad dreams do not fit Freud's existing model of dreams as wish fulfillment. The description of the small boy playing the *fort-da* game illustrates how a similar mechanism of repetition can lead to mastery of a seemingly banal event: the departure of the child's mother.[12] Both these events are concerned with the formation of subjectivity in the face of assaults on its coherence and in both cases, two factors are foregrounded: repetition leading to mastery, and therefore an active rather than passive relation to events; and the notion that preparedness or indeed predisposition will make a difference in the individual's response to trauma. Eric Santner points to another factor which is relevant to the present discussion: 'It was Freud's thought that the absence of appropriate affect – anxiety – is what leads to traumatization rather than loss per se. This affect can, however, be recuperated only in the presence of an empathic witness' (*Stranded Objects*, p. 25). In the child's case this witness is the parent or grandparent, whilst for the soldier, the analyst takes this role.[13] I will return to this suggestion, and in particular to the use of the word 'witness' to describe not the traumatized individual but the one who enables a successful re-enactment. This raises questions not only about where the limits of trauma lie, but also of whether this model is transferable to written narratives.

That these divergent examples – the shell-shocked soldier, the accident survivor and the child losing sight of its mother – can be used to describe a similar mechanism indicates some of the reasons why trauma has proved a capacious category.[14] A further factor which is relevant here is that in Freud's discussion of each of these cases, the symptoms of traumatic neurosis emerge only after a period of latency. This implies that the events are initially forgotten and that their significance becomes apparent only when they are later triggered. Ruth Leys has underlined the fact that latency was always part of Freud's definition of trauma and that this makes the traumatic experience 'irreducible to the idea of a purely physiological causal sequence' (*Trauma*, p. 19). I would stress here Cathy Caruth's description of trauma as that which 'is experienced too soon, too unexpectedly, to be *fully* known' (*Unclaimed*, p. 4, emphasis added). This implies not so much an absence of memory as a deficiency in comprehension, and this model of traumatic recall, consonant with Hartman's querying of 'experience' as an appropriate term to describe trauma, will prove helpful.[15] In relation to the issue of what constitutes knowledge of a traumatic experience, Lauren Berlant has identified the paradoxical fact that, 'a subject who identifies as post-traumatic is deemed both to have the most and least expertise over [the trauma's] significance – least because trauma definitionally dissolves the rules of continuity that stabilize self-knowledge over time and most because ultimately no one else can witness one's own story' (p. 43).[16] The question of authorizing, or indeed authoring trauma is one which is pertinent here, and it is also worth noting a further caveat expressed by Ruth Leys. She points out that Freud rejected a model of trauma in which 'the traumatic event assaults the subject from the outside' (*Trauma*, p. 20). This underlines Freud's insistence that predisposition lay at the root of traumatic neurosis, whatever the ostensible cause, which goes some way towards explaining why similar events can have different effects on different individuals. It also moves away from a conceptualization of the trauma survivor as simply a victim. However, while wishing to resist viewing the writers under consideration here as victims, it is not my intention to treat them as patients either. Whether any of these women would have been diagnosed as suffering from traumatic neurosis or some other related disorder (and Charlotte Delbo, for example, has been identified as displaying 'symptoms' of a dissociative disorder[17]) is less important than how they deal, in narrative terms, with recovering and recording the events through which they have passed.

With respect to the types of experience that I will be discussing, the 'shell shock' model of trauma could also be misleading because it downgrades the extent to which other aspects of war experience are traumatic. In Brittain's case I will be focusing on the effects both of repeated bereavements and of the prolonged uprooting from everyday life that took its toll on her and on her friends. This uprooting, followed by a period of intense uncertainty and fear, also characterizes Delbo's war experience, and like Brittain, Delbo finds it extremely difficult to readjust to everyday life after the war. The events witnessed cannot be fully understood as they are happening but, particularly in Delbo's case, spatial and temporal perspective do not necessarily lead to any fuller understanding. Frank's and Woolf's writings come from a different perspective. In Frank's case, as in Delbo's, the trauma is the trauma of incarceration, and this is shadowed by a scant knowledge of what might be going on outside. The effects of this are exacerbated if the reader knows what eventually became of Frank. The weight of what Frank's diary cannot encompass – her death – hangs heavily over this text. Woolf's experience of war seems to be a complete contrast to Frank's, albeit that neither lived to see the end of the Second World War. In Woolf's case too, however, part of the impact of the writing comes from the reader's knowledge that what the author fears during the 1930s – another war – will indeed come about. Woolf might seem removed from the events of both wars: air raids, comparatively speaking, are minor incursions. But Woolf's writings bear witness to both the shock waves of the First World War and to the disruptive effects on everyday life of the gathering clouds in the 1930s. The experiences of the writers discussed in my final chapter could seem to be even further removed, both temporally and spatially, from the Second World War. Part of my purpose here will be to explore both whether trauma can be 'transmitted' between generations, and if this is the case, what effects it has on usual conceptions of experience and memory.

Memory and testimony

How we conceptualize memory has profound effects on how we conceptualize trauma because the way in which an 'experience' is marked as traumatic depends largely on how it is remembered. However, remembering, here, is not simply about individual acts, or failures, of recall. It is also an adjunct to testimony, a term which has itself been disputed and redefined. The fact that I will be confining myself, in this study, to the examination of written testimony (under the rubric of the autobiographical), does not efface the question of what it means to testify to trauma. A further problem, however, is the suggestion that what was not known fully when it happened can be restored or completed some time after the event. This would imply the existence of an undamaged version of events somewhere within the unconscious which the survivor has only to find the means to access, and this raises ethical issues, not only in relation to 'recovered memories', where this model of anamnesia is most often deployed, but also, with resonance to the present study, in relation to the Holocaust, where factuality is deemed vital. This image of memory as an artefact to be uncovered is also in tension with a different type of memory, one which focuses on processes of narration. These two models, which are employed at various points by Freud, will bear further elucidation, as they can provide a bridge between memory as a psychic function, and the memorializing process of life-writing. Janice Haaken suggests that what she refers to as the 'storehouse model', which 'conceives of memory as discrete mental images accumulated over time and subject to decay or erosion' (p. 43) is essentially positivist in that it assumes the existence of an objective reality distinct from subjective perceptions. In this model, although there might be a recognition of the difference between factual and interpretative information, 'the interdependence of observer and observed tends to be minimised' (Haaken, p. 43). The second, the narrative-based model, which Haaken calls the 'storyteller approach', situates memory 'in the context of narratives and social relationships' and 'tends to focus on constellations of preserved knowledge – how things "hook together" – rather than on constituent elements of memory' (p. 43). This model, with its focus on possible social causes for the 'resurrection' (Haaken, p. 47) of traumatic memories in particular can be seen to avoid the congealing tendency of the 'storehouse' model; as Nicola King points out, it 'unsettles the belief that we can recover the past as it was and unproblematically reunite our past and present selves' (p. 12). Brittain's, Frank's and Woolf's reactions to re-reading their diaries show to varying degrees an awareness of this difficulty, even, or perhaps especially, when a textual version of the past self is in existence.

In tracing how these two models emerge throughout the course of Freud's career, King exposes the inconsistencies which can arise when attempts are made to use these models in the theorization of the analytical process. In Freud's work, the use of an 'analogy between the recovery of the buried past and the excavation of an archaeological site' (King, p. 11) would seem to be akin to the 'storehouse' model, whilst the concept of *Nachträglichkeit* or belatedness, like the 'storyteller' approach, places emphasis on the fact that 'operating as it does in the present, [memory] must inevitably incorporate the awareness of "what wasn't known then"' (King, p. 12). In practice, the apparently contrary notions of discovery and construction are not always confined to the two separate models, and are complicated by the fact that Freud's conception of the analyst's role necessarily implies that the task of overcoming repression cannot be carried out by the patient alone. In 'Constructions in Analysis' (1937), for example, Freud makes the following comments:

> The analyst [...] works under more favourable conditions than the archaeologist [...] the excavator is dealing with destroyed objects

of which large and important portions have certainly been lost, by mechanical violence, by fire and by plundering. [...] But it is different with the psychical object whose early history the analyst is seeking to recover. Here we are regularly met by a situation which with the archaeological object occurs only in such rare circumstances as those of Pompeii or of the tomb of Tut'ankhamun. All of the essentials are preserved; even things that seem completely forgotten are present somehow and somewhere, and have merely been buried and made inaccessible to the subject. (pp. 259–60)

The point here is not only that Freud seems to be implying that pristine memories can survive the passage of time but that they are 'inaccessible to the subject'. That is, it is not enough simply to identify the objects, for Freud seems here to be referring to the types of encoding of memory which he identifies in the cases of 'Dora' and the 'Wolf Man', where repressed memories emerge only in a transfigured form in the first instance. The burden then rests on the analyst to make what appears to be an appropriate construction. 'Only the further course of the analysis enables us to decide upon the correctness or uselessness of our constructions' (Freud, 'Constructions', p. 367); implicitly these remain open to further consideration or reconstruction.[18]

Such 'constructions' are, implicitly, narratives. On one level what is at stake is constructing a narrative about oneself. Peter Brooks' comments about narrative and repetition can also help to foreground the relationship between narrative and mourning. He suggests: 'Narrative always makes the implicit claim to be in a state of repetition, as a going over again of a ground already covered [...] This claim to be an act of repetition – "I sing", "I tell" – appears to be initiatory of narrative' (Brooks, p. 285). Alluding to the fact that in examples such as the *fort-da* game, repetition is a means of gaining mastery over particular events, 'an assertion of control over what man must in fact submit to', Brooks suggests that this is 'a suggestive comment on the grammar of plot, where repetition, taking us back again over the same ground, could have to do with the choice of ends' (p. 286). Brooks sees this form of structural repetition as characteristic of narrative in general; in relation specifically to the texts that I will be examining, the role of recuperative repetition as a means of overcoming loss and therefore as an adjunct to mourning will be important. In 'Mourning and Melancholia', Freud contrasts these two processes in the following way: 'In mourning it is the world which has become poor and empty; in melancholia it is the ego itself' (p. 246). I will suggest that narrative is the crucial means of representing this newly poor and empty world to oneself, and thus attempting to figure oneself within it, particularly in Delbo's and Brittain's work. As Eric Santner notes, 'The work of mourning is a process of elaborating and integrating the reality of loss or traumatic shock by remembering and repeating it in symbolically and dialogically mediated doses; it is a process of translating, troping, and figuring loss' ('History Beyond', p. 144). This is not to suggest that narrative per se will necessarily have a curative value, in the way that a psychoanalytic life-story might. Part of what characterizes the texts I will be examining here is the way in which they challenge the conventions of narrative, and expose the ways in which language fails as well as succeeds.

Although the notion of reinterpreting or revisiting past events in the continually changing contexts of the present, re-evaluating and reassessing our present subjectivity in the light of what has gone before, is one which has a certain plausibility and appeal beyond the context of the patient/analyst relationship, the positivist under-tow of 'what actually happened' still needs to be reckoned with. An encounter between the discourses of analysis and of history, described by Dori Laub gives one powerful example of how this might occur.[19] A female Holocaust survivor describes witnessing the Auschwitz uprising and says that she saw four chimneys being blown up. Later, when the video of her testimony is viewed at a conference, it is disputed:

> The testimony was not accurate, historians claimed. [...] Historically, only one chimney was blown up, not all four. Since the memory of the testifying woman turned out to be, in this way, fallible, one could not accept – nor give credence to – her whole account of the events. It was utterly important to remain accurate, least the revisionists in history discredit everything. (Felman and Laub, pp. 59–60)

Powerful though this argument is, particularly in its evocation, through its reference to the 'revisionists', of the spectre of Holocaust denial, there is another way of thinking about this misrepresentation, as Laub goes on to explain.

> A psychoanalyst who had been one of the interviewers of the woman profoundly disagreed. "The woman was testifying," he insisted, "not to the number of chimneys blown up, but to something else, more radical, more crucial [...] This woman testified to an event that broke the all compelling frame of Auschwitz [...] She testified to the breakage of a framework. That was historical truth." (Felman and Laub, p. 60)

Here, a middle way seems to have been found between the exigencies of history and of memory, although it should also be noted that it is the psychoanalyst here who pleads the witness's case to the historians. Oddly, despite the fact that the reader knows that Laub was himself present at the initial interview, it is only after transcribing this defence of the woman that he identifies himself as the speaker here. It is as though he feels it necessary to preserve the integrity of the part he himself played in this act of testimony, by distancing himself as the author from himself as the interlocutor. The implication of this vignette is that the testimony requires the supplement of interpretation, or else it remains, from the historians' point of view, simply an eye-witness account which contains factual errors. That is to say, its value quite apart from its evidentiary content has to be considered.[20] It lies somewhere between the therapeutic and the historical. In this later discussion, however the woman herself is absent; having delivered her story on video she afterwards remains mute. We have only Laub's account of what purpose this act might have served for her. In the written accounts that I will be discussing here, authors often supplement their testimony with a self-analytical or interpretative aspect; this means that, in relation to Laub's model of video testimony, authors are not restricted to the role of witness, but at times adopt, or attempt to adopt, the perspective of the analyst or indeed the historian.

The notion of testimony as an essentially performative process is explored further by Laub's co-author Shoshana Felman. Discussing another example of video Holocaust testimony, she suggests:

> The narrator herself does not know any longer who she was, except *through her testimony*. This knowledge or self-knowledge is

neither a given before the testimony nor a residual substantial knowledge consequential to it. In itself, this knowledge *does not exist*, it can only *happen* through the testimony: it cannot be separated from it [...] [I]t can never become a substance that can be possessed by either speaker or listener, outside of this dialogic process. (Felman and Laub, p. 51)

This notion of witnessing may seem helpful in moving from strictly clinical to literary notions of trauma, especially in view of the fact that Felman's conception of the performative implies written as well as spoken language. However, the broader context of Felman's discussion has led to criticism, largely because she implies that the listener or reader can in fact partake of the trauma through the very act of listening or reading. Felman describes a graduate class on literary representations of trauma which encompasses the poetry of Mallarmé and Celan, the novels of Dostoyevsky and Camus, as well as the video Holocaust testimony. Geoffrey Hartman, describing the Yale project which was the source for Felman's video material suggests that such testimonies, 'do not privilege the ocular or assault the eye. [...] [T]hey avoid the contagion of "secondary trauma"' (Caruth, 'An Interview with Geoffrey Hartman', p. 643). However, Felman describes her students' final essays as a 'profound statement of the trauma they had gone through and of the significance of their assuming the position of the witness' (Felman and Laub, p. 52). As Amy Hungerford points out, Felman here suggests that 'the significance of the students' feelings was to be found in the significance we accord to survivors' feelings. The students can experience trauma by listening to testimony about trauma' (p. 73). The students have been 'infected' by trauma, and what they have seen has become part of their own experience. There is also an ambiguity here about what constitutes witnessing. Is witnessing what the survivor does when he or she speaks? Or is listening to the survivor the act of witnessing? Put another way, does the conceit of 'bearing witness' imply the survivor delivering their story, or does it imply the student (or viewer or reader) taking this burden from them?[21]

Critics from a variety of disciplines have attempted to clarify how exactly trauma might be transmissable, but most are more cautious than Felman in attempting to draw boundaries around the traumatic experience. It will be worth briefly outlining some of these models of the relationship between survivor and interlocutor as this issue returns us to the question of what constitutes knowledge or understanding of traumatic events. In an essay which is critical of the use of historical knowledge implied in an analysis such as Felman's, Walter Benn Michaels suggests: 'It is only when it's reimagined as the fabric of our own experience that the past can become the key to our own identity' (p. 7). History conceived as simply the knowledge of facts is useless. When we believe we have some kind of personal investment in the events which those facts summarize, the past becomes meaningful, but appealing as this idea might be, its logical conclusion is the appropriative attitude ascribed to Felman's students. Other writers from a variety of disciplines have attempted to impose a certain distance between survivor and observer. Cathy Caruth, in an interview with the psychoanalyst Robert Jay Lifton, who has worked with survivors of Hiroshima and Vietnam veterans, encapsulates his approach: '[T]here's [...] a survivor and a proxy survivor, and it's the meeting of those two that constitutes the witness' (Caruth, 'An Interview with Robert Jay Lifton', p. 145). This retains the dialogic aspect of Felman's approach, but rooted as it is in a therapeutic context, it rethinks the analyst–analysand relationship whilst apparently avoiding a hierarchy whereby the analyst has the overwhelming interpretive power. This type of model also seems to underlie the approach of Dominick LaCapra, who writes as an intellectual historian and historiographer. He distinguishes between primary and secondary memory, where '[s]econdary memory is the result of critical work on primary memory, whether by the person who initially had the relevant experiences or, more typically, by an analyst, observer, or secondary witness such as the historian' (LaCapra, *History and Memory*, pp. 20–1). However, he also uses the term 'secondary memory' to describe 'what the historian attempts to impart to others who have not themselves lived through the experience or events in question' (*History and Memory*, p. 21). Here LaCapra makes the move from a face-to-face meeting between individuals to the textual transmission of the traumatic material. Elsewhere, he tackles the question of over-identification or potential appropriation when he suggests, in terminology that echoes Eric Santner's, that, 'Being responsive to the traumatic experience of others, notably of victims, implies not the appropriation of their experience but what I would call empathic unsettlement' (LaCapra, *Writing History*, p. 41).

Empathic unsettlement 'poses a barrier to closure in discourse and places in jeopardy harmonizing or spiritually uplifting accounts of extreme events' (LaCapra, *Writing History*, p. 41). It therefore vitiates against Benn Michael's scenario of the past as a 'key to our own identity'.

Both LaCapra and Marianne Hirsch cite the work of Kaja Silverman, which also shows a concern with retaining some boundaries between protagonists in the scenario of bearing witness. Silverman suggests that art can allow access to the subject positions of those considered socially marginal but that ideally this will not mean the 'occupation' of those positions, and the reinforcing of existing hegemonies that this would imply. '[T]hrough discursively "implanted" memories, we might be given the psychic wherewithal to participate in the desires, struggles, and sufferings of the other, and to do so in a way which redounds to his or her, rather than to our own, "credit" ' (Silverman, p. 185). Silverman calls this experience of memory which is not our own 'heteropathic memory'. Hirsch is especially interested in how the children of Holocaust survivors might 'remember' aspects of their family history that fall outside their own experience and describes a similar process which she calls 'postmemory'. This term 'characterizes the experience of those who grow up dominated by narratives that preceded their birth, whose own belated stories are evacuated by the stories of the previous generation shaped by traumatic events that can be neither understood nor recreated' (Hirsch, p. 22). However, despite the fact that the effect of the Holocaust on family histories, including Hirsch's own, is the focal point here, she also suggests that postmemory 'may usefully describe other second-generation memories of cultural or collective traumatic events and experiences' (p. 22). The implication here is that postmemory can exceed both the bounds of the family and the bounds of the Holocaust, and once again the boundaries of the traumatic begin to be blurred. Hirsch's exploration of her own family history, written in part as a response to Eva Hoffman's *Lost in Translation* will prove useful as a counterpoint to that text, but postmemory, like heteropathic memory, and the other formulations which have been devised to try and describe how trauma might be communicated, foregrounds a further problem. Memory, especially when conceived of as collective or cultural property, can become a shorthand for the depoliticization or sacrilization of history. Kerwin Lee Klein has recently noted '[t]he clustering of quasi-religious terms around *memory*' (Klein, p. 145, emphasis in original), and suggests that this vocabulary of memory has come to insinuate its way into historical and historiographic discourse. According to Klein, the use of terms such as '*sublime, apocalypse, fragment* [...] *redemption* [...] *cure* [...] *testimony*' (p. 145, emphasis in original) has a tendency to lead towards mystification. 'Memory talk' often falls into nostalgia, and like Michaels, Klein believes that the use of terminology such as 'haunting' to describe how the past might make its presence felt can downgrade individual agency. Memory itself is raised to 'the status of historical agent, and we enter a new age in which archives remember and statues forget' (Klein, p. 136).

Now because the texts that I will be examining are autobiographical, their use of figurative or 'literary' language, and their relationship to the 'official' discourses of history are not straightforward. Approaching this question from the historians' point of view, Jay Winter and Emmanuel Sivan suggest the term 'collective remembrance' which they define as 'a set of acts which [...] may draw from professional history, but [...] do not depend on it' (p. 8). They argue that this is a more nuanced approach than, for instance, Pierre Nora's, which they see as relying too heavily on an opposition between history and memory. With specific reference to the ways in which war might be represented they suggest that although individuals will have personal reasons for writing their stories, these 'were not only private matters, since they existed in a social framework, the framework of collective action' (Winter and Sivan (eds), p. 9). This formulation not only avoids setting history and memory up in opposition to each other but also distinguishes between such personally motivated acts of remembrance and those which may have ideological or political overtones. (One might think, for example, of Vera Brittain's reluctance to participate in the formal commemoration of Armistice Day.) I would wish to retain this sense of memory and history relating to each other, not simply as the part relates to the whole (with memory as an individual's personal experience of historical events) but in a way which acknowledges how different writers might themselves conceive of their historical situation (or even, as Anne Frank puts it at one point, historical duty). Locating texts in their contexts will be important here, not least because in the cases of both Virginia Woolf and Anne Frank, the potential reader is

at a distance in a way that is not the case for texts written for immediate publication. This necessarily changes the stakes for any reading
of these texts as being, like other testimonies, rooted in the act of dialogue. As Anne Whitehead has shown in her discussion of the letters
of Etty Hillesum, where the circumstances of a text's production put
in doubt that it will reach its destination, conceptualizing testimony
as a form of address, one side of a dialogue whose receipt is uncertain, can prove useful.

The autobiographical

My focus, then, is on examples of autobiographical writing which
each, in different ways, narrate the author's own sense of how her life
has been changed, often suddenly and shockingly but sometimes
gradually and insidiously, by the traumatic events of war. Here, I will
place my discussion in the context of some recent debates about, and
definitions of, autobiography, and specifically women's autobiography,
in order to explain my decision to include in the category of 'the
autobiographical' texts such as letters and diaries which do not necessarily conform to usual definitions of life-writing. Debates about
women's autobiography have developed rapidly since this form of
writing first became the subject of concentrated critical interest in
the early 1980s.[22] In some respects, the initial work of ground-
clearance mirrored earlier debates about women's literature in general. So, for example, Linda Anderson notes that it was initially
deemed necessary to recognize 'the absence of women writers from
the autobiographical canon' (*Women*, p. 2), in the same way that their
absence from the literary canon had been identified. This went hand
in hand with tackling 'the absence [...] of gender from critical
accounts of autobiography' (Anderson, *Women*, p. 2), and thus with a
reassessment of how autobiography might be constituted as a genre.
However as Anderson also suggests, 'If male critics had too easily
conflated the description of a genre with a narrative of the masculine
subject, feminist critics sought validation for women's experience in
a not dissimilar way, by using autobiographical texts as a reference for
life' (*Autobiography*, p. 86). Thus for example, normative models of
men's autobiography were brought into service as points of comparison. Important among these was the late nineteenth-century 'Life' of
a 'Great Man', which was seen as an endorsement of the ideological

precedence of men as the agents of (imperial) history. Women's lives (and women's 'Lives') could often therefore be characterized, broadly speaking, as occupying the domestic sphere and articulating the personal impact of political events, the course of which lay in the hands of men. However, to suggest that the distinction between men's and women's autobiography rests upon a split between public and private, and that by extension women's 'Lives' were more likely to be occasional or informal works, such as diaries, is to forge too wide a gulf between the two.[23] As Gillian Swanson has pointed out, representations of feminine subjectivity which focus on the 'rituals of domestic detail' downplay the extent to which 'it is in the *exchange* between masculinity and femininity that sexual difference is made' (p. 128). Any conception of femininity (and by extension 'female' writing) has to take into account a degree of cultural specificity which historical generalizations do not always allow. Laura Marcus also points to the dangers of falling into an essentialist position in which 'men's autobiography [is characterised] as ego-centred and progressive, and women's as discontinuous and associative' (*Auto/biographical Discourses*, p. 67).

However, although such culturally based and historically located conceptions of female subjectivity are important, the challenges posed by psychoanalytic ideas about subjectivity also need to be taken into account. It might be argued that autobiography necessarily rests on the presumption that there is a coherent self which can be narrated, but as Smith and Watson have pointed out, therorizations of subjectivity from writers including Kristeva locate 'the entrenched hold of patriarchal structures' in 'the subject's foundational relationship to language' (p. 20). The non-self-identity which follows the entry into the symbolic means, as Linda Anderson suggests, that the 'I' is 'a position in writing which the [female writer] cannot "naturally" assume' (*Women and Autobiography*, p. 2). However, for my own purposes here, such psychoanalytic conceptions of gendered identity and subjectivity can only be realized or understood through acts of writing (and reading). A writer such as Eva Hoffman, for example, develops within her work a conception of her own relationship to language which shows an awareness of the dislocating effects of losing one's mother tongue as a consequence of emigration. This is not of course to say that a text which displays self-critical characteristics therefore insulates itself against further critical analysis. In reading this selection of texts, I have attempted to show that interventions into autobiography, and specifically autobiography which is concerned with war experience, often see writers tackling not only issues of form and genre, but also the question of how their psychic and social subjectivity has been transformed by what they have gone through. This transformation is not only represented but enacted through the narration of these events, which is one of the reasons why I have found it useful to include discussion of texts which do not always 'count' in considerations of autobiography. It is often in less polished or 'finished' texts, that this process is most pronounced.

These works may also be seen to contribute to ongoing debates about where the limits of autobiography lie. Autobiography is worrying because, as the contrary positions of Philippe Lejeune and Paul de Man show, defining it seems to depend on either an act of faith on the part of the reader (Lejeune's 'autobiographical pact') or on a futile desire on the part of the author to write his or her way out of the shadow of death (which de Man encapsulates in the use of prosopopoeia as a figure for writing). My use of the term 'autobiographical' is intended partly as an acknowledgement of such debates, and of the open-ended nature of this category, but also as a way of recognizing that, for example, Vera Brittain's use of extracts from her diaries and letters within the narrative of *Testament of Youth* does not mean that these texts cannot also be considered in their own right. Although what is at stake in this example is, in part, the relationship between what is explicitly declared to be autobiography by the author and other writings, this will not simply be a case of distilling the autobiographical content from works of fiction. In Brittain's case, for instance, common narrative patterns of repetition and return recur, and in many respects it is useful to see her writings, whether explicitly autobiographical or not, as contributions to the ongoing project of attempting to understand war.

* * *

My first chapter, 'Vera Brittain and the "Lost Generation"', will be concerned in part with how Brittain situates her own experiences in relation to those of her male contemporaries. Brittain moves from an aspiration to somehow imitate her fiancé, her brother and their friends in their involvement in the war, to a deep disillusionment as she loses each of them in turn. Ironically, these losses are in part at least the spur to Brittain's adoption of feminism and pacifism in the interwar years. But although Brittain's 'conversion' to these causes might be seen as the ultimately positive outcome of a desperate situation, I will be questioning whether Brittain ever really succeeds in completely reconciling her anti-war stance with her desire to enshrine the men she has lost as heroes. Despite her own claims that writing *Testament of Youth* was a cathartic process which enabled her to 'come to terms' with her losses, I will be showing how these continue to cast their shadow in her other work. To give one example: Brittain was desperately disappointed that there was no final message for her among her fiancé's belongings. In a number of her novels, this absence is compensated for, as female protagonists receive letters in which their lovers predict their own demise and provide assurances of their love. The conceit of such a letter requires that the hero in each case should foresee his own death and, as the letter is only read afterwards, speak from beyond the grave. In many respects, this device stands for the broader intention of Brittain's project. She intends not only to write an autobiography, but also to provide a suitable memorial to those she has lost. This precarious intertwining of her life and their deaths is one of the characteristics of Brittain's writing which makes it worth revisiting.

My second chapter, 'Virginia Woolf between the Wars' will focus primarily on Woolf's writing of the 1930s. In particular, I will examine the relationship between the autobiographical piece 'A Sketch of the Past', and two biographical texts, the memoir of Julian Bell, written after his death in Spain in 1937, and *Roger Fry* (1940). Anna Snaith has suggested that the task of describing Fry's (non-combatant) First World War experience is likely to have led Woolf to consider how she might cope in a coming war; I also foreground the difficulty that Woolf had in constructing this life, and its relationship to 'A Sketch of the Past'. This text, part way between a diary and an autobiography, not only chronicles the encroaching war, but also shows Woolf attempting to record and preserve 'moments of being' from her childhood, thus creating a tension between a recuperative looking back and the impossibility of looking forward. 'A Sketch' is markedly a writer's life, as Woolf's focus is on what she sees as the development of her creativity. In this respect her meditation on the death of her nephew is a useful point of reference, insofar as it portrays Bell as having chosen the path of politics and war rather than that of art and peace, and also evidences regret on Woolf's part for not having exerted a greater influence on this choice. An act of personal reminiscence and mourning, this chimes with Woolf's wider concerns at this period, and can provide a useful point of comparison with Brittain's similar but differently realized project.

As I have already noted, Anne Frank's writings emerge from the fringes of the war. The aspects of the text which have most usually been highlighted are those which are apparently 'uplifting'. This, for example, is the burden of the popular stage adaptation of the diary, written in the 1960s by the Hacketts.[24] My intention here is to provide a reading of the text and its reception which foregrounds its distinctiveness as an example of Holocaust writing. In other chapters, I focus on how the writers themselves live through and narrate the traumatic events of war; here the emphasis will be slightly different. Although I will be paying attention to Frank's own portrayal of life in the Annexe, and, for example, reassessing incidents such as the 'love affair' with Peter van Daan, I am also interested in how the reader's knowledge of what eventually became of Anne Frank can render the text uncanny. I am referring here to Freud's formulation of the uncanny as that which is familiar and yet unfamiliar, that which is repressed but nevertheless comes to light in unexpected ways. The diary is a text about the Holocaust which does not confront us with the full horror of those events; but I would suggest that the pressure of that wider context is always shadowing the text, in an uncanny fashion.

Charlotte Delbo's *Auschwitz and After* approaches the Holocaust from a different perspective, and deals with the complexity of memory in a multifaceted way. I have already noted that Delbo's description of the workings of memory has led to her being 'diagnosed' as dissociative. I will place both this diagnosis and Delbo's own descriptions of memory in the context of a body of work written over a period of forty years. Not only does she attempt to write about what she can remember about the camps, but she also describes how memory worked when she was there. Thinking about her earlier life was not a consolation or source of hope, but rather increased the sense of desperation, and she decided it was better to avoid thinking about the life before. This means, however, that after her release, Delbo has the new problem of how to move forward when both her life in the camps and her life before that are, in different ways, estranging. Her accounts also bring to the fore the issues about 'factual' and 'creative' memory that I have already outlined, because Delbo not only uses her own voice but also speaks on behalf of others, interpolating herself into their experiences, particularly in the third volume of *Auschwitz and After, The Measure of Our Days*. This is in some respects similar to the way in which Brittain attempts to speak for those she has lost; it raises the question of whether memorialization of this kind is in danger of slipping into appropriation, or whether salvaging such a remnant is simply the only way for Delbo to retrieve something from these terrible experiences without falling back on increasingly hollow discourses of redemption.

The texts that will be the focus of my final chapter, 'Memory in a Foreign Language', will provide the opportunity to discuss issues around postmemory and other critical formulations of trans-generational life-writing. All the writers I am discussing here are the daughters of Jews who survived the Holocaust and then emigrated from Poland after the war. Lisa Appignanesi's *Losing the Dead* and Anne Karpf's *The War After* both combine memoirs of their own lives with accounts of their exploration of their parents' pasts. In each of these cases, this exploration involves a journey to Poland. In Appignanesi's case, this means travelling back to the country in which she was born but which she cannot remember clearly, whilst for Karpf, the trip is to a strange country which she nevertheless hopes will have some resonance for her. Eva Hoffman's *Lost in Translation* is principally concerned not with this type of family detective work but with the difficulties Hoffman experiences after arriving in Canada as a teenager. Many of her problems circulate around issues to do with language and, concomitantly, identity which are also present in Appignanesi's and Karpf's work. For each, exile and displacement are important topics. I will be questioning, however, whether the use of 'exile' as a means of describing a generalized post-traumatic, or indeed post-modern condition is necessarily helpful in this context. To suggest that the experiences of disturbed subjectivity and displacement which these women go through are simply a version of a universal malaise shears away the historical specificities which are at the core of each of these works.

1
Vera Brittain and the 'Lost Generation'

In *Testament of Experience: An Autobiographical Study of the Years 1925–1950* (1957), Vera Brittain describes the effects of writing her first, more famous, autobiographical volume: 'By enabling me to set down the sorrows of the First War and thus remove their bitterness, *Testament of Youth* became the final instrument of a return to life from the abyss of emotional death' (pp. 75–6). This view of autobiographical writing as facilitating the laying down of a burden is echoed in the 1947 text *On Becoming a Writer*, which combines practical advice on the submission of manuscripts with reflections on her own writing career: 'Between 1919 and 1933, I was handicapped, harassed and oppressed by recurrent memories of the first World War, which had brought me such personal tragedy. But after I had published my autobiographical story of that War, those memories never troubled me again' (p. 32). For Brittain then, writing this book about her experiences, and particularly her losses, appears to have been a means of coming to terms with them, controlling them and, ultimately, putting them to rest for good. Brittain does not emphasize here the other important intention of *Testament of Youth* (1933), which she states in its Foreword. Here she notes that she wishes to describe what the war meant to 'the generation of those boys and girls who grew up just before [it] broke out' (Brittain, *Testament of Youth*, p. 11), focusing on the middle class to which she herself belonged. This double focus on personal disburdening and on the experiences of a generation remains in tension throughout *Testament of Youth*, and the various claims which Brittain made for the text have been subject to vigorous critical scrutiny. Whilst it will be necessary to consider the apparent contradictions in Brittain's feminism that the text exposes, my principal focus here will be on *Testament of Youth* as an act of mourning and an attempt to compensate for different kinds of loss.

During the First World War Brittain lost, in rapid succession, her fiancé Roland Leighton, two close male friends, Geoffrey Thurlow and Victor Richardson, and ultimately her brother Edward. She also lost her initial enthusiasm for the war, which had been evidenced by her decision to leave her studies at Oxford and become a nurse. However, what she never lost completely, despite her disillusionment with the war, was a conception of the men as heroic. Imparting meaning to their deaths required a residual faith in a 'chivalric' ideal which eventually had to be reconciled with the strongly pacifist position to which Brittain moved during the 1920s and 1930s. A striking pattern of substitution and imitation becomes discernible within both *Testament of Youth* and Brittain's other works. In a diary entry written not long after she began nursing, in 1915, Brittain proclaims: 'I love the British Tommy! I shall get so fond of these men, I know. And when I look after any one of them, it is like nursing Roland by proxy. Oh! if only one of them could be the Beloved One!' (Brittain, *Chronicle*, p. 215). This comment both expresses the implicit wish that Leighton were injured, so that she could care for him, and also blurs the boundaries between her desire to serve her country, as represented by the 'British Tommy' and serving the individual 'Beloved One'. After Leighton's death, his friend Victor Richardson is temporarily identified as a replacement, and Brittain even goes so far as to consider marrying him in Leighton's stead. This plan, precipitated by Richardson's blinding, is foiled only when he too dies. Later, Brittain's friend Winifred Holtby identifies herself as a proxy for Brittain's brother Edward. This chain of substitutions has various complex effects. On one level, it seems to soften the blow of loss by providing alternative objects of affection, but on another it signals an inability to let go of earlier attachments. Brittain's claims to have written the events of the war out of her system, becoming in the process a proxy for the men by telling their story on their behalf, are belied by patterns which emerge in her fiction, which I will also consider here. The loss of a lover in the war is a recurrent trope in her novels, and Brittain frequently uses the narrative device of a letter received from the lover after his death which provides consolation.

This communication from 'beyond the grave' is striking because it suggests an alternative means of dealing with the gap which *Testament of Youth* also serves to fill. What is at stake in each of these examples is testifying on behalf of another.

Writing and mourning

As well as asserting its palliative qualities, *Testament of Experience* places *Testament of Youth* in the context of the numerous other war memoirs and novels that appeared in the late 1920s. Noting the publication of Robert Graves' *Goodbye to All That* (1928), Richard Aldington's *Death of a Hero* (1929) and Edmund Blunden's *Undertones of War* (1929), Brittain records: 'I began to ask: "Why should these young men have the war to themselves? [...] Who will write the epic of the women who went to the war?" [...] I intended to speak [...] for my own generation of obscure young women' (*Testament of Experience*, p. 77). Maroula Joannou has suggested that this post hoc attribution of feminist intent to *Testament of Youth* places in question the status the text has attained as a classic feminist account of war experience. This is not to imply that Brittain did not become a feminist. Rather, the shift to a focus on women in the comments from *Testament of Experience* shows Brittain herself colluding in the re-presentation of the earlier volume. However, Joannou also suggests that the status of the text as an autobiography 'is in its turn undercut by the weighty aim of representing a generation' (p. 51). In this regard, Claire Tylee has argued that *Testament of Youth* fails as an account of a generation because not only does Brittain 'not understand the men she writes about [...] she does not understand the experiences of women either' (pp. 214–15). I will suggest that the reasons why Brittain should have wished to identify herself with different groups at different times are as interesting as her failure to work through these identifications in her writing.

Although *Testament of Experience* foregrounds a desire to tell the female side of the story, Brittain's earlier description of her return to Oxford in *On Becoming a Writer* seems to efface this gender difference: 'During the next two years I was far from being the only lost soul who wandered around Boar's Hill and Christ Church Meadows, haunted by the War, and ferociously seeking that unknown catalytic process by which memories might be purged of their bitterness through embodiment in words' (p. 178). Graves and Blunden are the key points of reference here, and Brittain allies herself with the burgeoning (male) tradition of war-writing. This itself reflects the fact that Brittain writes extensively about the experiences of the men she has lost. But it also implies that her own experiences mark her as a war veteran. What interests me here is not so much an attempt to estimate whether Brittain's experiences were in any way comparable to those of Graves, for example, but the extent to which the losses she suffered compounded, or indeed constituted, her perception of herself as a survivor. Robert Jay Lifton suggests that the defining characteristic of the trauma survivor is that he or she 'has had a death encounter, and the death encounter is central to his or her psychological experience' (Caruth, 'An Interview with Robert Jay Lifton', p. 128). In Graves' case this is exemplified not only by the deaths of those around him in the trenches but also by the fact that he is at one stage believed to have died himself, an event which he uses to comic, or at least ironic, effect. 'People with whom I had been on the worst terms during my life, wrote the most enthusiastic condolences to my mother' (Graves, *Goodbye*, p. 187). In Brittain's case, witnessing the death of Richardson is shown to be less traumatic than not witnessing the deaths of other men. The other factor that links Brittain's work with that of a writer such as Graves, in her own description, is the fact that it is produced only after a temporal delay. Bernard Bergonzi, discussing Graves and other male writers, attributes this delay to the fact that writers were looking back on events which had taken place during their 'formative years' (p. 143). Implicitly, the writers had to have grown into men before they could 'trace a pattern in the scarifying events' (Bergonzi, p. 143) through which they had passed. From a different perspective, Adrian Gregory suggests that wider contextual issues can account for the popularity of the texts that appeared around 1929: 'The onset of economic crisis was partly responsible for the popular reception received by the literature of wartime disenchantment' (p. 119). Only by the end of the decade, according to Gregory, had it become acceptable to raise questions about the purposes of the conflict. This characteristic of temporal delay can also be related, in Brittain's case, to the way *Testament of Youth* functions as an act of mourning.

Linda Anderson suggests that in *Testament of Youth*, Brittain creates 'both a monument to the dead and a barrier against her own annihilation' (*Women*, p. 98). Preserving the memory of the dead by textualizing and therefore externalizing her recollections of them is here conceived as a means of self-preservation also. Whether Brittain actually manages to produce anything as discrete and self-contained as a monument is debatable; for the moment it will be useful to consider the tension between remembering and forgetting which is discernible in descriptions of the mourning process. Elisabeth Bronfen, citing the work of John Bowlby, suggests that in

> [s]uccessful mourning [...] a period of numbing, distress, and anger [is] followed by one of yearning and searching for the lost object, of thinking intensely about the lost person, calling for her or him [...] After a phase of disorganization and despair, based on the recognition that the lost love object cannot be retrieved, a last stage of reorganization concludes mourning. This closure is a healthy failure by the survivor to preserve a continuing sense of the dead person's presence, a detaching of memories and hopes from the dead. (p. 107)

This healthy trajectory of mourning, concluding with an admission that the future can no longer be structured around the dead person, can be either facilitated or stalled by the social situation in which the mourner finds him- or herself. Brittain does not only lose individuals; she loses a social group, which has been instrumental in shaping her future goals and aspirations. She therefore has to attempt to come to terms not only with the loss of people, but also with the loss of a value system. Although in Bronfen's description mourning is principally interior or psychic in nature, other writers on this topic stress the importance of social rituals in this process. Jay Winter has emphasized the significance of public ceremonials such as the interment of the Unknown Soldier as a means of compensating for the fact that many families were denied the consolations of either funerals or indeed graves to mark the passing of their loved ones. 'The need to bring the dead home, to put the dead to rest, symbolically or physically, was pervasive' (p. 28). However, Jane Littlewood suggests that such rituals are not always necessarily positive, and, in comments that echo Brittain's description of her feelings of isolation after the war, notes that '[m]ourners [...] may be expected to ignore, in terms of social interactions outside the group of mourners, the often devastating impact of their bereavement' (p. 34). Although Winter has indicated that many found comfort in 'fictive kinship' (p. 53) with those similarly bereaved, the nature of Brittain's attachments to those she has lost make it difficult for this to be a kinship she can establish. No such fictive community can salve the pain resulting from the loss of an actual community to which she felt she belonged with the men. Notable here is Brittain's description of the alienation she experiences during the Armistice Day celebrations, when her personal losses all but overshadow any sense of relief that the war is over. In *Testament of Youth* she describes herself wandering the streets and reflecting on the prospect of a 'brightly lit, alien world' (p. 462) where there will be no one left to 'share [...] the heights and the depths of [her] memories' (p. 463). The loss of so many significant contemporaries leaves Brittain feeling isolated and doomed to remember her past alone. The declaration of peace is therefore significant not as the end of the war but as the beginning of everyday life without her friends. She dismisses the two minutes silence in succeeding years as surplus to her requirements, writing to Winifred Holtby in 1921, 'I don't require two minute's silence to think of the dead. They're with me always; it's like putting two minutes aside in which to breathe' (Brittain and Handley-Taylor, p. 18).[1]

In this respect, Brittain's writing could be seen as an alternative form of remembrance and mourning; her use of repetition, which can be related to mourning, emphasizes this characteristic. Repetition compounds what Anderson identifies as 'the "excess" which disturbs Brittain's memoir' (*Women*, p. 100). It can account for the use of diary and letter extracts in *Testament of Youth*, for such an act of re-writing has to be preceded by an act of re-reading on the part of the author, initiating a further cycle of assimilation and re-presentation. Bronfen suggests that repetition is 'a double movement, both a return to something primary and the production of something new' (p. 105). In reference to Freud's description of the *fort-da* game, she describes repetition as 'an attempt to counteract absence, loss and death' (Bronfen, p. 106). In the *fort-da* game the departure of the mother is enacted more frequently than her return, as it is this aspect of the transaction which the child is attempting to master. However, in the case of the replacement of a love object, repetition can have the contrary effect of 'questioning the uniqueness of the first term and implying that the loss is not irrevocable' (Bronfen,

p. 106). This would help explain why substitutes or proxies do not necessarily aid the completion of mourning. In relation to Brittain's autobiographical writings, then, repetition occurs principally in the re-writing of events in different formats and contexts, in an attempt to gain mastery of them. For instance, *Thrice a Stranger* (1938) serves both to flesh out journeys abroad which are described in less detail in *Testament of Experience*, and to give another version of the composition and reception of *Testament of Youth*, and *On Becoming a Writer*, as I have noted, also recounts the genesis of *Testament of Youth*. This indicates the infinitely expandable nature of Brittain's autobiography: there are always more details that can be included, and events can always be told anew from a different perspective, in reflection of her shifting experience of her subjectivity. Brittain is therefore constantly returning, if not to the loss itself, then to the period at which she was most deeply concerned with it. Within *Testament of Youth*, as Anderson has shown, looking back on her earlier writings and attempting to close the gap between the earlier and later self through the use of irony is an uneasy business. The diary extracts 'conjure up a world which she both ironises and incorporates into her writing, which she distances herself from, even as she preserves [the men's] memory' (Anderson, *Women*, p. 95). This produces 'an "otherness" in terms of her self which cannot be assimilated into the order of events' (Anderson, *Women*, p. 100). I would suggest that this process can be seen writ large across the body of Brittain's work.

The road to war and the death of Roland Leighton

Following the death of Leighton, the deaths of Thurlow, Richardson and her brother Edward are experienced not just as personal losses but as factors which compound Brittain's diminishing faith in the war. Indeed, immediately after Leighton's death, she considers giving up nursing, reflecting that she had only been doing it for his sake:

> I had hardly realised how entirely it had been the eagerness to share Roland's discomforts which had made me shoulder the disagreeable tasks left over by everyone else, but now that he was dead [...] the increasing consciousness of loss and frustration filled me with impotent fury and resentment. (Brittain, *Testament of Youth*, pp. 246–7)

She decides to continue with her work only at the last minute, while packing to leave, after being

> overwhelmed by a passionate conviction that to give up the work and the place I hated would be defeat, and that Roland, and whatever in the world stood for Right and Goodness, wanted me to remain at the hospital and go on active service. (Brittain, *Testament of Youth*, p. 263)

Brittain recognizes, in *Testament of Youth*, the idealistic nature of this faith in Right and Goodness, and attempts to undercut the whiff of martyrdom contained in this decision. She also foreshadows here the sense of emptiness and lack of fulfilment which hits home at the end of the war, when she realizes that this faith was misplaced. However, the factors that influenced Brittain's decision to go to war in the first place are also relevant here. To identify these, it is necessary to trace the development of her attachment to Leighton, an attachment which although it took on the features of a romance, was initially based on imitation and aspiration.

In *Testament of Youth*, Brittain attributes the beginnings of her awakening into feminism to the good fortune of having met an unconventional teacher at her otherwise unprogressive boarding school. Notably, Miss Heath-Jones lends her a copy of Olive Schreiner's *Women and Labour* during her final term in 1911, and Brittain claims that this text helped her to envision 'a world in which women would no longer be the second-rate, unimportant creatures that they were now considered' (*Testament of Youth*, p. 41). However, Brittain was not immune to the contradictions that afflicted Schreiner and other feminists of that earlier generation. Cate Haste suggests that Schreiner 'experienced continual internal conflict between her background, and the shame then associated with female sexual feelings, and her search for an intellectual idea of companionate and equal relationships' (p. 8). This description could equally apply to Brittain during her relationship with Roland Leighton. Interestingly, his claim to be a feminist himself, and a shared interest in the writings of Schreiner, is one of the factors which draws the pair together, but it is Schreiner's tragic and pessimistic novel, *The Story of an African Farm* (1883) rather than *Women and Labour* which becomes a touchstone text for them. Not only does this signal a sublimation of the politico-sexual arguments of *Women and Labour* in favour of a more romanticized, literary vision: in the novel, Lyndall, with whom Brittain often identifies in her letters to Leighton, is punished for her sexual 'deviancy'.

By the time Brittain first meets Leighton she has already taken the decision to work, with little or no support, for the Oxford Entrance exam. Although this was a bold decision for a middle-class girl to take at this period, it is evident that her belief that women deserved equal reward for academic achievements was subsidiary to her belief that *she* deserved this. At one despondent moment she comments in her diary:

> I suppose it will be my lot to see Edward & his friends, who are as much or more to me than my own (as I can't really stand girls), going off to the university, while I, having failed in my exam., am left here once more to toil on drearily alone. (Brittain, *Chronicle*, p. 81)

This lack of fellow feeling with women seems less reprehensible when Brittain's account of her contact with the values and traditions of her brother's school, Uppingham, is considered. As Paul Berry and Mark Bostridge have noted, Uppingham had been the cradle of muscular Christianity during the nineteenth century, under the leadership of Edward Thring. By the time Edward Brittain was there, however, 'there had been a marked decline in standards' (Berry and Bostridge, p. 29) and athleticism and militarism had taken hold. Edward Brittain and Roland Leighton's involvement in the Officers' Training Corps (OTC) is one notable manifestation of this. Brittain herself seems to have been aware of the need to distance both her brother and Leighton from the taint of overt athleticism and to ally them with the more positive aspects of public school achievement. Edward was a violinist with aspirations to read music at university, whilst Brittain reports that Leighton's academic achievements contributed to a lack of popularity among some of his fellow pupils: 'very few people understand him, & merely think him haughty & conceited' (*Chronicle*, p. 79). The intersection of these portraits of sensitive individuals with Brittain's evident sense of the value of the public school system and ethos occurs when Brittain visits Uppingham with her mother for Prize Day in July 1914. *Testament of*

Youth is less effusive than Brittain's published diaries, *Chronicle of Youth*, on this subject, although the subtext remains.[2] In *Chronicle of Youth*, Brittain comments after her visit: 'For girls – as yet – there is nothing equivalent to public schools for boys – these fine traditions & unwritten laws that turn out so many splendid characters have been withheld from them – to their detriment' (p. 78). In the later account, she shows a sensitivity to the evident jingoism of the headmaster's speech, claiming not to be able to recall the martial ideals which 'were evidently considered entirely suitable for emulation by young English gentlemen' (*Testament of Youth*, p. 88). However, she does recall the headmaster's portentous conclusion and her use of juxtaposition reveals an awareness of the tension between Leighton as a 'sensitive individual' and as a victim of the 'Old Lie':

> "If a man cannot be useful to his country, he is better dead." For a moment [the words'] solemnity disturbed with a queer, indescribable foreboding the complacent mood in which I watched Roland, pale but composed, go up to receive his prizes. (*Testament of Youth*, p. 89)

Brittain here inscribes an earlier event with later knowledge, whilst also placing Leighton's academic achievements alongside what is essentially a call to arms. The question of how to reconcile these achievements with a sense of duty becomes a pressing one when war breaks out, not only for Leighton but, perhaps more surprisingly, for Brittain herself.

Shortly after this visit to Uppingham, Vera Brittain sits the final stage of her Oxford Entrance. Leighton and Edward Brittain were also destined for Oxford and their close friend Victor Richardson for Cambridge. These three boys were collectively referred to by the nickname 'The Three Musketeers' and in *Testament of Youth* Brittain writes of their friendship in terms which indicate that she herself had never experienced anything similar. She claims to have made only two friends at St Monica's: 'In neither case did the intimacy long survive our departure from school' (Brittain, *Testament of Youth*, p. 35). Although her relationship with Leighton rapidly becomes the key focus in *Testament of Youth*, there nevertheless remains the sense that Brittain saw the Three Musketeers' friendship and achievements as aspirational goals. The battle to get into Oxford is not just a battle against her own poor educational opportunities but a potential means of experiencing or sharing in their kinship. It can therefore only be seen as ironic that having equalled the boys academically by getting into Oxford, on the outbreak of war she is made to face the fact that they have quite other demands on their loyalties. In *Testament of Youth* she quotes from one of Leighton's letters, written while he was still trying to obtain a commission, having been rejected initially on account of his poor eyesight:

> I don't think in the circumstances I could easily bring myself to endure a secluded life of scholastic vegetation. It would seem a somewhat cowardly shirking of my obvious duty [...] You will call me a militarist. You may be right. (pp. 103–4)

These reflections of Leighton's, together with his speculation that war is 'if often horrible, yet very ennobling and very beautiful' (p. 104) reveal how well his headmaster has done his work.

In his discussion of attitudes to death at the outbreak of war, David Cannadine suggests that 'death on the battlefield was seen as something noble, heroic, splendid, romantic – *and unlikely*' (Cannadine, p. 196). This was partly a consequence of ignorance of what the war would be like. Abstract ideas about war took prevalence over actual knowledge, and the clash between ideals and practicality was a difficult one to reconcile. Eric J. Leed distinguishes between 'the military way', which defined war as a series of practical problems or goals, and 'militarism', which he describes as a 'system of images, symbols, and rituals designed to express the character of the "warrior" and the character of the community in which he is at home' (p. 57). The effect of Leighton's service in the OTC seems to have been a blurring of the two. Practical military knowledge was overlaid with the notion that war could be ennobling. Brittain also provides evidence of Leed's assertion that militarism was appealing to civilians. After quoting Leighton's letter, she quotes from her own reply: 'Women get all the dreariness of war, and none of its exhilaration' (Brittain, *Testament of Youth*, p. 104). She then attempts to deconstruct her own position by glossing this with an explanation: 'Obviously I was suffering, like so many women in 1914, from an inferiority complex' (p. 104). However, stronger than a wish to ally herself with other women, is a desire to emulate the Three Musketeers. Although Brittain does go up to Oxford, she only stays for a year before deciding to become a nurse. Brittain's own explanation for this decision in *Testament of Youth* again stresses the 'inferiority complex' as a factor, although she states this in rather stronger terms: 'Truly the War had made masochists of us all' (p. 154). Ostensibly her decision to give up her hard won place at Somerville results from a sense of duty which mirrors that of the Musketeers. Quoting from her diary she comments, 'He has to face far worse things than any sight or act I could come across; he can bear it – and so can I' (Brittain, *Testament of Youth*, p. 154). As Sharon Ouditt notes, Brittain 'longs to be heroic [but] the system permits her only to be auxiliary' (p. 34). For a woman, the nearest available alternative to active military service is nursing, an act which like soldiering involves sacrificing intellectual endeavour in favour of bodily duty, but which also draws Brittain into a gendered discourse of servitude.

Brittain implies that nursing opened her eyes and provided her with independence to an extent that would in other circumstances have been impossible for one of her class. She attributes to nursing an 'early release from the sex-inhibitions that [...] beset many of my female contemporaries, both married and single' (Brittain, *Testament of Youth*, p. 166), as well as freedom of movement.[3] There are dangers, of course, in overstating the positive, liberating qualities of war. Margaret R. Higonnet and Patrice L-R. Higonnet have suggested that although in wartime women might be able to take on 'roles previously reserved to men [...] [a]fter the war, the lines of gender can [...] be redrawn to conform to the prewar map of relations between men's and women's roles' (p. 35). Brittain herself notes that the 'sex-inhibitions' from which she was released did not disappear from society at large. Both Deborah Gorham and Claire Tylee have suggested, however, that the element of service in the nursing role encouraged Brittain's tendency to draw on romantic, chivalric models when describing her relationship with Leighton. Although Brittain did have intimate contact with injured men who she saw as proxies for Leighton, this type of contact, according to Gorham, 'drained sexuality [...] of eroticism' (p. 117). Tylee emphasizes the hero-worship aspect of Brittain's relationship with Leighton. She goes so far as to compare this to a 'religion in which letter-writing and nursing the wounded formed the ritual' (Tylee, p. 65). What is apparent to a reader of the diaries and letters, although rather less so, it would appear, to Brittain herself in *Testament of Youth*, is the extent to which, once he is on active service, Leighton discovers the mismatch between his idealism and the circumstances in which he finds himself.

There are some indications in *Testament of Youth* of the changes that Leighton undergoes. 'I wonder if your metamorphosis has been as complete as my own', he writes in October 1915. 'I feel a barbarian, a wild man of the woods, stiff, narrowed [...] I wonder what the dons of Merton would say to me now, or if I could ever waste my time on Demosthenes again' (Brittain, *Testament of Youth*, p. 216). The values which the war is intended to preserve are in stark contrast to the means by which it is being fought, but the realization that this is the case is gradual rather than sudden and emerges sporadically in comments such as these.[4] An incident that appears in Brittain's diary account of Leighton's final leave but which is excised from *Testament of Youth* gives a material indication of the 'barbarism' into which Leighton has apparently fallen. On a shopping trip in London, Leighton buys

> a vicious-looking short steel dagger – in case of – accidents. He handled it with great deliberation, and professional interest [...] The sight of this dagger in the hand of one of the most civilized people of these ironically-named civilized times depressed me to morbidity. (Brittain, *Chronicle*, p. 260–1)

Not only does Brittain here identify the gulf that Leighton also recognizes between the values being fought for and the means being used; as a nurse, she has a professional knowledge of the kind of damage such a weapon might inflict. Later, she finds herself nursing a German soldier and reflects on the paradoxical nature of this situation:

> [H]ow ridiculous it was that I should be holding this man's hand in friendship when perhaps, only a week or two earlier, Edward up at Ypres had been doing his best to kill him. The world was mad and we were all victims; that was the only way to look at it. (Brittain, *Testament of Youth*, p. 376)

Both these incidents signal a disturbance of the supposedly distinct boundary between civilization and barbarism. A similar sentiment is expressed in Freud's 'Thoughts for the Times on War and Death':

> We were prepared to find that wars between the primitive and the civilized peoples, between the races who are divided by the colour of their skin [...] would occupy mankind for some time to come. [...] But the great nations themselves, it might have been supposed, would have acquired so much comprehension of what they had in common, and so much tolerance for their differences, that 'foreigner' and 'enemy' would no longer be merged [...] into a single concept. (pp. 276–7)

Brittain still wishes to retain some sense of the chivalry of individuals, and thus distance them from the events in which they are constrained to participate. Freud, though, is bleaker: '[O]ur fellow citizens have not sunk so low as we feared, because they had never risen so high as we believed' ('Thoughts', p. 285).

A very different reaction to the sight of Leighton wielding a dagger is found in a text that provides an interesting contrast with *Testament of Youth*. Soon after his death, Leighton's mother, Marie Leighton, a prolific popular novelist, produced a memoir of his life called *Boy of My Heart* (1916). This text portrays the aftermath of bereavement in a painfully extravagant manner, but Mrs Leighton takes comfort from the noble nature of her son's sacrifice, which she portrays as the culmination of his upbringing and training. She describes being shown a dagger he has bought in this way: 'I took the newly bought thing in my hand and looked at it. "When it's done its work bring it back to me without cleaning it. I shall want to keep it always like that"' (Anon. [Marie Leighton], pp. 216–17).[5] For Brittain, the dagger is a taint on her romantic image of Leighton and a reminder of the alterity of war, as well as a sign of how different he may be when he emerges from the conflict. For Mrs Leighton, however, the dagger has a more thoroughly symbolic value. Throughout the text she stresses that heroism and physical prowess can exist alongside sensitivity, and indeed do so in her son. The changes he has undergone during the war are essentially contingent, and examining the dagger is on a par with admiring the prize books he won at Uppingham. It is a sign of his ability and achievement in a particular field. Mrs Leighton is not completely locked into a chivalric view of the war and in fact comments that 'this war of machinery might as well be carried on by women, for all the good that male muscle can do in it' (p. 209). These sentiments, however, go alongside a knowledge that he must go to war alone and she must relinquish him. Berry and Bostridge have noted that this text appeared in the same year as the infamous 'Letter from a Little Mother', reproduced by Robert Graves:

> [T]he bugle call came, and we have hung up the tennis racquet, we've fetched our laddie from school, we've put his cap away, and we have glanced lovingly over his last report which said "Excellent" – we've wrapped them all in a Union Jack and locked them up, to be taken out only after the war to be looked at [...] Women are created for the purpose of giving life, and men to take it. (*Goodbye*, p. 190)

Like the Little Mother, Mrs Leighton both stresses her adoration of her son and emphasizes her own role in building his character. 'I thought he had too much brain power for the Army [...] And yet I was making him a soldier every day' (Anon [Marie Leighton], p. 39) she writes, citing the patriotism she encourages during the Boer War. She also promotes 'manliness' by warning her son that he must hide his 'great love for flowers and colour and poetry' when he starts at school and instead 'go in for boyish plainness' (Anon [Marie Leighton], pp. 72–3). For Mrs Leighton to throw herself into mourning her son seems a straightforward task, notwithstanding her sorrow, because she can create a narrative of his life in which Leighton grows up and grows into a soldier. This essentially provides a rationalization of his death, no matter how difficult it might nevertheless be to accept.

An incident which occurs in the aftermath of Leighton's death but which is not dealt with directly in *Boy of My Heart*, is the arrival of his uniform and kit, sent back from the front. Brittain recounts this in a letter to her brother Edward, extracts from which are included in *Testament of Youth*, and in her diary. To me it provides the most startling image for the gulf between Leighton's experience and Brittain's understanding of it. This is also the most grim substitution; instead of Leighton himself, or indeed his dead body, Brittain is faced with the paltry remainders. According to her accounts, Brittain arrives to visit his parents and sister just as they are examining the various items.[6]

> I had arrived at the cottage that morning to find his mother and sister standing in helpless distress in the midst of his returned kit, which was lying, just opened, all over the floor. The garments sent back included the outfit that he had been wearing when he was hit. I wondered, and I wonder still, why it was thought necessary to return such relics – the tunic torn back and front by the bullet, a khaki vest dark and stiff with blood, and a pair of blood-stained breeches slit open at the top by someone obviously in a violent hurry. [...] "Everything," I wrote later to Edward, "was damp and worn and simply caked with mud. And I was glad that neither you nor Victor nor anyone who may some day go to the front was there to see. If you had been, you would have been overwhelmed by the horror of war without its glory. For though he had only worn the things when living, the smell of those clothes was the smell of graveyards and the Dead." (*Testament of Youth*, pp. 251–2)

Gilbert and Gubar consider this incident as expressive of the estrangement from their homes which was experienced by young men such as Leighton once they entered the 'polluted realm of the trenches' (Gilbert and Gubar, p. 267). This reading is supported by Brittain's thankfulness that Edward and Victor Richardson, neither of whom have been to the front at this stage, were not there to see the 'remains'. It is ironic that Brittain takes it upon herself to protect them from knowledge of the fate which might await them in the trenches. She here becomes the custodian of Leighton's front-line experience. What Gilbert and Gubar do not consider, though, is the extent to which the uniform is not only a symbol of Leighton's estrangement, but also, more disturbingly, is itself *polluting* as well as polluted. The uniform brings death into the domestic sphere. In this respect, it stands as a metonym for Leighton's corpse and presents many of the characteristics which Trudi Tate, following Kristeva, attributes to the abject.

> [T]he corpse as abject marks the threshold between subject and object and threatens to contaminate or dissolve the subject [...] on

the other hand, the corpse marks the border which confirms the living person as alive, and can thus be a source of strength and affirmation to the subject. (p. 69)

But the uniform, sent unasked for, is not so liable to perform this affirmative function. The clothes, which they have hitherto associated with Leighton's living body, can now only signal his absence. The significance of Leighton's uniform has been noted by Brittain on earlier occasions. When he comes home from France for the first time, she records: 'At that stage of the War it was fashionable for officers who had been at the front to look as disreputable and war-worn as possible in order to distinguish them from the brand-new subalterns of Kitchener's Army' (Brittain, *Testament of Youth*, pp. 177–8). However, this idea of a uniform as a badge of honour is difficult to preserve and this is especially apparent in the text of the letter to Edward, where Brittain attempts to ascertain the nature of Leighton's wounds through an examination of his garments, some of which she cannot even name. Mrs Leighton, as I have noted, does not describe the return of the uniform directly. This can partly be accounted for by the fact that *Boy of My Heart* is framed by her wait for Leighton to arrive home on leave, and ends when the news of his death is received. But it is interesting that Mrs Leighton nevertheless describes a neighbour going through the same ordeal, thus displacing onto another the events which she herself will experience, in fact has experienced at the time *Boy of My Heart* was written, but which fall outside its narrative ambit. She describes being shown, 'the [...] pitiful clothes with the bullet holes in them' (Anon [Marie Leighton], p. 201). Here we see, as in Brittain's writing, an attempt to cushion herself against a blow which was not expected when it actually arrived, by persuading herself that it was expected, or that, at least, had she read the runes she could have predicted it.

In the aftermath of Leighton's death, Brittain attempts to reanimate the uniform. She wishes to know exactly how the damage to the garments and, by extension, Leighton's death were caused, but she also expresses a need to find out whether he had any final message for her. This double task is important not just as a signal of Brittain's desire to somehow gain possession of Leighton's death, to make up for not having been there. Her failure in the second aspect is a reminder, if one were needed, that the dead cannot speak.

Leighton's is not an especially heroic or glorious death: not having been warned by his predecessors that a gap in a hedge had a German machine gun trained on it, he is mortally wounded while passing the gap in the moonlight. Brittain reports what she eventually manages to learn, reconstructing the event as though she herself were an eye-witness: 'As soon as Roland reached the gap, the usual volley was fired. Almost the first shot struck him in the stomach, penetrating his body, and he fell on his face' (Brittain, *Testament of Youth*, p. 242). Leighton does not die immediately but has to undergo an operation, and the reconstruction of events between his injury and his death is of particular concern to Brittain. Only after contacting 'his colonel, and his company commander, and his servant, and the Catholic padre, and a sympathetic officer who, in order to satisfy me, made a special journey to Louvencourt and catechised the doctors' (Brittain, *Testament of Youth*, p. 244) does Brittain finally accept that he left no message for her. Indeed, as far as she can ascertain, neither his fellow officers nor any of the men knew of her existence. This is a blow to Brittain, not least because it means she is denied any final assurance of his love, and indeed any third party proof of his feelings towards her. There is only the poem 'Hédauville', found in an exercise book among his things which she puzzles over but which is not direct enough to provide any immediate reassurance. Later, Brittain uses the poem as an epigraph to the final chapter of *Testament of Youth*, imbuing it with prophetic power and seeing it as bestowing a bless-ing on her relationship with George Catlin who she is about to marry at the end of the volume: 'And when the thrush sings in your wood, / Unknowing you may meet / Another stranger, Sweet' (p. 606). Berry and Bostridge point out that this poem is open to a quite contrary reading and that Leighton 'could be gently suggesting that their own relationship is cooling and that Vera will eventually find happiness elsewhere' (p. 95). The fact that Brittain does not make more of the discovery of this poem perhaps indicates her own doubts and it did not stop her from making extensive attempts to find other less ambiguous assurances of his affection.

Further losses: Victor Richardson and Edward Brittain

Although, as I have noted, Brittain for a time considers giving up nurs-ing in the immediate aftermath of Leighton's death she eventually decides to enrol for overseas service and is sent to Malta. During the year following Leighton's death she continues to correspond with her brother, with Victor Richardson, and with Geoffrey Thurlow, a friend Edward Brittain made when he enlisted. The bond between Brittain and Richardson is precipitated by the loss of Leighton. Richardson comments of the friendship between himself, Leighton and Edward Brittain: 'It was the more strange because any two of us were linked more closely by affection for the third. [...] [N]ow that you are His representative it seems natural to talk to you about it' (Bishop and Bostridge, p. 229). For Richardson, Brittain becomes an intercessor, or a proxy for Leighton. Soon, Richardson begins to express his disillusionment. Brittain comments that in one letter Richardson speculated on 'why they were all out there', only to conclude that, the protection of Belgium notwithstanding, the best answer was 'to be found in the words of an Army marching song to the tune of "Auld Lang Syne": We're here because/ We're here because/ We're here because/ We're here...' (*Testament of Youth*, p. 335). In a letter which is not quoted in *Testament of Youth*, he stresses a sense of isolation:

> [T]he Army is like a freezing mixture. One shuts oneself up from people, and when one comes among people to whom one may speak what one really feels one either can say nothing at all or else one gives utterance to a heap of conventional shibboleths in which one does not believe. (Bishop and Bostridge, p. 261)

The lack of romantic involvement between himself and Brittain seems to facilitate Richardson's openness; she takes on a role she had earlier envisioned for herself, as the Fourth Musketeer, but this comes only at the price of losing Leighton. The ongoing memorialization of Leighton and the cold comfort it provides are all too short-lived, however. In April 1917, comes a double blow: Geoffrey Thurlow is killed in action, and Richardson blinded. Brittain is in Malta when this news arrives and her reaction, as described in *Testament of Youth* has a particular kind of internal logic: 'There was nothing left in life now but Edward and the wreckage of Victor – Victor who had stood by me so often in my blackest hours. If he wanted me, surely I could stand by him in his' (p. 344). The comment 'there was nothing left in my life now' indicates not merely masochistic altruism but a sense of the utter impossibility of ever extricating herself from the cycle of mourning and remembrance. Devoting herself to Richardson would serve the symbolic function of giving her own life, as Leighton gave his.

However, as Trudi Tate points out, in accounts of interaction between soldiers and nurses, '[t]he difference between viewer and spectacle – or between subject and damaged object – is frequently more important than the difference between men and women' (p. 84). Richardson is depersonalized when he is wounded; he becomes a potential means by which Brittain can bring into line her identity as a nurse and her identity as a lover-in-mourning. Fixing on the injured man as an object makes him a proxy for Leighton but also desexualizes the replacement relationship, not because of any necessary connection between injury and emasculation, but because Brittain approaches him, in part, as a nurse, a role which, as I have suggested, tends to neutralize her contact with men.

> So much human wreckage had passed through my hands, but this...well, this was different. [...] I took his fingers in mine and caressed and kissed them as though he had been a child. [...] His fingers, I noticed, were damp, and his lips very cold. (Brittain, *Testament of Youth*, p. 357)

Richardson is first infantilized, and then viewed with a professional eye. His condition begins to deteriorate and within a week he is dead. However, this death, a relatively peaceful one, in hospital in England, does not appear to provide an opportunity for Brittain to attain a better grasp on Leighton's death: '[T]he husband of my imagination was always Roland, and could never now be Victor' (Brittain, *Testament of Youth*, p. 358). This comment does at least indicate a realization that such an act of replacement or repetition will not be an adequate way of coming to terms with her loss. Aside from other factors, the act of viewing Richardson's body seems to provide a degree of closure that is not possible with either Leighton or Edward Brittain. The body is 'familiar, but in its silent unfamiliarity so terrible an indictment of the inept humanity which condemned its own noblest types to such a fate' (Brittain, *Testament of Youth*, p. 358). Paradoxically, then, seeing the body reinforces Brittain's belief that it might be possible to separate her friends' public school-instilled nobility from the goal – war – towards which it was propelling them.

When Edward Brittain is killed in Italy in June 1917, Brittain wishes to discover all she can about the circumstances of his death: '[T]hough I dreaded more than death whatever I might be self-condemned to learn, I was driven and impelled [...] to find out as much as I could' (*Testament of Youth*, p. 441). Fleshing out the circumstances of Edward's death is, as it was in Leighton's case, both a means of compensating for her own absence from the scene and, perhaps, an attempt to cushion the blow inflicted by the news. To place this death within a narrative, however ghastly, can help to rationalize and control it, even if it makes it no easier to bear. In Leighton's case the uniform served as a series of clues; in Edward's C.O., Brittain hopes to have found an eyewitness who can initiate her, turn her into a proxy witness. This is important in relation to Brittain's intention to recount the experiences of a generation. In attempting to construct a narrative of Edward's death, she inscribes a place for herself within it. This is not necessarily an act of appropriation, or an attempt to somehow bathe in reflected glory. Adrian Gregory suggests that in the immediate post-war, '[t]he concept of knowledge being the distinction between combatant and non-combatant is central. It is what the soldier has seen, sensed and felt that marks him out' (Gregory, p. 81). Edward will never be able to speak about his own experience and Brittain is impelled to somehow approximate this knowledge. However, Gregory also notes that this knowledge was often presumed to have a mystical aspect, and this is reflected in the way that Brittain's 'quest' becomes a search for truth and redemptive meaning. In fact, what is revealed is the unbridgeable gap between simply knowing about an event and the actual experience of it.

Although Brittain manages to elicit from the C.O. a description of how Edward died (she is told that he was shot through the head), she fears that this might simply be a way of protecting her by indicating an immediate death rather than prolonged suffering. Only a second testimony from Edward's Colonel, confirming the C.O.'s report, assures her that this was indeed how Edward died. Brittain notes in *Testament of Youth* that she 'haunted the colonel quite shamelessly' (p. 442), unable to find out any more about Edward's death, eventually realizing that the Colonel was 'nervously afraid that every young woman he met might want to marry him' (p. 443). Her pursuit of knowledge is misread as a romantic pursuit, but after Edward's death, Brittain seems disinclined to seek another proxy. 'It was Edward's death rather than Roland's which turned me into an automaton ... I could have married Victor in memory of Roland, and Geoffrey in memory of Edward but the War took even the second best. It left nothing' (qtd in Berry and Bostridge, p. 136). She remains disappointed that she is unable to discover whether Edward's part in 'the vital counter-attack [...] really involved some special act of heroism' (Brittain, *Testament of Youth*, p. 444). Again there is a desire not so much to romanticize Edward's sacrifice but to see him as having died a death worthy of the regard in which she holds him. This at least would provide some purpose to the loss.

Afterwards

In the post-war section of *Testament of Youth*, describing her return alone and disillusioned to Oxford, Brittain notes her preoccupation with the twin figures of Leighton and her brother, who come to stand, in her mind, for her general sense of displacement. 'The two of them seemed to fuse in my mind into a kind of composite lost companion, an elusive ghost which embodied all intimacy, all comradeship, all joy, which included everything that was the past and should have been the future' (p. 485). Bereft of these companions, but haunted by their memory, Brittain finds it impossible to pick up where she left off at Oxford, and this is compounded by her perception that those who have remained there for the duration of the war are unwilling to acknowledge that anything particular might have happened in the interim. As I have noted, Brittain portrays herself as thoroughly traumatized when she returns, and eventually blames herself for alienating those around her, as much as she blames them for their lack of understanding.

The beginnings of the friendship with Winifred Holtby are one sign if not of recovery then of a growing belief in the possibility of a future without the men. In many respects, Holtby, Brittain's first really close female friend in her adult years, allows Brittain to realize that female companionship can be based on the type of intellectual interaction she had envied in the Musketeers. Concomitant with this friendship is a new set of beliefs, feminism and eventually pacifism, to replace those she shared with the men. However, Holtby also has a role to play in the continuing acts of mourning performed by Brittain in the years following the war. In 1921, Holtby travels with

Brittain on her first visits to Leighton's and Edward's graves. Although Brittain makes further visits, including one while on her honeymoon with George Catlin, it is clearly significant to her that Holtby is present on this first occasion. In *Testament of Youth*, Brittain comments, 'I knew of no one with whom I would rather share this pilgrimage than Winifred, who had identified herself so closely in imagination with Edward and Roland that they almost seemed to be her dead as well as my own' (p. 521). Notwithstanding speculation over the precise nature of the relationship between the two women,[7] it would appear that it was with Edward rather than Roland Leighton that Holtby principally identified. (The syntax in the above quotation in fact blurs the distinction between Holtby feeling akin to the dead men and her feeling akin to Brittain in her loss.) Marion Shaw cites a poem written by Holtby in 1925 that reflects Holtby's 'wishful belief, ever since the Italian holiday in which she and Vera visited Edward Brittain's grave, that she was linked to this dead brother, perhaps had in some sense taken his place' (*Clear Stream*, p. 202). Later Edward comes to mind while Holtby is at a concert: 'the words came into my head "I am his deputy"' (qtd in Shaw, *Clear Stream*, p. 202). Another link is added to the chain of substitutes and proxies, although what is striking here is that Holtby interpellates herself into this role, and indeed that she chooses Edward rather than Leighton to identify with. By the time Holtby makes these comments, Brittain is already involved with her future husband, George Catlin. By identifying with Edward in this way, Holtby secures herself against any possible diminution of Brittain's affection and friendship by presenting herself as fulfilling the supporting and encouraging role which had been Edward's, adjacent to any romance.

Brittain's relationship with Catlin begins when he writes her a fan letter after the publication of her first novel, *The Dark Tide* (1923). Engaging with her intellectually, via her work, seems to have been an indication to Brittain that this man would not expect her to sacrifice this work at any stage in the relationship. But in view of her continued sense of loss throughout the early 1920s it is also particularly appropriate that, just as the relationship with Leighton became principally an epistolary one before its untimely end, with Catlin there is a reversal of this movement. If Leighton's experiences became inexorably more distant, the correspondence with Catlin, on the contrary, gradually draws them together. This reverse trajectory means that with Catlin the meeting of minds precedes any other type of attraction, although in *Testament of Youth* she is glad to eventually receive a photograph of him: ' "Nice looking," I concluded' (p. 613). The ultimate consequence of this was a marriage of a semi-detached kind, with both parties pursuing careers and travelling independently. For Brittain, then, marriage was not simply a case of finding a substitute for Leighton. She later claimed, in a letter to Catlin, that a marriage between herself and Leighton would not have been successful: 'unsophisticated, romantic, physical enchantment is seldom a quality which survives more than a few weeks of marriage. Unless it becomes something else, the marriage soon fails – as Roland's and mine might have failed' (qtd in Berry and Bostridge, p. 96). Nevertheless he continues to shadow the marriage. In *Testament of Youth*, Brittain records a dream in which 'news came that Roland had never really died, but had only been missing with a lost memory [...] In the dream his family invited me to their house to meet him; I went, and found him changed beyond recognition by cruel experience but unchanged towards myself, [and] anxious to marry me' (p. 650).[8] Two aspects of Brittain's hesitancy over the marriage to Catlin are encapsulated here: it will mean finally letting go of Roland; and it will also mean ceasing to define herself solely by her involvement in the war. She reflects: 'So long [...] as I remained unmarried I was merely a survivor from the past' (p. 651). However, what gains prominence in both the concluding pages of *Testament of Youth* and throughout *Testament of Experience* is the other aspect of Brittain's uncertainty. Marrying will require not only the renunciation of past attachments but will rob her of the independence she has won since leaving Oxford – not that she has ever been financially independent of her parents, but rather has enjoyed a life more or less free from responsibilities, sharing a flat with Holtby and writing her first novel. Although at the conclusion of *Testament of Youth* some resolution seems to have been reached, the dual task of attempting to complete the story of the war whilst dealing with the new challenges of married life continues to loom large throughout Brittain's post-war writing.

Echoes of war in Brittain's fiction

Before *Testament of Youth*, Brittain published two novels, *The Dark Tide* (1923) and *Not Without Honour* (1925). *The Dark Tide* contains a version of Brittain's post-war experiences at Oxford, and *Not Without Honour* draws on Brittain's pre-war life in Buxton.[9] It would seem then that Brittain only felt ready to describe the war itself after framing it in this fashion. I have suggested some of the reasons why Brittain might have delayed tackling her own war experience head on, but even in these earlier fictions Brittain can be seen to be restaging her losses, and particularly, attempting to complete the correspondence with Leighton and her brother which was truncated by their deaths. This is a way of grasping the actuality of their loss not by simply reiterating the loss itself but by affirming, albeit textually, their survival. They themselves are lost but their final thoughts, in Brittain's version, are with her. The persistent use of the device of the letter from 'beyond the grave', which first appears in the novels of the 1920s, encapsulates the tension apparent in Brittain's writing between repetition as a means of putting to rest or forgetting and repetition as a means of perpetuating the earlier attachment.

In *The Dark Tide*, Virginia Dennison, in deep mourning for most of the narrative, returns to her wartime occupation of nursing after rejecting an academic career on the grounds that '[i]ntellectual success goes to [her] head like cheap champagne' (p. 230). This self-martyrdom is coupled with a deep disdain for the vapidity of the post-war world, induced by her losses during the war. 'I did have friends once, and a brother [...] they died because you and your like had to be saved from the fate you deserved' (Brittain, *Dark Tide*, pp. 38–9), she tells the vacuous Daphne Lethbridge at one point. Having rejected a proposal of marriage from her tutor, Sylvester, who immediately makes a successful bid for Daphne's hand instead, Virginia retreats to re-read a letter from her dead fiancé. We learn that, like Leighton, he was due to come home for Christmas:

> I can hardly believe that in forty-eight hours I shall have you beside me, dear. Just one more night in the trenches and than a dash for the first lorry that comes along, to take me straight to our wedding-day [...] There's a Christmas feeling in the air [...] Just twelve hours more, and then! (Brittain, *Dark Tide*, p. 86)

For Virginia the memory of this love affair, symbolized here by the letter, is enough. By the end of the novel, there is no sign of her changing her mind and the disastrous union between Daphne and

Sylvester seems to prove that Virginia has made the right decision. But there is another model for marriage within the novel, in the relationship between Patricia O'Neill and Mr Stephanoff. As Kennard points out, this meeting of minds shows the extent to which Brittain was unable to envision 'a positive life without heterosexual love' (p. 49). Even the self-sacrificing Virginia sustains herself on the memory of such a love, her intransigence about its possible renewal or replacement notwithstanding.

A second version of Virginia Dennison appears in *Not Without Honour*. In the body of the text, Brittain returns to the pre-war, and focuses on a romance between Christine Merivale and the Reverend Albert Clark. The epilogue, however, is set at Oxford in the early years of the war. Ironically, in view of Brittain's own experience, Christine has been sent there as a punishment after becoming romantically involved with Clark, who is married, and meets Virginia Dennison, who, in her brief appearance is portrayed as a 'dark other' to Christine. '[R]umour said that she was writing a satire about war and a provincial town [...] she was engaged to some boy at the front. Her brother was out there, too' (Brittain, *Not Without*, p. 294). This wartime Virginia has all the anger and mystery of the post-war version who appears in *The Dark Tide*. However, in *Not Without Honour* the losses are divided between the two protagonists. Virginia receives news that her brother has died and Christine learns of this only a moment before she receives a letter bearing the news that Clark too has been killed in action. Enclosed is a letter from her former lover, written the night before he went into action, and containing not only some final affectionate words to Christine but also a prediction: 'I do not believe that I shall ever see England or you again [...] I must bid you farewell' (Brittain, *Not Without*, pp. 311–12). Here we see the difficulty raised by the use of a letter as a device to convey a final message to a loved one. For it to be successful, Clark has to predict his own death. His belief that he will die is the spur to breaking a long silence and bringing closure to the relationship with Christine, and hence to the novel. This can be contrasted to the letter Virginia receives in *The Dark Tide*, which serves little purpose in terms of the plotting of the novel, except to assure us that she was once loved. The hopeful, forward looking letter in *The Dark Tide* does not release Virginia but serves to perpetuate her attachment to her lover. Christine, on the other hand, is released, and this is evidently a more satisfactory state of affairs, despite the logical contradiction that it entails: that the author of the letter foresees his own death.

Clark's prescience has a mystical aspect which tallies with how he has been presented throughout the novel, but in *Honourable Estate* (1936), which Kennard describes as 'in part a fictionalization of *Testament of Youth*' (p. 177), the letter Ruth Alleyndene receives from her brother Richard is a thinly disguised suicide note. Although this is a logical means of having a final message delivered after death, it produces problems as regards the morality of suicide. Richard Alleyndene is revealed to have been romantically involved with one of his fellow officers, but his 'death wish' is transmuted into reckless bravery and the question of whether his death was deliberate is left in suspension. Ruth asks the American officer Eugene Meury, '[D]o you believe Richard killed himself to escape the disgrace that might have come to him?' (Brittain, *Honourable*, p. 338) 'I guess that's a thing we'll never know' (Brittain, *Honourable*, p. 338), is Eugene's reply. If there are echoes here of the death of Brittain's own brother,[10] the relationship between Ruth and Eugene refigures the relationship with Leighton in a more radical way. Despite knowing that he has a fiancée waiting at home, Ruth decides to sleep with Eugene before he goes into battle, but takes precautions to prevent pregnancy. After his death she regrets this, wishing that she could have had his child so that 'something of him would have been left' (Brittain, *Honourable*, p. 403). However, this cannot simply be read as regret on Brittain's part that she did not have a similar opportunity with Leighton, because Ruth's actions also become an example of substitution, or action taken by proxy. Touring America as a political speaker (as Brittain did), Ruth meets Dallas Lowell, Eugene's American fiancée, who has remained unmarried: 'Somehow it's never been possible to switch over to someone else' (Brittain, *Honourable*, p. 533). Dallas guesses that Ruth and Eugene were in love and confides her regret at not having 'given him all of [her]self, body and soul' (Brittain, *Honourable*, p. 537) before his death, provoking Ruth to confess the nature of her own involvement with him. 'Ruth Alleyndene,' Dallas responds, 'you can be sure I'll always remember you with gratitude for giving him what I couldn't give' (Brittain, *Honourable*, p. 538). Brittain can thus explore both denial and submission, and Dallas and Ruth complement each other, the former romantically dedicated to Eugene's memory, the latter married to another. Dallas's assertion that it was better for Eugene to have found himself an alternative lover before his death than to have remained faithful to her not only absolves Ruth of any blame within the narrative, but also asserts the importance of such sexual knowledge (sanctified, necessarily by love) in the face of death. Notably, the woman who did not share this knowledge with him is the one who perpetuates her attachment to him, and as Diana Wallace argues, 'Dallas's sublimation of her desires is presented as a second-best' (p. 155), her successful career providing no consolation.

Even in her final two novels, published during the 1940s and addressing from a pacifist perspective the progress and legacy of the Second World War, Brittain continues to address the aftermath of the First World War. This could suggest that she viewed the Second World War as a doomed repetition, as much as a continuation or a completion, of the 1914–18 conflict; certainly, for the protagonists, the two cannot necessarily be separated. Francis Halkin, in *Account Rendered* (1944), murders his wife while in a 'fugue' state and is unable to remember having committed the crime. Halkin is a veteran of the First World War who has never been able to discuss his experiences and the murder signals the inappropriate intrusion of battlefield behaviour into the domestic sphere. Brittain here comments, implicitly, on the nature of civilian involvement in the Second World War, with the 'Home Front' eroding the distinction between combatants and others. Halkin's inability to integrate his First World War experiences into his later life also recalls the anxieties expressed by Leighton and Richardson, that having lived through and adapted to war, it would be impossible to readjust to peace. Halkin eventually achieves recovery of sorts, and goes to work for the Red Cross, his new wife's pregnancy signalling hopes for the future.

The possibility that the next generation will be able to learn the lessons of the war is also the burden of *Born 1925* (1948), Brittain's last novel. But although Adrian Carbury and Carol Brinton have no personal experience of the First World War, Brittain implies that their task is not only the promotion of peace (specifically through Carol's work as a journalist) but also the salvaging of the romantic aspirations of Adrian's parents, Sylvia and Robert, whose story forms the body of the narrative. Sylvia marries Robert,[11] the local vicar despite never having recovered from the death of her first husband, Lawrence, who was summoned to the trenches on the day of their wedding. (Notably, whilst Ruth in *Honourable Estate* can console herself with a last message of love from Eugene, passed on by a fellow officer, Sylvia has to make do with the traditional telegram.) When Robert dies after a Second World War air raid, Sylvia finds herself mourning not for him, but for her first husband. Only through this repetition are Sylvia's feelings released, although she takes little comfort from this: 'She was weeping [...] for the death of love, and its obstinate refusal to rise again' (Brittain, *Born*, p. 335). When Adrian and Carol agree to marry, in the ruins of post-war Germany, we are told: 'They would be able to put together Robert's love for Sylvia and Sylvia's passion for her first husband [...] Lawrence' (Brittain, *Born*, p. 378). The completion of Sylvia's mourning is here displaced in favour of a (successful) repetition of her love affair, and it is to the next generation that the burden of closure must fall.

Conclusion

Testament of Youth can be read as an assertion of the author's survival in the face of the deaths that surround her. Only in the fiction do we find models for the resolution of acts of mourning. However contrived they might be, fictionalized deaths are controllable, can be plotted, predicted, managed and mourned. In the autobiography, despite Brittain's attempts to impose her own voice and deliver the shock to the reader with the control of the novelist, what underlies this procedure is its actual uncontrollability. Brittain shields the reader from the shock she experienced by foreshadowing her losses before they occur. This is not just a case of making the text less shocking and therefore more palatable. It seems to show that for Brittain there can be no access to events before the deaths except through the lens of the deaths having occurred. It also indicates the ultimate impossibility of truly sharing such moments. The original shock can never be replicated. Brittain might be able to guide the characters in her novels through their losses in a way she could never guide herself; but the overwhelming sense is that the novel cannot make up for the inadequacy of autobiography as a means of completing the act of mourning.

Testament of Experience (1957) shows, like much of the fiction, that hope for the future can be embodied in children. Of her son John,

Brittain notes:

> Whenever he played the Beethoven Violin Concerto [on the gramophone] he brought back the ghost of Edward, whom in a dark emphatic fashion he strongly resembled. The rough Norfolk jacket, brown eyes, black eyebrows, and slight stoop of the shoulders [...] carried me to the distant past in which Edward for me was never a soldier, but a tweed-coated musician permanently aged sixteen. (p. 324)

This is a very different presentation of the workings of memory to that contained in *Testament of Youth*. There, looking back and reconstructing a narrative of the past becomes a way of giving past events some meaning. Here, the past emerges into the present. The figure of John simultaneously provides a means of looking forward, because he belongs to the next generation, and is a means of conjuring the ghost of Edward and of the past. He stands as a proxy for Edward, but Brittain herself seems to realize that the match can never be a precise one. Her son is playing records on the gramophone, rather than playing the violin as Edward did, and preserving this image is an acknowledgement that John will grow and change. Here too Brittain points to the ultimately personal nature of her loss. In her writings, Edward is commemorated as a soldier, whilst in her memory he remains a schoolboy. This is a reverse of what happens in, for example, *Honourable Estate*, in which different courses of action are played out by attributing them to different characters. Here, as in *Born 1925*, the hopes of the previous generation are collapsed into those of the succeeding one.

Brittain's faith in writing as a means of catharsis is therefore belied by the proliferation of alternative and more satisfactory models of mourning shown in the fiction, models which rely not only on the assimilation of her own testamentary archive but on the closure effected by others. An incident such as the description in *Testament of Youth* of the return of Leighton's uniform, combining as it does an eye-witness account and later reflections, seems also to combine authenticity and immediacy with assimilation and understanding. In fact the disjunction between memory and understanding is shown up. The uniform retains its status as an unassimilable remainder and the retranscription of the contemporary account only underlines the sense that Brittain can get no further in her understanding of it. What is also played out here is a clash between two aspects of the writing process that are identified in *On Becoming a Writer*. There, Brittain sees the writer as equally, if not more, important than the historian in preserving traces of the generation to which he (sic) belongs: 'His work must tell generations to come of the hopes, fears, griefs and loves of the ordinary men and women whom he has studied and knows. He is the recorder of their experiences, the instrument of their immortality' (*On Becoming*, p. 34). Brittain indeed gives her friends the status not just of examples, but of exemplars, worthy indeed of 'immortality'. However, at the end of the text, a much more personal aspect of writing is described. Even if one remains relatively obscure, the process of writing itself can provide fulfilment, she suggests:

> You recall those radiant moments, having nothing to do with money or success, which come with the sudden enlarging of your consciousness, and the breathless capture of the right word in which to convey your illumination to others. Because of those brief intervals of strange glory, in which perhaps you did for once create something first-rate, you realise that if you could re-live your life and be presented with the same series of alternatives, you would make exactly the same choices all over again. (Brittain, *On Becoming*, pp. 200–1)

Work and life are oddly conflated here: small moments of perfect expression or insight can be reward enough, even if one's success is not as great as one might have hoped. The work in effect becomes a compensation for the deficiencies of the life. Perhaps this is the root of many of the difficulties which present themselves when Brittain's work is examined, either as 'women's writing' or as wartime testimony. The constant self-reflection, rewriting and memorialization give a new twist to the notion of 'life's work'. It becomes impossible to approach one without the other but the boundaries between the two seem to refuse to remain stable. Moreover, the proliferation of autobiographical content, which could point to some stable sense of self on the part of the author, is, on closer examination, riven by uncertainties.

2
Virginia Woolf between the Wars

In her 1932 study of Virginia Woolf's writing, Winifred Holtby notes a preoccupation with the First World War and its aftermath on Woolf's part. 'She has given little direct indication of its effect upon her, but into almost all the work she wrote after 1919 she introduces some reference to it, as though its memory were the scar of an old wound she could not hide' (Holtby, p. 82).[1] Earlier, however, Holtby suggests that because Woolf was ill for much of its duration, '[t]he war passed over her' (p. 34). The contradictory nature of these statements is striking; according to Holtby, despite the fact that 'the war passed over' Woolf, it wounded and scarred her. What Holtby seems to be attempting to acknowledge is that the impact of the war on Woolf was an indirect one, which could be accessed only in mediated ways in her writing, and only after a lapse of time; she also seems to allow that one who is not a combatant can indeed be wounded. Woolf, in this analysis, is a survivor who deals not in the action of the war but in 'its effects' (Holtby, p. 83); it is the *memory* of the war that is like a scar. Holtby ultimately seems unsure of quite how to describe Woolf's relationship to the First World War: is she a victim, a survivor, or merely a commentator?

Holtby's uncertainty here is striking not least because the debate about Woolf's attitude to both wars, and specifically her involvement (or lack of involvement) in politics and the anti-war movement in the 1930s, has not gone away. Woolf's position cannot be neatly categorized, and as Phyllis Lassner has commented, discussing Woolf's Second World War writing, 'we owe it to Woolf to understand her responses [...] as not only theoretical and polemical but as personal and ambivalent' (pp. 29–30). In what follows, I will not attempt to smooth over the ambiguities of Woolf's position but rather to show how these might yield meaning. As Jacqueline Rose has noted (echoing Holtby), 'the whole of [Woolf's] writing life passes across the two world wars' ('Virginia Woolf', p. 8). I intend to examine how Woolf dealt with both the aftermath of one war, and, centrally in this chapter, the approach, and outbreak, of another, whilst acknowledging that, in her analysis (as in Brittain's), the two were not always clearly separated from each other. Woolf was not alone in predicting that the second war would involve a repetition and intensification of the dangers of the first;[2] as David Cannadine has noted, by the 1940s, 'the two wars were [widely] seen as different episodes in the same conflict' (p. 233).[3] However, a third conflict, the Spanish Civil War, was also important to Woolf both in its political implications and for personal reasons. Woolf's memoir of her nephew Julian Bell, who was killed while serving as an ambulance driver in Spain, is not only an elegy for a young man of whom she has personal fond memories. It can also be placed alongside *Three Guineas* (1938), as it is in many respects a case study of the deleterious effects which a particular (patriarchal) educational and social system could have even on an individual from a supposedly 'civilized' or progressive background.

In this chapter, as well as the memoir of Bell, which was written immediately after his death in July 1937, I will be examining two other examples of life-writing produced by Woolf as the Second World War approached: her biography of Roger Fry and the autobiographical piece 'A Sketch of the Past'. *Roger Fry* (1940) and 'A Sketch' (1939–40) present strongly contrasting models of life-writing; in both, however, Woolf not only reflects in a self-conscious fashion on the task she is undertaking, but also considers the impact of war on the creative artist. Woolf's experiences of war, loss and trauma were very different from, for example, Vera Brittain's, as was her aesthetic. Reading *Testament of Youth*, Woolf commented that it was, 'A very good book of its sort. The new sort, the hard anguished sort, that the young write; that I could never write. [...] Why now? What urgency is there on them to stand bare in public?' (*Diary IV*, p. 177). Woolf is here making a differentiation not just in terms of content (she could not write that book because she has not had those experiences) but also in terms of its implications for the relationship between reader and writer (she could not write that book because it would involve standing 'bare in public'). I am concerned to consider not only Woolf's attitude towards such self-exposure, but also the tension between the difficulty of looking back and the impossibility of looking forward. In the mid- and late-1930s, Woolf uses life-writing to deal not only with the continuing aftermath of the 1914–18 conflict, and with the loss of Bell in Spain, but in an attempt to protect herself against the reopening of wounds which seems inevitable by the end of the decade.

War, death and mourning

Considering the relationship between the emergence of modernism during the First World War, particularly as exemplified by *The Voyage Out* (1915), and Freud's wartime writings on the conflict, Jacqueline Rose identifies certain differences between Freud's and Woolf's atti-tudes to death and mourning. These differences, she suggests, char-acterize how death is considered in modernist writing, although the effects of gender have also to be taken into account. Citing Freud's comments in 'On Transience' (1917), that 'the riches of civilization' can still be valued, even after their 'fragility' has been exposed in war, Rose argues that, 'Leonard and Virginia Woolf, and their famous group, did not believe in "civilization" any more indeed than in his better moments, many commentators would insist, did Freud' ('Virginia Woolf', p. 7). For Woolf in particular, the notion of going to war to preserve civilization exposes the contradictory nature and violent basis of that civilization. Specifically, in the 1930s, the prospect of (patriarchal) society heading towards self-destruction, which, on one level, she might be expected to welcome, is troubling because that society seems likely to be superseded only by a more extreme version of itself. This is the imperative that underlies *Three Guineas*. As Sharon Oudit suggests, Woolf's 'vision of the world that led to, and recovered from, the catastrophe of the First World War is fragmented, multiple-visioned, detached, ironic [...] fuelled [...] by the desire to expose the series of false constructs and dangerous values that produced one war and that underpinned the same social system that was heading relentlessly towards another' (pp. 169–70).

The Freudian model of mourning, involving working-through and a return to an earlier equilibrium, is also, in Rose's view, rejected by the modernist project. For Rose, Woolf's attitude to death and its aftermath is formed by personal experience and compounded by the events of 1914–18: 'Private and public trauma, death for Virginia Woolf is, one could say, more than elegy, more than mourning [...] it is something through the eyes of which [...] she *sees'* ('Virginia Woolf', pp. 8–9, emphasis in original). I will argue that war becomes the nexus of this private and public trauma in Woolf's writing through the 1920s and 1930s, particularly insofar as death is what it either brings in its wake or heralds. This is not to say that the prevalence of loss of life in war is simply an intensification of personal, peacetime losses. Not only is the manner of death in war quite different – violent, random and mechanized – but its meaning is also complex. With regard to the First World War in particular, this seemed to be a kind of death that non-combatant women would be unlikely to suffer or to witness directly,[4] but these losses were nevertheless being sustained for the salvation of a society and for principles in which Woolf for one had little faith. Woolf's letters and diaries give the lie to Holtby's impression that she remained completely detached from the events of the war. Ouditt has noted that one comment in particular, from a letter Woolf wrote to Margaret Llewelyn Davies in January 1916, can be seen to illustrate the estrangement Woolf experienced during the conflict: 'I become steadily more feminist owing to The Times, which I read at breakfast and wonder how this preposterous masculine fiction keeps going a day longer' (Woolf, *Question*, p. 76). Ouditt is keen to point out that Woolf is not referring to the war itself as a 'masculine fiction' but rather to the way it is presented and indeed promulgated in the newspaper. This attitude resurfaces in Woolf's use of men's self-presentation in newspapers as damning evidence for the prosecution in *Three Guineas*. The gender divide here is not an absolute one, of course; Woolf's letters and diaries from the war years also detail the struggles of both Leonard Woolf and various of their friends to register as non-combatants or conscientious objectors.[5] Although Woolf's non-fiction is my main focus here, it is relevant to consider certain continuities of theme between these writings and her fiction. An awareness of the complexities of masculine attitudes towards war is also evident in her novels, especially in the portrayal of the shell-shocked Septimus Smith in *Mrs Dalloway* (1925).

Karen De Meester has suggested that Woolf intends Septimus Smith's and Clarissa Dalloway's experiences to show different ways of dealing with a similar problem, '[f]or Clarissa is a trauma survivor herself' (p. 663). De Meester here refers to the fact that Clarissa has witnessed the death of her sister, and this opening up of the category of trauma is consonant with De Meester's description of the shell-shocked soldier as the 'ultimate paradigm of the trauma survivor and hence modernist man' (p. 652). Although I would to an extent agree that '[i]nstead of presenting in Clarissa a positive alternative to Septimus's failure to recover from his war trauma, Woolf presents another inappropriate method of dealing with trauma' (De Meester, p. 663), it is wrong to view the two characters solely as different varieties of victim, not least because Clarissa ultimately survives both the trauma of her sister's death and the war, which has very different consequences for her than it does for Septimus. So far as De Meester's parallel between the shell-shocked soldier and modernist man is concerned, then, it is important that such a comparison does not blind us to the particularities of cause and effect. That much modernist writing displays the fragmentation, confusion and dismay of the discourse of shell shock is as much a testament to the power of that discourse as it is to the ability of modernist writers to identify with it.[6]

Hermione Lee has pointed out that, 'Though almost all [Woolf's] novels are dominated by a death, in almost all the death is not written in' (qtd in Rose, 'Virginia Woolf', p. 8). Death itself is resistant to representation; deaths are reported indirectly rather than narrated directly. This is not simply an evasion on Woolf's part; rather it is a means of acknowledging that the corollary of death is survival, a task which, in Woolf's novels of the 1920s, often falls to women. Woolf is not implying that surviving a war as a bystander or observer is directly comparable with taking active part in it and risking or succumbing to death; more relevant is the powerlessness the survivor experiences. In this respect, the climax of *Jacob's Room* (which echoes Brittain, faced with Leighton's 'remains') is telling. ' "Such confusion everywhere!" exclaimed Betty Flanders [...] "What am I to do with these, Mr Bonamy?" She held out a pair of Jacob's shoes' (p. 176). A woman, specifically a mother, is left to make sense of this confusion. In *Mrs Dalloway*, having witnessed the death of Evans, and haunted by the fragmented memories of his impotence in the face of this event, the only means for Septimus to regain a sense of agency is to take his own life. In contrast to Jacob, Septimus does not die 'offstage', although Woolf has to pull away from the articulation of his thoughts at the very moment of his death:

> He did not want to die. Life was good. The sun hot. Only human beings? Coming down the staircase opposite an old man stopped and stared at him. Holmes was at the door. "I'll give it you!" he cried, and flung himself vigorously, violently down on to Mrs Filmer's area railings. (*Mrs Dalloway*, p. 164)

The words 'vigorously, violently', together with the contrast between the staccato syntax of Septimus's reflections and the longer final sentence here mark the point at which identification with Septimus, on the part of narrator and reader, have to halt.[7] Immediately, though, Dr Holmes's simplistic condemnation of Septimus as a 'coward!' (Woolf, *Mrs Dalloway*, p. 164) forces the reader to consider the complexity of the causes that have brought Septimus to this point. Holmes wishes to shut down the possibility for any more nuanced interpretation of Septimus's actions. In *To the Lighthouse* (1927) Woolf uses the euphemistic language of journalism as another means of indicating how the nature of war, and specifically, the nature of death in war, can be mediated and masked: '[A shell exploded. Twenty or thirty young men were blown up in France, among them Andrew Ramsay, whose death, mercifully, was instantaneous.]' (p. 207). In this novel, Woolf does not counter this 'masculine fiction' of the 'mercifully instantaneous' death with anything more accurate; after Bell's death, as I will show, she is in a position to hear a fuller account, but does not find this a consolation for the fact that her nephew was among those who ' "Gave their lives" as they call it' (Woolf, *Diary V*, p. 108).

Woolf's rejection of the compensatory Freudian model of mourning, coupled with her scepticism towards the notion of the 'just' or necessary war, could have left her stranded in a position of hopelessness and powerlessness during the 1930s. Instead, Woolf uses writing as a means carving out an alternative position for herself. One manifestation of this is the 'Society of Outsiders', suggested in *Three Guineas* as a means of countering the kinds of political campaigning from which Woolf was feeling increasingly distanced. In relation, more specifically, to the issue of death and mourning, Woolf's biographical and autobiographical life-writing is important. Writing the lives of Julian Bell and Roger Fry is not only a means of attempting to preserve some impressions of lives that have now ended; it also, particularly in the case of Bell, functions as a means of assessing the impact of the loss on her own life, in a way that is not possible in *Three Guineas*. Acknowledging the difficulty of adopting the position of an objective narrator is not evidence of simple ego-centricity on Woolf's part; rather it illustrates Woolf's rejection of more generalized compensatory narratives. Conversely, much of the ostensibly autobiographical piece 'A Sketch of the Past' involves discussion not of Woolf's own experiences, but of the impact of others on her personal history. Writing is the means by which Woolf attempts to gauge this impact, but what is also revealed in 'A Sketch' is the impossibility of analysing the past in isolation from the present. When political events in the present seem to herald destruction, the desire to assert an understanding of cause and effect within her own life story becomes all the more pressing.

The death of Julian Bell

'Mrs Ramsay dead; Andrew killed; Prue dead too' (Woolf, *To the Lighthouse*, p. 227). In view of the juxtaposition of these deaths, a parallel that Woolf draws at the time of Julian Bell's death in July 1937 is striking:

> When Roger died I noticed: & blamed myself: yet it was a great relief I think. Here there was no relief. An incredible suffering – to watch it – an accident, & someone bleeding. Then I thought the death of a child is childbirth again; sitting there listening. (*Diary V*, p. 104)

Julian's death is like his birth, for Woolf, because of how she herself is positioned in relation to it; she is an outsider, an impotent observer who can only watch or listen. Yet the phrase 'an accident, & someone bleeding' is also significant in that it transforms the witnessing of her sister's grief into an echo of witnessing the death itself. The news of the death has the impact of an accident, which, like childbirth, has to be suffered, essentially, by the mother alone, and this impact is compounded by the fact that, like Andrew Ramsay, Bell does not simply die: he is killed. In October 1937 Woolf compares her feelings to those she had after the death of her brother Thoby: 'It is an unnatural death, his [Bell's]. I cant make it fit in anywhere. Perhaps because he was killed, violently. I can do nothing with the experience yet. It seems still emptiness: the sight of Nessa bleeding: how we watch: nothing to be done' (*Diary V*, p. 113). Here, as in the earlier entry, despite feeling the loss of Bell keenly, Woolf positions herself as an empathic witness to the grief of his more immediate family, particularly Vanessa Bell. A principal means of accessing or understanding his death is through their reaction to it, although, Woolf had already, by the time of these diary entries, attempted to materialize her loss through the production of her memoir of Bell. This becomes a means of both preserving her memories of him and attempting to analyse the forces that led him to go to war.

The memoir of Bell was written within days of his death. Woolf comments near the start, 'I am so composed that nothing is real unless I write it' ('Virginia Woolf', p. 255). This statement could apply either to the fact of Bell's death, or to his life (which is, after all, what she is writing); it also suggests that the 'real' resides in writing rather than in experience as such, a notion that appears particularly suited to the description of traumatic events. Woolf asserts that it is important to her to preserve some record of Bell's 'actual personal presence' ('Virginia Woolf', p. 255). In this respect, the memoir stands as an immediate memorial, a means of gathering together and retaining her impressions of his physical being, and an attempt to give his life, if not his death, some meaning. Woolf claims: '[S]ubconsciously I was sure he would be killed; that is I had a couchant unexpressed certainty, from Thoby's death I think' ('Virginia Woolf', p. 256). In the light of this comment, the memoir is a retrospective means of preserving what she knew (subconsciously) would be her final encounters with him. The piece is also shot through, as Lee notes, with the anger Woolf felt towards Bell 'for what seemed to her the wastefulness of his death' (*Virginia Woolf*, p. 699). In particular, Woolf considers Bell to have displayed a lack of consideration towards his mother in placing his life at risk, despite the partial concession he made by going to Spain as an ambulance driver rather than a soldier.[8] She asks: 'What made him feel it necessary, knowing as he did how it must torture Nessa [...]?' (Woolf, 'Virginia Woolf', p. 258) His decision to go may have been made in the light of his own principles, but for Vanessa Bell and for Woolf herself, the cause cannot justify the sacrifice. Woolf does attempt to gain some comfort from Bell's own determination to act on his convictions; in a letter of 26 July 1937, she comments: '[I]t had become necessary for him to go; and there is a kind of grandeur in that which somehow now and then consoles one' (Woolf, *Leave*, p. 150). But this consolation is immediately undercut in the next sentence: 'Only – to see what [Vanessa] has to suffer makes one doubt if anything in the world is worth it' (Woolf, *Leave*, p. 150). Woolf here rejects the consolation, albeit a chimerical one, that Brittain, for example, falls back on. Brittain, and indeed Mrs Leighton, manage to separate out the nobility of the ideals in which Leighton believed, and to which he was educated, from the brutal conflict in which he lost his life. Such doublethink is inimical to Woolf. Her attitude might be seen as displaying a greater awareness of political realities, but it does not make the death itself any easier to conceptualize.[9]

As Michele Barrett has noted, 'Woolf's writing of [*Three Guineas*] had, literally, been interrupted by her nephew's death' (p. xxxix). A month before Bell's death, Woolf notes in her diary that she is 'at work on the Second Guinea' (*Diary V*, p. 100) and the bulk of the final part, which deals most directly with war and belligerence, was written up in August and September 1937. Woolf herself commented of the essay, in a letter to Vanessa from August 1937, 'I'm always wanting to argue it with Julian – in fact I wrote it as an argument with him' (*Leave*, p. 159). This implies a vision of *Three Guineas* as a conversation between the generations and between the sexes, characteristics it shares with *The Years* (1937). Bell's death is both a personal loss and a signal of the particular kinds of failure of post-First World War society. In the novels of the 1920s these failures are already implicit: in *Three Guineas* they are placed in the foreground, with particular attention being paid to the persisting rhetoric of war. Woolf expresses the conviction that to go to war can never be an appropriate solution to a political or social problem; the means will never justify the end: 'Obviously there is for you [men] some glory, some necessity, some satisfaction in fighting which we [women] have never felt or enjoyed' (*Three Guineas*, p. 14). In this regard, the decision of young men such as Bell to support the war in Spain in defence of a particular set of ideals is doomed to failure because it will necessarily involve the imposition of those ideals by brute force. Bell's own reasons for supporting the war should, however, be considered. In an open letter to E.M. Forster, composed in January 1937 on the journey back to England from China, where he had been working as a university lecturer, Bell states clearly that he knows 'the pleasure and value of a peaceful civilisation' ('War and Peace', p. 337). Nevertheless, he has come to a belief that an approach to international relations, based on, for instance, a strengthened League of Nations, displays 'deliberate ostrich ignorance' (Bell, 'War and Peace', p. 338) of the need to 'choose war, not peace' (Bell, 'War and Peace', p. 337). Bell goes on to argue in favour of 'beneficient engineering socialism' ('War and Peace', p. 354), suggesting that, with the failure of post-1918 restructuring measures in Europe, and '[w]ith three great powers in the hands of murderers and gangsters' ('War and Peace', p. 357) war must be resorted to. He also offers a critique of varieties of pacifism, suggesting that many such attitudes boil down to squeamishness: 'I think the militarists are right in insisting on men being disciplined, "blooded" and inured to horror' (Bell, 'War and Peace', p. 365), and he does not shrink from 'the comparative barbarism of a socialist society' (Bell,'War and Peace', p. 387), seeing this, like war, as a necessary evil. Finally, Bell reflects that his experiences in China have led him to be sceptical about the allegedly civilized qualities of the west:

> Nor is it strange that the foundation of European literature should be the "Iliad." For in a sense hardly any Europeans have ever been civilised, the Greeks least of all. [...] I do not feel that the attitude to which I would persuade my fellows is cut off from "civilisation" in the common European meaning [...]: it is an attitude opposed to the contemplative and reflective virtues. ('War and Peace', p. 389)

This scepticism about the value of civilization is also a concern of Woolf's, as I have indicated, although Bell's own solution is inimical to her own.

Responding to Bell's letter when it was published in 1938, Forster himself was not slow to identify its shortcomings. Bell, he suggests, 'had a vigorous mind, and had been brought up in Cambridge and places where they argue, so it came natural to him to pop in a bunch of reasons. [...] [S]till, it does seem to me that as a reasoned exposition the letter is all over the shop' (Forster, p. 391). Woolf had seen Bell's letter before its publication. In her diary for September 1937 she notes that she has been 'reading, how strangely – to hear his voice so clear from the other side of the grave – Julian on War' (Woolf, *Diary V*, p. 110). In the manuscript of the memoir, to a greater extent than in the shortened, published version, she, like Forster, notes the effects of 'Cambridge' on Bell. If not always explicitly negative, her comments in this regard tend to emphasize a sense of estrangement from her nephew. At one point, attempting to express the differences in attitude between them, she comments, 'He was very Cambridge. He would wrinkle up his face in a very queer way, the Cambridge way' (Woolf, 'A Memoir', p. 3). Later, 'Cambridge' more explicitly stands for a gulf both of age and of gender. Describing a minor difference of opinion, she explains: 'I had again the feeling that he resented a woman's interfering with his plans. [...] An odd feeling. Half that I was a woman, and older, and would not stand for rudeness from him. [...] Damned Cambridge insolence I said to myself' (Woolf, 'A Memoir', pp. 6–7). Here, as in *Three Guineas*, and indeed *Jacob's Room*, there is an allusion to the power of the university as an institution to instil a self-confidence not necessarily matched by the consistency of one's argument, as much as to foster particular attitudes to women or to politics.[10]

It should be noted that Bell was a campaigning pacifist for a time while at Cambridge. As Tom Buchanan notes, however, many of those who began the 1930s as pacifists found that:

> the Civil War forced them to modify their pacifism and to accept that war was a valid response to aggression in certain circumstances. The change was particularly apparent among the young. The Duchess of Atholl [a campaigner on behalf of the Republican cause] observed that meetings in support of the Spanish Republic were largely attended by "young men who, a year or two ago, might have supported the notorious Oxford peace resolution" [of 1933]. (p. 68)

Bell's change of heart had begun before the outbreak of war in Spain in July 1936. Invited to edit the volume *We Did Not Fight 1914–1918: Experiences of War Resisters* (1935) by David Garnett, Bell provided an introduction that is a striking contrast to the foreword written by Canon Dick Sheppard, founder of the Peace Pledge Union. Whilst Sheppard warns against 'militant pacifism' characterized by 'bitterness and violence' (p. x), Bell argues that war must be put down 'by force if necessary' (p. xix). As his biographers point out, Bell 'blurred the distinctions between war resistance and pacifism' (Stansky and Abrahams, p. 116) and came out in favour of civil conflict as a means of overturning dictatorship. Stansky and Abrahams point to Bell's 'almost obsessive interest' (p. 118) in the Irish revolutionary leader Michael Collins as one manifestation of this, but Bell's conviction that the way to prevent a global conflict was to attempt to establish a socialist government helps provide a rationale, however flawed, for his decision to go to Spain. In a letter to John Lehmann written in 1934, Bell comments, 'All my instincts make me want to be a soldier; all my intelligence is against it' (qtd in Stansky and Abrahams, p. 117); despite his upbringing in 'civilized' pacifist circles, Bell here describes the desire to fight as an irrepressible, visceral one, that intelligence cannot overcome. At the climax of *Three Guineas*, Woolf implicitly addresses such a point of view when she describes the image of the dictator: '[W]e cannot dissociate ourselves from that figure but are ourselves that figure. [...] [W]e are not passive spectators doomed to unresisting obedience but by our thoughts and actions can ourselves change that figure' (*Three Guineas*, p. 258). Woolf here demands a reimposition of intelligence over instinct, as well as an acknowledgement that the supposedly public world of war can never be kept separate from the private world of everyday life. Later, in 'Thoughts on Peace in an Air Raid'(1940), Woolf draws an explicit parallel between the instinct to fight and the instinct towards motherhood, and suggests that the even the latter could be suppressed 'for the sake of humanity' (p. 170), but underlying this startling parallel is the fact that the instinct to fight is ultimately destructive, the maternal instinct creative.[11]

In her memoir, Woolf describes the last time she saw Bell alone before his death, an incident that seems to encapsulate many of the differences between them. Woolf also returns to the question of whether Bell could have been persuaded, or indeed educated, towards a different course of action:

> I had just come in with the Evening Standard in which The Years was extravagantly praised, much to my surprise. I felt very happy [...] the bell rang. [...] [H]e came up; it was to ask for Dalton's telephone number [...] I went & looked for the number. When I came back he was reading the Standard. I had left it with the review

open. But he had turned, I think to the politics. I had half a mind
to say, Look how I'm praised. And then thought No, I'm on the
top of the wave: & it's not kind to thrust that sort of thing upon
people who aren't yet recognised. So I said nothing about it.
('Virginia Woolf', pp. 257–8)

Woolf was always extremely uneasy about how her books would be
received and her anxiety over *The Years* was particularly pronounced;
a positive review would obviously be a fillip.[12] Her decision not to
draw Bell's attention to it is overlaid with a sense of guilt, to which
she has already alluded, at not having encouraged him enough: 'This
is the one thing I regret in our relationship: that I might have
encouraged him more as a writer' ('Virginia Woolf', p. 256).[13] Woolf
blames this omission on the fact that at the time when he was starting to write her own attitude towards art had turned towards 'hating
"personality"; desiring anonymity' ('Virginia Woolf', p. 257). That
Bell turns from the book reviews to the political reports is thus a
reminder to Woolf that she might have been a greater support to her
nephew, could have helped him to choose art rather than politics, or
at least have been more explicit in passing on her scepticism about
the 'masculine fiction' to which he is drawn. Bell's own account of
his attitudes makes it clear that he had long passed the position of
believing that an intellectual or artistic struggle could be adequate.
The edition of the *Evening Standard* containing praise of *The Years* as
well as reports of the Spanish Civil War does not simply stand for a
gendered split between art and politics, however. The newspaper is
able to encompass both, offering, perhaps, a sign that there is the
possibility, and the need, for an interchange between the two.

In *Three Guineas*, Woolf alludes to another means by which events
in Spain were communicated to the British public. The civil war
intrudes into the text in her description of photographs sent out
'with patient pertinacity about twice a week' (*Three Guineas*, p. 20) by
the Spanish government. Elena Gualtieri notes that although no
such photographs survive among Woolf's papers, Woolf does mention, in a letter to Bell from November 1936, receiving 'a packet of
photographs from Spain all of dead children, killed by bombs' (qtd,
Gualtieri, '*Three Guineas*', p. 167). Indeed, in the rest of this letter,
Woolf is rather more specific in attributing these deaths to masculine
aggression, if only by her use of juxtaposition: 'Lord Cecil [President
of the League of Nations Union] is coming to tea, to talk about Spain

I think. He [...] is a nice man – there are many nice men; why are men in the mass so detestable? This morning I got a packet of photographs from Spain all of dead children, killed by bombs – a cheerful present' (*Leave*, p. 85). Gualtieri, who notes that Woolf began writing *Three Guineas* shortly after receiving these photographs, describes the likely provenance, and reproduces examples, of those Woolf might have been sent as part of a propaganda campaign by the Spanish Communist Party. Patricia Laurence, pointing out that *The Times* newspaper featured photographs of the civilian impact of the conflict during the winter of 1936–7, suggests that these might be the originals of the 'dead bodies' and 'ruined houses' (Woolf, *Three Guineas*, p. 126) referred to in *Three Guineas*. Woolf chooses not to reproduce these photographs, perhaps presuming their familiarity to her contemporary readers, but also allowing them to take on a symbolic role in the text.[14] She acknowledges that 'those photographs, are not an argument; they are simply a crude statement of fact addressed to the eye' (Woolf, *Three Guineas*, p. 21), alluding to their visceral communicative power. By not including the photographs, Woolf avoids the a-rational or purely 'shocked' reaction which contemplation of the images might provoke in the reader, but instead uses references to them as a reminder of how the horrors of war can come to be quotidian, their initial shock blunted. Elena Gualtieri suggests that Woolf makes the reader aware that 'the more powerful [...] the impact of the photographs, the less effective language becomes in conveying it', and connects this to the 'failure of language [...] when faced with the enormity and monstrosity of war' ('*Three Guineas*', p. 173). The photograph is a means, however brutal, of representing death in a way that language could not. Laurence suggests that the images of the dead Spanish children prefigure Bell's death (p. 234); the memoir can therefore be seen as an attempt to counter these images of death with images of his life. This suggestion is supported by the fact that the manuscript of the memoir culminates with Woolf describing a number of miscellaneous visual memories of Bell, which she likens to snapshots.

In this regard, and indeed as a further echo of Brittain's experience, the following diary entry from August 1937 is notable:

[O]ne must act. In London yesterday, I began: & saw Dr Hart & Archie Cochran [who had been with Bell in Spain] about Julian.

Rather a physical distress than mental; about his wounds: as if one felt them bodily. Nothing new: only that he was conscious when they got him to hospital, & anxious to explain that the road was dangerous: then anxious to get on with the operation. He became unconscious, talked in French about military things apparently ... & died 4 hours later. Why do I set this down? It belongs to what is unreal now. What is left that is real? Angelica in a yellow hand-kerchief picking dahlias for the flower show (Woolf, *Diary V*, pp. 108–9).

If Woolf, like Brittain earlier, is attempting here to gain greater understanding of a death through the acquisition of factual infor-mation, she is under no illusions about the efficacy of this as a tac-tic. Woolf states that she has learned '[n]othing new', only to recount a number of details which evidently were unknown to her, implying perhaps that this knowledge could yield no new understanding of the events described. Consigning these events, or perhaps even Bell's death, to the 'unreal' seems an admission of the failure of writing to give reality to them, but her turn to the image of Angelica is a further reminder that one important function of the memoir of Bell was to preserve similar images of him as a child and therefore to focus on him living rather than dead. This is especially important because his own physical presence can no longer guarantee or supplement her memories. The image of Angelica, inconsequential and innocent, is also a contrast to the effect on Woolf of the description of Bell's injuries, which impacts at a visceral rather than rational level. The phrase 'as if one felt them bodily' seems, in this context, not so much to indicate identification with Bell's suffering on Woolf's part, but to increase her sense of divorcement from it. These bodily shocks have a numbing effect which language is only partially able to alleviate and for which it cannot compensate.

Roger Fry: writing lives

Once *Three Guineas* was completed in early 1938, Woolf began work in earnest on her biography of *Roger Fry*, which had hitherto been fit-ted into 'the crannies of other writing' (Woolf, *Leave*, p. 9). In March 1939, she notes in her diary that she has 'set the last word to the first sketch of Roger. And now I have to begin [...] to revise & revise'

(*Diary V*, p. 207). In April, she starts 'A Sketch of the Past', commenting that she is 'sick of writing Roger's life' (Woolf, *Moments*, p. 64). Like the memoir of Bell, then 'A Sketch' was not written with a view to immediate publication; like the memoir, it was written alongside other, 'official' projects. The informal structure of 'A Sketch' contrasts strongly with the marshalling of source material required by *Roger Fry*, but both, in different ways, encompass the impact of war, as well as allowing Woolf to reflect on the process of life-writing. Whilst in the Bell memoir Woolf both records her own memories and attempts to explain Bell's attitudes, relying in each case principally on her own experiences and contact with Bell, such subjectivity is complicated in the case of *Roger Fry*. Woolf has to 'make a life out of Six Cardboard boxes full of tailor's bills love letters and old postcards' (*Leave*, p. 374), and she might have reflected ruefully on the blithe treatment of the factual in the mock-biography *Orlando* (1928):

> Just when we thought to elucidate a secret that has puzzled historians for a hundred years, there was a hole in the manuscript big enough to put your finger through. We have done our best to piece out a meagre summary from the charred fragments that remain; but often it has been necessary to speculate, to surmise, and even to use the imagination. (p. 110)

The paucity of documentary evidence notwithstanding, the narrator goes on to describe in detail Orlando's daily routine: 'About seven, he would rise, wrap himself in a long Turkish cloak, light a cheroot, and lean his elbows on the parapet' (p. 111). In contrast, in June 1937, Woolf wrote to Janet Case, 'I'm looking at boxes of Roger Fry's letters and wondering how anyone writes a real life. An imaginary one wouldn't so much bother me. But oh, the dates, the quotations!' (*Leave*, p. 135). It might seem surprising that Woolf despairs of facts, in view of the raw material which is corralled in *Three Guineas*. Perhaps the difference is that in that instance, she was able to pick and choose the evidence which would best reflect and support her argument, creating the necessary illusion that the argument had been waiting there to be discovered. *Roger Fry* presents an opposite problem: a man's life can never simply be the sum of factual knowledge about him. Recording in her diary Marjorie Strachey's suggestion that Fry had 'no life that can be written', Woolf decides, 'I will

go on doggedly till I meet him myself – 1909 – & then attempt something more fictitious' (*Diary V*, p. 155). This seems a paradox: at the
point at which her own testimony would come into play, the fictitious will be introduced; however, it could be an acknowledgement
that Woolf has to write not only as a witness to Fry's life, but also as
a writer. She cannot pretend to be simply a neutral observer or a hack
hired to process the raw material into something suitable. The point
being made here is about her own practice and about her attitude
towards biography: that the truth cannot lie in evidence alone, however much that evidence proliferates. As Woolf reflected in the 1939
essay 'The Art of Biography' the biographer's 'sense of truth must be
alive and on tiptoe. [...] [H]e must be prepared to admit contradictory versions of the same face' (pp. 149–50).

The biography deals with these problems in part by foregrounding
them. Discussing Fry's criticism of the 1890s, for example, Woolf
notes: 'The muddle in which these old newspaper cuttings lie is perhaps symbolical – they are mixed up with passports, with hotel bills,
with sketches and poems and innumerable notes' (*Roger Fry*, p. 116),
placing the reader, momentarily, in the position of the researcher.
Later she comments of Fry's study of Cezanne that 'Like most
books that appear seamless and complete, [it] cost its author much
drudgery and despair' (Woolf, *Roger Fry*, p. 286). This reminds the
reader that any published piece of writing is shored up by practicalities and raw materials, and is a further muted expression of the kinds
of sentiments that Woolf made more explicitly in her letters to
friends. Similarly, in the opening chapter, Woolf introduces a range
of specifically biographical and autobiographical source materials
which she places in dialogue with each other and which serve as a
further testament to the complexity of her task. She begins with an
extract from Fry's own memoir, which is then supplemented by his
father's, but the most striking example of unconventional life-
writing cited here is Fry's mother's attempt at autobiography, 'a list
of "Things that were not -: Things that were: when I was a little
child." [...] Among the things that were not, she counted lucifer
matches; hot-water bottles; night-lights; Christmas trees [...] Among
the things that were, she counted flint and steel; rushlights; prunes
and senna [...] snuff-boxes and Chartists' (Woolf, *Roger Fry*, p. 17).
This citation compounds the impression of this early part of *Roger Fry*
as an implicit exploration of both biographical and autobiographical

life-writing as a practice, and makes it less surprising that Woolf was composing a memoir of her own around this time.

Anna Snaith points to a different example of how Woolf might have been influenced in her own practice by her exploration of Fry's life and work. She suggests that Woolf's description in the biography of Fry's life during the First World War shows her working through her own possibilities for sustaining creative work during the conflict which began while she was still working on the text: 'Woolf elaborates on Fry's division of his life into "the hurried and distracted life" and "the still life" [...] In noting Fry's success at dealing with the First World War, Woolf reinforces her own similar strategy' (Snaith, pp. 141–2). This notion of using Fry as an example of how the artistic life might be maintained goes hand in hand with the actual construction of the text serving, during the Czechoslovakian crisis of 1938, as 'a help [...] in this welter of unreality' (Woolf, *Diary V*, p. 167). The stylistic change that occurs in the wartime section of the text is also notable. In an amalgamation of fragments from Fry's letters and other accounts of the period, Woolf creates the impression of a life being lived day to day in a kind of suspense. This effect is compounded by the fact that, because of the use of quotations from the letters, large portions of the text at this point are written in the present tense: 'Back in England he finds the Omega languishing. Can it be revived by "doing hats and dresses as being things which people must have quand même"? No sooner is that scheme set on foot than air raids begin' (*Roger Fry*, p. 203). The war cannot be conceived as simply a contingency, a backdrop against which life must continue as usual. The danger in describing Fry's war years in this way is that they could seem to be simply a caesura, after which pre-war life will be resumed. The climax of this chapter strikes a note of optimism: 'Whatever the theory, whatever the connection between the rhythms of life and of art, there could be no doubt about the sensation – he had survived the war' (Woolf, *Roger Fry*, p. 215); but neither life nor art can be immune to the war's after effects.

If, as Snaith suggests, Woolf sought in Fry a model of how her own artistic life might be sustained during wartime, there are two factors which should be borne in mind. One is Holtby's suggestion that Woolf bore the scar of the First World War, despite its having 'passed over' her, that is, although her own present experience of war undoubtedly must have affected her portrayal of Fry's earlier experiences, she too lived through the earlier conflict. As Karen L. Levenback notes, throughout the 1930s, 'distinct echoes, conscious memories, and secondary remembrance from the Great War were blurring her daily experience, her reading and her writing' (p. 144). But there is also the fact that in reconstructing Fry's war she reconstructs it as a completed, past event. It cannot simply be a case, for her, of imitating his earlier strategy of survival, not only because of changed historical and political circumstances (and the increased danger of invasion, the earlier commencement of aerial bombardment and so on),[15] but because the current conflict is, precisely, current. The pattern, or strategy for coping that is discovered in her account of Fry's war is a retrospective one, and one which is to an extent belied by her own earlier experiences. The question remains then, of how to maintain a perspective on current threats. This is one function of 'A Sketch of the Past'.

'A Sketch of the Past' and the dangers of the present

In her diary, Woolf described *Three Guineas* as 'autobiography in public' (*Diary V*, p. 141), provoking the question of what might constitute 'autobiography in private'. 'A Sketch', unpublished at the time of Woolf's death, might seem to fit into this latter category. However, as Linda Anderson argues, issues of gender also enter the equation: 'For Woolf the question of a life and its written form – whether in biography, autobiography or fiction – were inseparable and often made her blur the boundaries of genre, disputing the authority enshrined in masculine convention' (*Women*, p. 47). Sidonie Smith also identifies such conventions as the structuring of the life around patriarchal lineage or career development as problematic for Woolf (p. 84). What is at stake is both a challenge to formal distinctions of genre, and a specifically gendered development of the self. This is not only apparent in, for example, Woolf's meditations on her early feelings towards her mother: she also returns to the issues that were of concern in *Three Guineas*. What are the effects on the individual of formal education or the lack of it? What challenges might the oncoming war present to the individual in society? Like *Roger Fry*, 'A Sketch' does not present a thorough-going theorization of life-writing, but reflecting in a self-conscious fashion on what she is producing is nevertheless an important part of the task for Woolf.

She begins by asserting that she will not attempt to enumerate the 'merits and faults' of 'the number of different ways in which memoirs can be written' (Woolf, *Moments*, p. 64) but will, rather, allow her memories to find their own form. This desire to proceed immediately without setting up any over-arching framework for the piece is, in part at least, a result of the fact that 'A Sketch' is initially written in time borrowed (or stolen) from *Roger Fry*. The memoir frees her from the formal strictures of the other project and Woolf is therefore constructing an antitype to *Roger Fry*, perhaps also aware that at some point in the future another writer will be at work on *Virginia Woolf*.[16] As Anderson suggests, 'A Sketch' can therefore be seen as part of an ongoing development of Woolf's relationship to a life-writing tradition: 'Whilst "Reminiscences" [1908] seems to embody Woolf's desire to incorporate herself into an already established tradition, the "Sketch" was written literally in the spaces between, in time that could be liberated form the more conventional ordering of a life of Roger Fry' (*Women*, pp. 67–8).[17] Like the memoir of Bell, it is a provisional gathering of material.

Despite this relative informality of approach, Woolf did not simply spill the memoir out in an unthinking fashion. For instance, her diary contains meditations on how the memoir ought to progress, as in this entry from August 1939.

> Oh yes. I thought of several things to write about. Not exactly diary. Reflections. Thats the fashionable dodge. Peter Lucas & Gide both at it.[18] Neither can settle to creative art (I think sans Roger, I could). Its the comment – the daily interjection – that comes handy in times like these. I too feel it. But what was I thinking? (Woolf, *Diary V*, p. 229)

A week previously she had commented, in similar vein, 'Its queer that diaries now pullulate' (Woolf, *Diary V*, p. 227). This helps to explain the diary element of 'A Sketch', its dated entries and the inclusion of brief reflections on current events; it is also notable that Woolf seldom writes diary entries and passages of 'A Sketch' on the same day, perhaps implying that these two types of writing served a similar function. Anna Snaith has suggested that Woolf's references to the war can be seen as 'invasions of the text' (p. 140) of 'A Sketch', but Woolf is not simply dealing with present political threats in a dutiful way before retreating into the safety of personal reflections on the past. As she comments, the 'past is much affected by the present moment' (*Moments*, p. 75). Providing a context for her recollections emphasizes that she is suspended between an uncertain and unpredictable future and a past that is no less mercurial. What, and how, she remembers will be influenced by both political and personal circumstances. When Woolf resumes the piece after the declaration of war – there is a gap in the writing of the text between July 1939 and June 1940 – she feels, as she suggests in a letter to Smyth, that she is writing in a 'vacuum' (*Leave*, p. 430), a comment also relevant to her work on *Between the Acts*. This is not to say that 'A Sketch' becomes a narcissistic or escapist project, more that the question of an eventual audience is deferred, in part by the urgency simply to continue, but also by the practical difficulty of planning any future publications in wartime.

Woolf's reflections on the influence of her present mood on her writing would seem to indicate that she understands memory as being constantly retranscribed rather than 'archaeologically' preserved in an unchanged state, and, for example, she rejects the comparison of her childhood to a 'great hall' (Woolf, *Moments*, p. 79) or 'Cathedral space' (Woolf, *Moments*, p. 81) as too static. However, there are points at which the archaeological model is implied, and Woolf appears to suggest that different types of experience are registered in different ways. Early on in 'A Sketch', she asks:

> [I]s it not possible [...] that things we have felt with great intensity have an existence independent of our minds; are in fact still in existence? And if so, will it not be possible, in time, that some device will be invented by which we can tap them? [...] I shall fit a plug into the wall; and listen in to the past. (Woolf, *Moments*, p. 67)

This description applies, principally, to the earliest childhood memories, which Woolf describes as being sensuous and pre-rational: 'I am hardly aware of myself, but only of the sensation' (Woolf, *Moments*, p. 67). Other incidents, although preserved intact, can be subjected to later interpretation: 'Later we add to feelings much that makes them more complex' (Woolf, *Moments*, p. 67). The example Woolf gives here is her feeling of guilt when looking at herself in a mirror, a sensation she connects to her memory of being interfered with by her stepbrother Gerald Duckworth. Woolf attributes the discomfort she felt at the time of this incident to the fact that 'a feeling about certain parts of the body; how they must not be touched; how it is wrong to allow them to be touched; must be instinctive. It proves that Virginia Stephen was not born on the 25 January 1882, but was born many thousands of years ago' (*Moments*, p. 69). The particular way in which this event impresses on her memory, as an unchanging 'snapshot', is therefore attributed, by Woolf, to the instinctual roots of her reaction rather than to any personal conception she might have had of the event as traumatic; she includes this incident as an example of how difficult it is to locate the first causes for feelings of shame. Placed in this context, it can be made comprehensible to herself in a way in which other events from her childhood cannot. In a letter to Ethel Smyth of January 1941, Woolf again alludes to this incident, in the context of a discussion of what can and cannot be dealt with in autobiography. Here, she notes that 'as so much of life is sexual – or so they say – it rather limits autobiography if this is blacked out' (Woolf, *Leave*, pp. 459–60). Again, however, her feelings of shame over the incident with Gerald Duckworth are given as an example of 'subterranean instincts [...] Why should I have felt shame then?' (Woolf, *Leave*, p. 460). Thus while acknowledging that issues to do with sexuality ought to be included in autobiography, Woolf here admits a barrier to her own discussion of such matters; again, though, as in 'A Sketch', the reasons for this are presented as historical (or indeed primeval) rather than personal.

The manner in which Woolf contextualizes this event in 'A Sketch' can be interpreted as a strategic means of protecting herself from its full impact. Sue Roe suggests that Woolf displaces her feelings onto 'thousands of ancestresses' (Woolf, *Moments*, p. 69) because 'language has deserted her' (Roe, p. 49). Introducing the historical, and, indeed, discussing herself in the third person, becomes a means by which she 'screens herself' (Roe, p. 49) from confronting these feelings anew. Similarly, Sidonie Smith argues that this incident shows that Woolf 'seems to have no words for talking about her own sexualized body and no personal narratives for conveying her response' (Smith, p. 91). Despite apparently choosing to include this distressing incident, Woolf uses it not as a way of beginning to discuss her own feelings towards sexuality, but rather to make a more general point about the functions of memory. Both Roe and Smith argue that Woolf shies away from discussing the ramifications of the incident for herself as a sexualized individual; yet what Woolf does seem to grapple with, both here and elsewhere in the memoir, is the difficulty of unravelling the influence of particular individuals or indeed historical events from more deeply rooted, genealogical factors. The apparent lack of emotional engagement with this episode also characterizes Woolf's description of 'moments of being'. In these passages too, Woolf attempts a structural as much as emotional assessment of the importance of what she remembers.

This unpleasant experience, then, is not the only one that preserves its initial force for Woolf. She presents a typology of memories that continue to have an impact even in the wake of post-facto rationalization, and attributes her creativity to her ability to receive and transform such shocks: 'I [...] suppose that the shock-receiving capacity is what makes me a writer. [...] I make it real by putting it into words' (Woolf, *Moments*, p. 72). Of the examples she gives of such moments from her childhood, two 'ended in a state of despair' (Woolf, *Moments*, p. 71): after fighting with her brother Thoby she is overcome with 'hopeless sadness' (Woolf, *Moments*, p. 71) and an apple tree in the garden at Talland House becomes associated with the suicide of Mr Valpy. 'The other [incident] ended, on the contrary, in a state of satisfaction' (Woolf, *Moments*, p. 71). Looking at a plant in the flower bed she experiences a sense of completeness and understanding, rather than intellectual paralysis. Indeed Woolf goes on to suggest that 'these sudden shocks [...] are now always welcome' in that they are a signal of 'some real thing behind appearances' (*Moments*, p. 72). Anderson, citing Julia Kristeva's definitions of the abject and the sublime, suggests that the experiences Woolf describes appear to vacillate between the two. This is not simply a case of discomfort opposed to pleasure. In the abject, associated by Kristeva with the transition between the pre-symbolic and symbolic, 'the abyss threatens', whilst the sublime is a moment of 'expansion and spaciousness' (Anderson, *Women*, p. 71). Two different concepts of subjectivity and its relation to the world are therefore indicated. The subject can either be engulfed by the abyss, or achieve mastery. The sense of a 'real thing behind appearances' can be either a threat or a promise, but in both cases, the boundaries between subject and object are disturbed. Writing, and specifically in this instance, autobiographical writing, is the principle means through which this disturbance can be approached, even if this involves acknowledging the tenuous nature of any equilibrium that might be created.

Elena Gualtieri suggests that Woolf's transformation of shocks into a source of creativity poses problems for the relationship between memory and writing:

> [T]his making (up) of scenes to stave off the assault of traumatic events also has the effect of eroding the distinction between memories of past events and their fictional re-elaboration, turning writing into a substitute for the act of remembering itself. If it is true that scenes survive the onslaught of time because they are real, it is also true that for Woolf "reality" is an attribute that belongs more properly to art than to life. (*Virginia Woolf's Essays*, p. 104)

For Woolf, according to this argument, the written takes priority over the remembered; or the remembered only gains meaning insofar as it exists in written form. Yet to preserve a distinction between memories and their written form would seem to be self-defeating for the author of an autobiography. In interpreting remembered events from her childhood as signs of her creative capacity, Woolf both presents those events and, simultaneously, demonstrates that capacity. The notion that an artistic representation might take on greater 'reality' than life is a problematic one, but Gualtieri implies that these two realms – art and life – are for Woolf completely divorced. In contextualizing 'A Sketch' in terms of both the progress of the war and the progress of her other projects, Woolf implies that her autobiography is not a means of escaping present realities but an attempt at finding a way in which these may be better understood. What eventually seems to be revealed, however, is that the kind of traumatic shock of creativity central to 'A Sketch' is difficult, if not impossible, to weigh against the shocks of war.

As she progresses with 'A Sketch', Woolf explores further the idea of memory, and the writing of memoirs, being influenced by both past and present circumstances. In an entry from July 1939, she comments that: '[T]he present when backed by the past is a thousand times deeper than the present when it presses so close that you can feel nothing else, when the film on the camera reaches only the eye. But to feel the present sliding over the depths of the past, peace is necessary' (Woolf, *Moments*, p. 98). The rather imprecise image of the 'film on the camera' reaching only the eye recalls the use of photographs and photographic imagery in *Three Guineas*. Woolf here reinforces the importance of perspective, a perspective often elaborated by writing, to her understanding and indeed perception of events. The notion of the present pressing close implies events which assault the subject in the way that the photographs of dead children did, and although Woolf refers to moving house as the kind of event that upsets her, there is perhaps an underlying anxiety here that home may not long remain a peaceful refuge. Initially an escape from the 'antlike meticulous labour' (Woolf, *Moments*, p. 100) of *Roger Fry*, when that book is completed, the memoir serves a similar purpose in relation to *Between the Acts*: 'I continue, for I am at a twist in my novel' (Woolf, *Moments*, p. 126). At this stage, in the summer of 1940, 'the Germans fly over England; [the war] comes closer to this house [Monk's House] daily. If we are beaten then – however we solve that problem, and one solution apparently is suicide (so it was decided three nights ago in London among us) – book writing becomes doubtful' (Woolf, *Moments*, p. 100). Thus the war is not seen only as a threat to life itself, but as a threat to a way of life that allows writing. Partly because it does not present the structural problems of *Roger Fry* or *Between the Acts*, the memoir becomes a means of attempting to preserve, in writing at least, the sense of 'the present sliding over the depths of the past'.

But although Woolf was freed from certain formal constraints in writing the memoir, and although reflecting on the past might, temporarily, forestall contemplation of imminent danger, she finds herself obliged to examine many incidents of unhappiness and personal loss from throughout her childhood and youth, as well as the more positive 'moments of being'. Thus for example, in describing her brother Thoby, she shies away thinking about his life in the years following the deaths of 'the two people who should have made those years normal and natural, if not "happy". I am not thinking of mother and Stella; I am thinking of the damage that their deaths inflicted' (Woolf, *Moments*, p. 136). Describing the aftermaths of these deaths is as difficult, if not more so, than describing the deaths themselves. Woolf comments that she was only able to cease being 'obsessed' (Woolf, *Moments*, p. 80) by her mother with the composition of *To the Lighthouse*, many years later, and that the 'tragedy' of her mother's death was that 'it made her unreal' (Woolf, *Moments*, p. 95). This echoes her reason for producing the memoir of Julian Bell: nothing is real until she writes it. Writing is again characterized not as a means of escape from the world but as a way of attempting to gain an understanding of it. Yet if *To the Lighthouse* was, by Woolf's own account, effective as a means of incorporating her mother's death, any attempt to forestall the possible future shocks of war by reliving earlier shocks either of loss or of creativity will inevitably fall short. Woolf's juxtaposition of the ongoing war with her childhood memories cannot provide a shield against the shocks of a physical as much as psychic nature that seem imminent, but which can never be fully prepared for or predicted.

Conclusion

Although I have referred to 'A Sketch' as unfinished, insofar as it has aspects of the diary it is in fact complete in itself. (One might suggest that the only absolute completion point for a diary is the death of the author although as I will show in the next chapter this is not invariably the case.) This form of narrative (non) completion has a consonance with Rose's suggestion that an important characteristic of Woolf's writing is its refusal to endorse the quiescent trajectory which is apparently implied by Freudian mourning. 'A Sketch', necessarily, evades any redemptive development or working through of present fears. This, however, is not an indictment of the piece, but an indication of the strength of Woolf's resistance to the ephemeral reassurance that might be provided by narrative archetypes of a more consolatory nature. Throughout the writings I have been examining here, Woolf is caught in the double bind of anxiety that Lyndsey Stonebridge has identified: 'Anxiety cuts in two directions [...] On the one hand, it is a "signal", a protective action which warns the ego of a potential danger to come [...] But this warning [...] is efficacious because it is predicated on the repetition of a past trauma: anxious anticipation, thus, has the potential to plunge the ego into traumatic anxiety anew' (p. 57). The consequent '[d]reading forward' (Stonebridge, p. 57) can be either protective or shattering; in Woolf's case, attempting to prepare for the future by looking back to the past could not disguise the fact that the future might ultimately bring the intensification rather than the repetition of what had come before.

'We pour to the edge of a precipice,' she writes on 27 June 1940, '... & then? I cant conceive that there will be a 27th June 1941' (Woolf, *Diary V*, p. 299).

After Woolf's death, Brittain, in one of the fortnightly newsletters she produced in the war years under the auspices of the Peace Pledge Union, gave the following analysis:

> How far [Woolf's suicide] was a deliberate protest against the sorry situation to which war has brought literature and its exponents throughout Europe, we shall probably never know [...] It may be that Virginia Woolf felt that the war, for too long, had put an end to all she cared for; that she had no contribution to make to the "tough" society which is in the process of evolving. Her end was perhaps a kind of protest, the most terrible and effective that she could make, against the real hell which international conflict creates for artists. (*Testament of a Peace Lover*, pp. 69–71)

Brittain simultaneously portrays Woolf as a figure not fitted for life in the contemporary world and appropriates her death as a political gesture. For Brittain, Woolf's death is the ultimate culmination of her life's work, a gesture more meaningful than any of Woolf's writings could ever be. Regardless of other explanations that have been given for Woolf's decision to end her life,[19] Brittain's analysis obscures the fact that for Woolf, her writing was, precisely, the contribution that she *could* make, and continued to make, even when the nature of her work came to be subject to the vicissitudes of war. Woolf's own writings, I would suggest, are in large part testament to the dangers of attempting to give meaning to death and death encounters in such a straightforward fashion.

3
Anne Frank: The War from the Annexe

Anne Frank died in Bergen-Belsen in early 1945, a victim, in all probability, of the typhus epidemic that was sweeping the camp at that time. In recent years, a number of texts, notably Jon Blair's documentary *Anne Frank Remembered* and biographies by Melissa Müller, Mirjam Pressler, and Carol Ann Lee have served as a reminder that Frank's story continued, and concluded, after the end of her diary. However, *The Diary of a Young Girl* still occupies a paradoxical position; the exemplary text of the Holocaust, it portrays a life secluded from those events. This is not to deny that the Franks' situation was an aspect, albeit an unusual one, of what constituted experience of the Holocaust.[1] Rather, it is interesting that a text that, as Alvin H. Rosenfeld notes, has become a 'metonymy' (p. 243) for the Holocaust necessarily looks at those events awry. As I have suggested, notions of witnessing become complicated when the witness in question is placed in what would appear to be a peripheral situation. In the case of Frank's diary, the apparent non-inclusion of the more familiarly harrowing aspects of the Holocaust is part of what has contributed to its iconic status. Karein K. Goertz suggests that the diary has functioned as 'a bearable, collective screen memory', masking 'the more widespread experiences of children in ghettos and concentration camps' ('Writing', p. 655), but believes that the continuations of Frank's story that I have mentioned have served as a corrective to this. However, these other texts are essentially adjuncts to the diary, which in itself can still function as a 'safe' or 'clean' version of the Holocaust. This, together with the fact that it was written by a teenager, is part of what has made this text seem particularly suited for use with children. What this reading evades is the very fact that Frank's diary is only available to us, and only has this metonymic force, precisely because she did not survive. Even if it not always explicitly acknowledged, Anne Frank's death shadows and inflects any reading of this text.

Critics including Rosenfeld, Tony Kushner and Tim Cole have considered the process by which the diary gained its current status, and this process, including the tangled publication history of the text, will be considered here. I will also return to the diary itself. This is not to say that a close reading of the text can yield the 'true' Anne Frank. Rather, there are aspects of the diary that make it a still compelling example of Holocaust autobiography. Some existing interpretations presume that its force comes from Frank's honesty and openness about her emotions, implying, perhaps, that because she was a child, she was less inhibited than an adult would be. For example, writing on the publication of the 'Definitive Edition' of the diary, Julia Neuberger described Frank's as an 'authentic voice [...] by no means mealy mouthed, or saintly' ('Why Anne Will Live', p. 1), whilst Natasha Walter noted Frank's 'clear, resonant voice', judging her 'an unsentimental writer who still breaks our hearts' (p. 11). However, whilst such comments may provide the key to the image of Anne Frank as a basically uncomplicated figure with whom we can all identify, they downplay the extent to which optimism and hopefulness in the text are countered, or perhaps even necessitated, by fear and uncertainty. Frank's own redrafting and reworking of the text, spurred by a radio broadcast from the Dutch government in exile, is important not only because it adds an element of retrospection to a supposedly spontaneous text, but also because it gives the diary a self-consciously testimonial aspect. Frank expresses a desire to bear witness, and this forward looking, and indeed outward looking, aspect of the text is in tension with what might more usually be considered the characteristics of a diary as a private account of inner feelings.

Discussing recent revelations about the Holocaust, such as the 'Nazi gold' scandal, Leak and Paizis cite the definition of the uncanny that Freud borrows from Schelling: it is *the name for everything that ought to have remained (...) secret and hidden but has come to light* (Freud, 'The "Uncanny"', p. 224, ellipsis and emphasis in original), but they suggest that 'the return of this particular repressed is more predictable than uncanny' (Leak and Paizis, p. 2). New information about the implementation of the Holocaust is revealed not through 'some mysterious capacity of the events themselves to resurface autonomously' (Leak and Paizis, p. 2) but through the efforts of historians and other scholars. If reinserting the diary into its historical context, as Frank's biographers have done, is a case of revealing what was always there on its margins, there are other aspects of the text itself that are also uncanny, but have less frequently been acknowledged as such. The uncanny as a means of expressing the return of repressed and its disquieting un/familiarity, not only has resonance for the way in which the Holocaust shadows the diary, but can also be helpful in the exploration of its other uncertainties.

In his 1919 essay, 'The "Uncanny"', Freud begins with an exploration of the etymology of the word, in German 'das Unheimliche', literally the unhomely; this underlines the instability of the concept, particularly as it relates to its apparent opposite, the 'Heimliche', the homely or familiar. The uncanny, Freud suggests, 'is that class of the frightening which leads back to what is known of old and long familiar' ('The "Uncanny"', p. 220). That which is familiar and homely is also, from another point of view, hidden and concealed; uncanny effects can arise from the exposure of this ambivalence. I will be discussing the uncanny both as it is represented within the diary, as something which Frank herself appears to experience, but also as it is produced through reading the text. Ellen Wayland-Smith has noted that, '[a]ny attempt to locate the uncanny, to pinpoint its place in articulated time and space, is [...] bound to fail, as it signals precisely what never *takes* (its) *place* as an identifiable present' (p. 185, emphasis in original). This not only stresses the notion of the uncanny as an *effect* (of reading or writing) rather than an object, but is also useful in terms of the consideration of states, such as displacement or estrangement, as themselves uncanny.[2] The Secret Annexe is a home which is distinctly unhomely; the Franks and the others in hiding are not only Jewish but have also suffered an earlier displacement from Germany; and during her time in the Annexe, Frank passes through adolescence, becoming in the process estranged from herself. This type of analysis can usefully defamiliarize the text, and restore the referential force that has slipped away in the process of Frank's elevation to exemplary status.

The diary as testimony

Before moving on to explore these aspects of the text in greater detail, it will be useful to indicate some of the ways in which it, and, by extension, Frank herself, have typically been considered. Rosenfeld notes that the first piece of critical writing on the diary, an article by a Dutch journalist Jan Romein that appeared before Otto Frank had been able to find a publisher for his daughter's work, reads it as an 'admonitory text' (p. 247). Indeed, Romein sees Frank's death as evidence that 'we have lost the fight against human bestiality' (qtd Frank, *Critical Edition*, p. 68). Rosenfeld contrasts this initially pessimistic reading with later reviews which 'preferred to see the diary as [...] a work of bright adolescent spirit' (p. 249). However, Rosenfeld is also drawing a contrast here between a reading (Romein's) that views the text as a 'historical document' and one that views it as 'a moving personal testimony' (p. 249). From this point of view, attempts at continuing Frank's story that rely on personal testimony from others, such as the documentary *Anne Frank Remembered*, are similarly problematic. These two functions – of historical documentation and personal testimony – need not necessarily be mutually exclusive, but Rosenfeld's concern is that focusing on the optimistic aspects of the text ultimately leads to the events described taking on a general or 'existential' (p. 266) rather than specifically historical meaning.

A further consequence of this 'existential' reading is the downplaying of the fact that Anne Frank's fate was a result of her being Jewish. As Tony Kushner has noted, this was also the reading of the diary promoted by the stage version, written by Frances Goodrich and Albert Hackett and first produced in 1955 (p. 12).[3] The question of the precise nature of the Franks' Jewishness is problematic, although what of course is not in doubt is that however they might have defined themselves religiously or racially, they ultimately had no choice but to submit to inclusion within the category of 'Jew' as employed by the Nazis. As Yasmine Ergas comments in an essay on Anne Frank and Etty Hillesum, another Dutch victim of the Holocaust, '[a]s Nazism casts them, they must cast themselves: first and foremost as Jews' (p. 85). However, the Anne Frank Educational Foundation has as one of its aims the promotion of anti-racism and tolerance, not specifically anti-Semitism, and the contextual material displayed at the Anne Frank House in Amsterdam has a similarly wide focus. Tim Cole notes that the ' "liberal" message of the "Universal Anne" ' (p. 41) was the burden of an exhibition, 'Anne Frank in the World 1919–1945' which toured during the late 1980s and early 1990s, and argues that such a liberal understanding of Anne Frank's story, and by extension the Holocaust can be overly reductive. '[I]f we ask ourselves "had Anne Frank – an ordinary young Jewish girl – lived next door, could she have counted on us for help during the Nazi occupation?" and simply answer "yes", we betray a lack of humility which confrontation with the Holocaust demands' (Cole, p. 43). Kushner suggests further that for a post-war generation who 'were ambivalent to the precious and untouchable memory of the war presented by their parents, *The Diary* offered a new perspective and one which they could identify with through the adolescent struggles of a young girl – in spite of her being imprisoned in an Amsterdam attic' (p. 14).[4] For Kushner, as for Cole, such generalized identification – the notion that anyone who has been, or is, an adolescent can find something to relate to in the diary – is simply another means of stripping away the historical and cultural particularities of the text.

Reinstating the context is one possible way of remedying this situation, as both Cole and Kushner point out. Through a reading of the text which is attentive both to its status as a work of autobiography and to the exigencies of its production, the Holocaust can be brought to bear on the diary in such a way as to defamiliarize what has become, effectively, an empty signifier. Knowledge, however generalized, of contemporaneous events occurring outside the walls of the Annexe, and of events after the end of the diary, has to be held in abeyance if the diary is to be interpreted, as it still commonly is, as being about 'the triumph of the human spirit over evil and adversity' (Karpf, 'Let's Pretend', p. 10). Going back to the diary, however, serves not to 'flesh out' the reality of Anne Frank so much as to underline the ambiguities implicit in her own attempts at self-representation, ambiguities which are compounded by issues such as her attitude towards her Jewishness and her national identity, as well as by the particular characteristics of the diary as a form of autobiographical writing.

Felicity Nussbaum notes that diaries can pose particular challenges that are not present in more usual autobiographical forms. 'The diarist […] may record himself in order to produce an enabling fiction of a coherent and continuous identity; or he may record himself and recognize, to the contrary, that the self is not the same yesterday, today and tomorrow' (p. 134). A diary might seem to offer the chance of tracing, at a microscopic level, the growth and development of one's personality, but it can also disturb such notions of coherence. Thus, for example, in November 1942, Frank notes her excitement when she realizes that she is soon to begin menstruating. In January 1944, however, she annotates the earlier entry with the comment, '*I wouldn't be able to write that kind of thing any more. Now that I'm rereading my diary after a year and a half, I'm surprised at my childish innocence*' (Frank, *Definitive Edition*, p. 60, emphasis in original). The fact that Frank is passing through adolescence during her time in hiding exacerbates this sense of self-estrangement and this self-reflexivity recurs throughout the text. Frank, as both reader and writer, illustrates that the diary cannot simply be considered a straightforward decanting of the self into textual form. However, if Nussbaum's comment foregrounds the notion of the diary as a potentially unending attempt at self-exploration, Werner Hamacher points to a different but no less troubling characteristic of this form:

> The diarist's every word could be his last. Thus in the form of the diary [...] absolute skepticism about the durability of the written word and its meaning is intertwined with an astonishing optimism that demonstrates itself more in the compactness and conciseness of its linguistic expression than in its contents: since each entry could be the last, everything that comes together in it must appear under the aspect of its perfection, that is, of closure and finality. (Hamacher, p. 438)

Frank provides this element of closure by signing her name at the end of each entry, continuing the conceit that the account of the day's events is being sent as a letter to Kitty. There is, however, always the possibility of starting a new letter to fill the next gap for her imaginary correspondent. Hamacher's comment that the diarist's 'every word could be his last' thus seems particularly apt in the case of a diary written *in extremis*. The diary provides Frank with a means of asserting her own ongoing survival in the face of threatening circumstances, and it is misleading to focus on her optimism at the expense of the uncertainties with which it is countered. Frank expresses not only the disturbances of subjectivity described by Nussbaum, which can have the effect of estranging the author from herself, but also the pressures of the historical situation that provides the context and, to some extent at least, the pretext for the production of the diary. In this regard, Frank's diary shares some of the characteristics Barbara Foley identifies in Ghetto diaries, in which the '[p]rivacy and particularity [that] are characteristic of the traditional diary' are supplemented by a desire to 'register [...] the fate of a whole people' (p. 336).

Frank begins keeping a diary in a check-covered autograph album she receives as one of her birthday presents when she turns 13 in June 1942. The earliest entries are addressed to the diary itself: 'I hope I will be able to confide everything to you, as I have never been able to confide in anyone' (Frank, *Definitive Edition*, p. 1).[5] However, Frank soon begins to write in epistolary form, addressing the entries to 'Kitty', and explains her reasons for this decision: 'I want the diary to be my friend' (*Definitive Edition*, p. 7).[6] The unusual conceit of addressing a friend she has never met necessitates the inclusion of descriptions of her family history as well as of the incursions into everyday life that have been made by anti-Jewish legislation. Very occasionally, Frank even implies that she is writing in response to a specific request from Kitty. The entry for Thursday 6 April 1944, for example, begins, 'You asked me what my hobbies and interests are' (Frank, *Definitive Edition*, p. 249). However, in March 1944, when the Franks have been in hiding for almost two years, a radio broadcast from London by Gerrit Bolkestein a member of the Dutch government in exile prompts Frank to reconsider the function of her diary:

> [Bolkestein] said that after the war a collection would be made of diaries and letters dealing with the war. Of course, everyone pounced on my diary. Just imagine how interesting it would be if I were to publish a novel about the Secret Annexe. The title alone would make people think it was a detective story. Seriously, though, ten years after the war people would find it very amusing to read how we lived, what we ate and what we talked about as Jews in hiding. (*Definitive Edition*, p. 242)

Although diaries and letters are the forms of writing cited by Bolkestein, Frank does not immediately seem to make the connection to her own diary, mentioning instead fictionalizations. In the light of the broadcast, she began to recopy her existing diary onto loose sheets of paper, making stylistic amendments and fleshing out the original account, as well as continuing to write new entries. Neither version survived in totality, and this is important for several reasons. The most commonly available editions of the diary are pieced together from the two drafts,[7] and present it as a much more discrete text than it actually is; this has itself been used as a means of questioning the diary's authenticity by Holocaust deniers. But Frank's rewriting also means that her diary defies the usual definitions of that form. Not only does the date at the head of each entry not necessarily match the day on which the entry was actually (re)written, but Bolkestein's request foregrounds for Frank the possibility that this document or its contents may at some point enter the public domain, a possibility which is already implicit in an entry written two days before the broadcast: 'At least one long chapter on our life in hiding should be about politics, but I've been avoiding the subject, since it interests me so little. Today, however, I'll devote an entire letter to politics' (*Definitive Edition*, p. 237) Notable here again is Frank's implicit reference to a projected further re-telling of her 'life in hiding', told in chapters rather than diary form. Thus although Bolkestein's broadcast provided the impetus for reworking the diary, leading, as Goertz suggests to a 'new status' for the text, 'as historical and public document' ('Writing', p. 652), it is by no means clear that Frank was, even at this point, writing with a direct view to publication. A tension therefore remains between the diary as a personal record and as a self-conscious attempt at producing an historical document.

Exile, displacement and the haunted Annexe

Even in its early draft, the diary is not solely the record of day-to-day events but also invokes other conventions of autobiography, not least because, as I have indicated, Frank details her genealogy, ostensibly for the benefit of Kitty. The history of the family prior to the start of the war is a history of displacement; Anne and her older sister Margot were both born in Germany and the family only moved to Holland in 1933. Especially as the war progresses, this complicates not only Frank's sense of her own identity within the family group but also her sense of their religious and national affiliations. Indeed, these two factors are implicated in each other and it is useful to consider Frank's own understanding and projection of her Jewishness in the context of her comments on her national identity. The tension between being Dutch and being German is evident. For example, Frank comments that both her mother and Mrs van Daan[8] 'speak abominable Dutch' (*Definitive Edition*, p. 34), and that her father asks her for help with his Dutch. These relatively neutral references to the question of nationality are not the only ones that Frank makes, however. After she unintentionally insults Mrs van Daan, she receives 'a tongue-lashing: hard, Germanic, mean and vulgar, exactly like some fat red-faced fishwife' (*Definitive Edition*, p. 46). The issue of language is also introduced in the 'regulations' issued to the dentist Dussel when he arrives. Here it is declared, albeit as a joke, that '[o]nly the language of civilized people may be spoken, thus no German' (Frank, *Definitive Edition*, p. 70). There is therefore an uneasy separation between the adults' previous identity as Germans and their new status as Dutch. To describe Mrs van Daan as 'Germanic' is clearly intended as an insult, but the continued use of German by her father, in the poem he writes for her on her birthday, for instance, is seen more in the light of a personal quirk than as a marker of race. Any acknowledgement of possible differences between individual Germans as regards political belief is therefore implicit rather than openly expressed.

Frank at one point surprises herself by falling back into speaking German when water is spilled over her scrapbooks: 'I nearly cried, and I was so upset I started speaking German' (*Definitive Edition*, p. 297). The implication here is that the extremity of the emotion causes her to revert to a more fundamental form of expression, one which associated in her mind with early childhood; despite retaining this vestigial language, however, she evidently considers herself more Dutch than German.[9] It is only as her anxieties about attitudes towards Jews in Holland grow that she increasingly falls back on her Jewishness as a means of self-definition. Shortly before D-day brings renewed hope of an end to the conflict, rumours of an anti-Semitic backlash provoke further reflections on the issue of nationality. Frank records that there are suggestions, in 'underground circles', that German Jews who emigrated to Holland before the war should be sent back to Germany once Hitler is defeated:

> We too will have to shoulder our bundles and move on, away
> from this beautiful country, which once so kindly took us in and
> now turns its back on us. I love Holland. Once I hoped it would
> be a fatherland to me, since I had lost my own. And I hope so still!
> (*Definitive Edition*, pp. 300–1)

De Costa cites this passage as evidence that, '[t]he position of exile
was one of the most dominant aspects of the life and work of Anne
Frank' ('Anne Frank', p. 215). Frank understands that it will be
impossible to simply leave the Annexe and return to normality, as
though awakening from a state of suspended animation. The Annexe
dwellers are not only sequestered from the outside world, incapable
of effecting changes in their own economic or political situation but
are also subject to the exigencies of the type of public opinion Frank
describes. Having felt 'at home', albeit in an increasingly segregated
Holland, Frank realizes the impossibility of returning to Germany.
The only option would be a further stage of exile.

'We too will have to shoulder our bundles': the image evoked here
is that of the wandering Jew, eternally displaced and never able to
assimilate. In later life, Otto Frank described himself as a political
rather than religious Jew, but as I have noted, defining oneself was,
during the war, secondary to the effects of interpellation. Edith
Velmans, who survived the war in Holland by going into 'open'
hiding – she was taken in by a Gentile family who claimed that she
was a visiting relative – notes in her autobiography that with the
introduction of anti-Jewish laws she and her friends, '[s]uddenly [...]
discovered who was Jewish and who was not. We had never been
aware of any differences in our crowd' (Velmans, p. 64). By the time
she began the diary, Frank had already had to move to an all-Jewish
school, and, like Velmans, she describes the impact of the anti-Jewish
decrees. After listing many of the restrictions imposed, she
comments, 'Jacque [a schoolfriend] always said to me, "I don't dare
do anything any more, 'cause I'm afraid it's not allowed"' (Frank,
Definitive Edition, p. 8).[10] To be Jewish is to be marked as Other; in
this context it is an identity defined by restrictions on one's behaviour. Going into hiding, separating themselves from a society which

has stripped away their civil rights is thus, paradoxically, a means of attempting to assert their freedom by depriving themselves of their liberty.

What reach their apogee in this decision are the self-contradictions of the assimilatory project. Refuse to assimilate and your differences remain a threat to the 'natives': assimilate too well, and you become the enemy within, passing as the genuine article. Susan Shapiro's discussion of the Jew as uncanny interrogates this paradox. Shapiro takes the figure of the wandering Jew, condemned to eternal life and therefore 'occupying an indistinguishable and undecidable borderline between life and death' (p. 64) as an archetype for the contradictory and even ironic position in which Jews were placed during nineteenth-century moves to assimilate. Following Alain Finkielkraut, Shapiro suggests that the assimilated or 'invisible' Jew was perceived as an even greater threat to the nation-state than those who remained unassimilated: 'Mimicry did not ultimately empower the Jew as subject but made the Jew who would be emancipated in the modern nation-state even more threatening and threatened' (p. 64). Shapiro invokes the image of the stateless Jew, capable only of rendering the homelands of others unheimlich. One solution to this would of course be the restitution of a Jewish nation-state, but Shapiro suggests that this itself raises a difficult question: '[C]an Judaism and/or Jewishness separate itself from the metaphysics of Europe and its anti-Semitism?' (p. 75). Put another way, is it ever feasible for negative images to be reappropriated by the group to which they have been applied? This is not a question that those in hiding were in a position to answer, of course.[11]

In view of the Frank family's earlier displacement from Germany, the move to the Annexe can be considered as a form of internal exile, during which attempts were made to continue a semblance of everyday life. Two hundred and sixty three Prinsengracht, where the Annexe was located, became an unheimlich house, an uncanny double of a family home. Bruno Bettleheim argues that the attempts which were made to continue with school lessons in the Annexe, and even the decision to go into hiding as a family group, were in fact a tactical blunder on Otto Frank's part:

> We gather from the diary [...] that the chief desire of the Frank family was to continue living as nearly as possible in the same

fashion to which they had been accustomed in happier times.
[...] Choosing any other course would have meant not merely
giving up living together, but also realizing the full measure of the
danger to their lives. [...] Anne, her sister, her mother, may well
have died because her parents could not get themselves to believe
in Auschwitz. (pp. 248–50)

Bettelheim does not deny that 'open hiding' posed its own dangers,
but he also argues that even in their chosen situation, the Franks
could have been better prepared for their eventual discovery if, rather
than studying literature and history the girls had been taught 'how
to make a getaway' (p. 253). Of course, such suggestions are all very
well at a temporal distance; more relevant to the current discussion
is that although the Franks decided to try and continue in something
resembling their former way of life, what they achieved was, by
Frank's account, only ever an uncanny echo of that earlier pattern.

In his study *The Architectural Uncanny: The Modern Unhomely*,
Anthony Vidler returns to a very literal understanding of 'das
Unheimliche', but, as its subtitle suggests, Vidler connects this to what
is essentially the alienation of modern life. He thus quotes Marx on
the estrangement of the individual from his or her home which is the
effect of renting property: ' "Here I am at home" – but [...] instead
he finds himself in *someone else's* house, in the house of a *stranger*
who always watches him and throws him out if he does not pay his
rent' (qtd Vidler, p. 5, emphasis in original). Iain Sinclair similarly
notes that:

> Doors represent status: those who possess them are allowed a mea-
> sure of privacy. They can remove themselves from their servants,
> supplicants or creditors. The door is a border, framed and pre-
> sented. The impoverished [...] know them only from the outside.
> Spaces to which they are granted access have no doors (unless
> they are doors to keep them in, doors of prisons or madhouses).
> (Lichenstein and Sinclair, p. 184)

Although these observations could, and indeed are intended to,
apply to modern life beyond the confines of the Holocaust, their resonance is increased when they are applied to the Annexe.[12] The door
to the Frank's 'house' is hidden behind a bookcase. Their ownership

of it cannot be freely acknowledged and for much of the time they can make no use of it. When they can, they can only enter other, restricted, parts of the building. This incarceration, as Bettelheim maintains, was chosen, but of course it was barely a choice at all – and was still incarceration.[13] Some of the diary's most tense moments for the present day reader are those when the families have to take precautions not to be heard by workers, or indeed intruders, in the rest of the building. One example of this is Frank's description of the second attempted burglary.

> It was ten-thirty, then eleven. Not a sound. [...] Up above you could hear the whole family breathing. [...] Footsteps in the house, the private office, the kitchen, then ... on the staircase. All sounds of breathing stopped, eight hearts pounded. Footsteps on the stairs, then a rattling at the bookcase. This moment is indescribable. (Frank, *Definitive Edition*, p. 253)

What such an incident foregrounds for the reader is a usually submerged awareness that the families in the Annexe are carrying out a semblance of everyday life on one side of the wall whilst on the other their presence goes unnoticed. In so far as this is the case, they haunt the building.

On another occasion, after she has been down to the lower part of the Annexe alone to use the lavatory, Frank comments:

> There was no one down there, since they were all listening to the radio. I wanted to be brave, but it was hard. I always feel safer upstairs than in that huge, silent house; when I'm alone with those mysterious muffled sounds from upstairs and the honking of horns in the street, I have to hurry and remind myself where I am to keep from getting the shivers. (*Definitive Edition*, p. 304)

Detached temporarily from the family unit, Frank has to remind herself that this is, for the time being her home, and that the 'mysterious muffled sounds', seemingly a sinister threat, are actually being made by her family, who provide her only form of protection. The alternative, signalled by the sound of car horns outside, is a return to the outside world, currently an impossibility. In this passage, the emptiness of the rest of the building is itself a threat, and this, of course is an archetypal trope in the haunted house story. Emptiness and darkness can never be benign absences: there is always a possibility of another presence announcing itself. Even the 'ghosts' can feel themselves to be haunted. Immediately prior to the passage quoted above, Frank prevents herself from considering the possibility that the police, having got into the office downstairs to investigate the break-in, could just have easily have got into the Annexe. What might happen next if such an incursion occurred is not explicitly stated. The fear generated by simply being in the Annexe serves only to mask the fear of what could follow.

Here Frank briefly expresses a degree of estrangement from her family. This not only connects to her recurring discussion of the problems of growing up and establishing her own identity in these circumstances but also, perhaps, to a more fundamental sense that the family unit in fact offers little in the way of protection. The sounds she hears are made by her family, but could be made by ghosts. Such defamiliarization is apparent at other points also, in particular when Frank presents images of the older inhabitants of the Annexe. In early 1944, for example, Frank apologises to Kitty for retelling the same news stories, but protests that she herself is 'sick and tired' of 'hearing the same old stuff. […] Mother or Mrs van D. trot out stories about their childhood that we've heard a thousand times before' (p. 176). Even news brought into the Annexe by their helpers is recycled in a similar way:

> [T]he grown-ups [are] in the habit of repeating the stories we hear from Mr Kleiman, Jan or Miep, each time embellishing them with a few details of their own, so that I often have to pinch my arm under the table to keep myself from setting the enthusiastic storyteller on the right track. (Frank, *Definitive Edition*, p. 177)

Such comments have been interpreted as illustrating that the stultification of life in the Annexe ultimately did not dampen Frank's spirits, or as a typical adolescent complaint about her elders. Norma Rosen, for example, sees it as a sign of Frank's 'innate style and unfailing wit' that '[w]hen all the adults in their hiding place grow impatient with her "cheeky" high spirits, this girl so starved for the feel of the outdoors can write: "The rain of rebukes dies down to a light summer drizzle" ' (pp. 82–3). Jenny Diski, meanwhile, suggests that the 'horrible honesty' (p. 11) of Frank's criticism of her mother could be liberating for a teenage reader. But although focusing on how such incidents reveal Frank's creative side (and her desire for the story to continue on the 'right track' could be read as revealing her sense of narrative structure) a particular kind of debilitation is shown to be at work among the adults. Frank might dream of new experiences, but for the older generation, there is a logic in retreating into the past when the future is so uncertain and the present essentially the marking of time. The making-over and retelling of news from outside is a means of absorbing and controlling this information, rendering it non-threatening. Repetition has to take the place of action and becomes a tactic for avoiding the detailed consideration of the present circumstances. This is repetition as a means of masking the loss of one's agency and in this respect it echoes one of the functions of Frank's diary.

Growing up in hiding

In an essay which considers the extent to which Frank's diary illustrates its author's passage through typical stages of adolescent growth, Gracie K. Baruch suggests that diaries can in fact be instrumental in, rather than just illustrative of, attempts to establish a sense of identity. Paradoxically, according to Baruch, 'the impoverished environment may have been responsible for the great richness of Anne Frank's diary' (p. 426), because Frank had few other possible channels through which to express her thoughts and feelings, being deprived of, for example, female friends of her own age. Baruch therefore argues that even in these unusual circumstances, Frank goes through identifiable rites of passage. The attitudes Frank expresses towards the older inhabitants of the Annexe, and particularly her parents, are, in this analysis, as much a symptom of her age as of being in hiding. The danger with this interpretation is that focusing on Frank as an exemplary adolescent can downgrade other important aspects of the text.[14] However, it will be worth giving some consideration to the diary's account of growth and development. As Baruch shows, Frank passes through, and knows she is passing through, many recognisable stages of adolescence, including 'detachment from old love objects in the family [and the] establishment of an independent identity, vocational as well as sexual' (p. 425); but the effects of these processes are intensified both by her situation and by the manner in which she records them. This means that the uncanny aspects of adolescence, such as the increasing unfamiliarity of the supposedly familiar body, are intensified. Two key factors will be considered here: Frank's awareness of her own physical and emotional growth, and the function of the 'romance' between Frank and Peter van Daan.

Frank's indictment of her mother and Mrs van Daan for telling 'the same old stories' is symptomatic of her belief that the adults in the Annexe refuse to acknowledge that she is growing up. In early 1944, Frank records discussing this matter with her older sister Margot, and suggests that, given the circumstances, they have both in fact had to grow up more quickly than would otherwise have been the case:

> [E]verything's out of kilter here. By that I mean that we're treated like children when it comes to external matters, while, inwardly, we're much older than other girls our age. [...] [T]hough it may sound odd coming from a teenager, I feel I'm more of a person than a child. (*Definitive Edition*, p. 220)

This notion of being 'out of kilter' is an important one. Frank implies, here and elsewhere, that because of the lack of external points of reference, her parents' treatment of her has essentially remained unchanged during the time in hiding. This chimes with the sense that the adults are, to some extent, marking time. Frank herself initially appears to regard the stay in the Annexe in a similar way. In March 1943, she describes the courses that she and Margot are encouraged to follow as 'time killers' (Frank, *Definitive Edition*, p. 96), little more than a means of passing the time until their release, even though the date for this cannot be predicted. However, the longer the stay in the Annexe lasts, the greater her anxiety about whether, and if so how, she will be able to resume her previous life once the war has ended. In April 1944, for example, she decides that unless the war is over by September, she will be too old to rejoin school. Projecting forward to the distant future, imagining becoming a journalist, for instance, does provide some degree of consolation, but looking to events in the more immediate future, such as the end of the war, tends only to foreground the parlous nature of her current situation, and is troubling rather than a source of hope. Frank wants the time to pass because each passing day brings the end of the war closer, but it also marks another day lost in the dead time of the Annexe.

Frank also draws attention to the physical changes she undergoes during the time in hiding. Photographs of Frank as a schoolgirl are so familiar as to have taken on an iconic status, and it is of course impossible to imagine what she might have looked like after two years in the Annexe. The gap between the earlier visual image and the later, textual figure is impossible to bridge. The diary might seem to promise to animate the photograph, but in fact the gap between the two widens. For example, when it is suggested that she be taken out of the Annexe to see an optician, a year into her time in hiding, Frank tries on her coat but finds she has grown out of it: 'it looked as if it might have belonged to my little sister' (Frank, *Definitive Edition*, p. 110). This use of the image of the 'little sister' stresses Frank's sense of estrangement from her own body, emphasizing the distance from the outside world and 'normal' time created by the stay in the Annexe. The mis-fitting coat redoubles the distance between her current life and what might have happened before, or might happen after, in the outside world. Eventually the plan to go to the optician is cancelled, ostensibly in the hope of a breakthrough in the war, but it could almost be implied that the unwearable outdoor clothes are themselves the deciding factor. Passing back unnoticed into everyday life is an impossibility.

The incident with the coat is a minor one, which I interpret as a metonym for the anxieties provoked by the passage of time in the Annexe. The interface between life in the Annexe and everyday life is interrogated in a different way by Frank's description of her romance with Peter van Daan. This romance is structurally as well as emotionally important. For the reader it is almost the only element of 'plot' in the text as a whole, and it could have served a similar function for the author.[15] Frank seems at times to acknowledge that her growing affection for Peter is almost inevitable in the circumstances. In January 1944, having reflected on the changes that have occurred since her arrival in the Annexe (principally the onset of menstruation), she wishes that she had a girl friend. In the next entry, however, she records:

My longing for someone to talk to has become so unbearable that I somehow took it into my head to select Peter for this role. [...]

You mustn't think I'm in love with Peter [...] If the van Daans had had a daughter instead of a son, I'd have tried to make friends with her. (Frank, *Definitive Edition*, pp. 161–2)

That night, however, she dreams about another Peter, a former sweetheart called Peter Schiff. Retrospectively, she comes to realize the strength of her feelings towards this other Peter, and for a number of days is unable to stop thinking about him, imagining conversations with him and lamenting what might have been. Within a couple of months, this longing has dissipated into an abstract state of near-ecstasy: 'I think spring is inside me. I feel spring awakening [...] I'm in a state of utter confusion [...] I only know that I'm longing for something...' (Frank, *Definitive Edition*, p. 184). Just as the earlier longing for a friend finds its object in Peter, it comes as little surprise to the reader that after recording these sentiments, Frank begins to sense that he is paying her extra attention. A courtship of sorts begins and Frank eventually admits that, 'Peter Schiff and Peter van Daan have melted into one Peter, who's good and kind and whom I long for desperately' (Frank, *Definitive Edition*, p. 197). The imagined or remembered Peter, a figure standing for unrealized hopes in the past, becomes superimposed upon Peter van Daan and Frank's abstract desires, centred initially around the spectral Peter, ultimately direct themselves to the Peter of flesh and blood.

At one point, when Frank has a dream about kissing Peter van Daan, another Peter apparently materializes: 'Peter's cheeks were very disappointing: they weren't as soft as they looked. They were more like Father's cheeks – the cheeks of a man who already shaves' (*Definitive Edition*, p. 211). Anxiety about male sexuality is apparent enough here, but this comment is also relevant to more generalized uncertainties about the future which permeate the diary. Frank will never be able to fit back into her 'little sister's' coat: Peter will never be a man with a rough face like Otto Frank's.[16] As well as this doubling and re-doubling of Peters, Frank also evokes a double of herself in an attempt to convey the unfamiliarity of the feelings she experiences when in proximity to Peter van Daan:

We were sitting on the divan, as usual, in each other's arms. Suddenly the everyday Anne slipped away and the second Anne took her place. The second Anne, who's never over-confident or amusing, but wants only to love and be gentle. [...] Did he realize he had two Annes at his side? (*Definitive Edition*, p. 272)

In conjuring this 'second Anne', Frank conveys her own confusion in the face of unfamiliar feelings. Having grown accustomed to particular, delimited kinds of social interaction during the time in the Annexe, the arousal of such emotions distances her from herself. The new, sexualized Anne seems to be an emanation from, rather than an integral part of, the first. This image expresses the sense that Frank is in a stage of transition, unable yet to incorporate the second, mature Anne, who is experienced as an uncanny double of herself. Frank is therefore caught between being the 'little sister' whose coat won't fit, and becoming the grown-up 'second Anne'. Later in the same entry, having admitted that she could never marry Peter, Frank worries that she might be giving in 'too soon. How can it ever go right with other boys later on?' (*Definitive Edition*, p. 274). On the one hand, this is a moment which has to be grasped; on the other, to give in now effaces the possibility of it happening 'properly' later. Frank is once again caught between wanting the time in the Annexe to be merely an interlude, and acknowledging that ordinary life can never simply be resumed afterwards.

Thus the romance with Peter is not only a case of two lonely teenagers taking comfort in each other: it is also a further reminder that the usual rites of passage have been denied them. An incident that could be cited as evidence that Frank was an 'ordinary girl' serves instead to emphasize that she is stranded permanently in abeyance. A conjunction of her concerns about the way in which she is perceived by the adults in the Annexe, and her anxieties about the future, occurs when Frank records the adults' comments about the friendship:

> I can't tell you how often the conversation at meals has been about an Annexe wedding, should the war last another five years. Do we take any notice of this parental chitchat? Hardly, since it's all so silly. [...] [T]hey laugh at us when we're serious, and they're serious when we're joking. (p. 233)

There is something distinctly queasy about the notion of an 'Annexe wedding', perhaps because of the paradoxically public nature which its consummation would have in the close confines of the Annexe. Frank here seems to want to resist the labelling of her relationship with Peter that this suggestion implies, thus evading the implication that the relationship is a 'grown up' one. Simultaneously, she wants it to be considered as serious in its own right. Perhaps what underlies these sentiments is a desire to believe, despite possible evidence to the contrary, that there will be more to her life than this, that like the romance with Peter, the time in the Annexe is a phase that will pass.

Writing in the shadow of the Holocaust

At several other points in the diary, Frank tentatively wonders what life might be like after the war. Looking forward to freedom should provide some form of psychological sustenance in these circumstances, but optimism is difficult to maintain because Anne knows that the war could continue indefinitely. News that is brought into the Annexe by the families' helpers or heard on the radio therefore has contradictory functions. When the news is good, it builds up hopes, but these are all too easily dashed; when it is bad, those in hiding have the compensation of being out of the way of immediate peril, but only at the cost of knowing that the net might close in at any stage. The reports on the progress of the war that Frank inserts into her diary have a variety of functions, then; in the light of Bolkestein's broadcast, they contribute to Frank's sense of her present predicament being a consequence of external historical events, events to which her diary can provide oblique testimony. These external events, whether interpreted by the Annexe dwellers as good or bad, are made sense of by being written. Their possible consequences can be explored. Writing these events is the only form of active relationship that Frank can have with them, but this positive function comes at the price of having to consider the possible negative consequences such events might bring in their train.

It is not my intention here to fill the gaps in Frank's account of the progress of the war and the Holocaust in Holland;[17] however in terms of the dual historical and testimonial function of the diary, Frank's incorporation of specific pieces of news from outside is notable. The rumours about Westerbork transit camp provoke the following reflections:

> It must be terrible in Westerbork. The people get almost nothing
> to eat, much less to drink [...] Escape is almost impossible; many
> people look Jewish, and they're branded by their shorn heads.
> If it's that bad in Holland, what must it be like in those faraway
> and uncivilized places where the Germans are sending them? We
> assume that most of them are being murdered. The English radio
> says they're being gassed. Perhaps that's the quickest way to die.
> (Frank, *Definitive Edition*, p. 54)

Ostensibly, of course, the news is being recorded for Kitty; but it is
also interesting that this letter full of bad news is followed, a week
later, by one that is full of what might seem to be, in comparison,
trivia, in the form of a record of books Frank has been reading.[18]
Marshalling the account of Westerbork into a discrete section of narrative could be seen as a means of containing both the rumours and
the reflections that they provoke (and which are indicated by the
comment 'Perhaps that's the quickest way to die'). This is not to say
that such narrative containment is always achievable; but it does
appear to reflect the contradictions in Frank's position. On the one
hand, she believes it important to record this information, but on the
other, it frightens and depresses her to consider it. In an entry from
January 1943, also largely devoted to recording news about the conditions outside, she goes so far as to acknowledge that the Annexe
dwellers are '[l]uckier than millions of people' (Frank, *Definitive
Edition*, p. 83). She concludes this entry by commenting: 'I could
spend hours telling you about the suffering the war has brought, but
I'd only make myself more miserable. All we can do is wait, as calmly
as possible, for it to end' (Frank, *Definitive Edition*, p. 84). These
remarks illuminate both the complexities of Frank's position and the
source of some of the popular misconceptions about the diary.
Despite realizing the importance of reporting these events, she here
acknowledges that it would be easier not to dwell on them; but the
final sentence quoted here is also significant. This is the type of comment which, taken out of context, can be seen to imply a stoical and
brave attitude to her predicament on Frank's part. Within the context, it comes across more as an attempt to persuade herself that
such a strategy is plausible. Viewing the situation objectively, things

could be worse than they are; but this cannot disguise the fact that, subjectively, they are as bad as they have ever been.

It is from this tension between looking out and looking inward, and, concomitantly, looking forward with, alternately, fear and hope, that the traumatic aspects of this text arise. Like Woolf, Frank finds herself in a situation in which death and loss are always at one remove, but could, by dint of this, always become an immediate threat. Looking back to the life before is painful because, as Frank realizes through the course of the text, it will never be possible to return to that life, not only because of possible hostility towards Jews in Holland after the war, but also because of irrevocably altered family dynamics. Looking forward, and attempting to develop plans for the future is impossible for similar reasons. An attitude of taking one day at a time would appear to be the most psychologically helpful one in such a situation but the physical and emotional changes of which Frank is all too aware, and that her diary heightens her awareness of, vitiate against this. Rachel Feldhay Brenner distinguishes between writing produced during the Holocaust and that produced afterwards in terms of the functions such writing serves for the author:

> Through her post-Holocaust testimony, the survivor attempts to return to the experience and to relive it, often as an attempt to exorcise the haunting past. But at the time of the unbearable suffering, the victim records the horror in an attempt to distance herself from it. (p. 131)

Placing current events at arm's-length, through writing, is here seen as a means of protecting oneself from their full impact. The Holocaust survivor, on the other hand, might feel impelled, paradoxically, to draw closer to the events again as a preliminary to placing them, finally, at a distance. Brenner's point seems to be that it is only when the survivor knows the experience has ended that the return to it can be safely made. While events are in train, they cannot be fully grasped, and writing serves as a delaying tactic, holding them in abeyance. I would suggest that Frank in fact attempts to render earlier events complete, through rewriting them, whilst continuing to benefit from the diary's properties as a shield against present dangers. However, I would also reinforce Brenner's use of the verb 'attempt' here. The failure to achieve these ends can be as revealing as success. Despite the different temporal relationships that the two authors have to the events they describe, the disturbance of the relationship between past, present and future is also a marked characteristic in the writings of Charlotte Delbo, the subject of my next chapter. In Delbo's work, a complex relationship to the workings of memory is established through writing. For Frank, rewriting the diary could be seen as a means of forestalling the type of traumatic self-estrangement described by Delbo, but as I have been indicating, the success of this strategy only ever appears to be partial.

Towards the end of the diary, the news reaching the Annexe begins to improve; after the D-day landings, Frank writes, 'A huge commotion in the Annexe! [...] Will this year, 1944, bring us victory? We don't know yet. But where there's hope, there's life' (*Definitive Edition*, p. 309). These hopes are not unalloyed, however, as food shortages become an increasingly pressing problem. It is not until the end of July that Frank writes, 'Now, at last, things are going well! They really are! Great news! An assassination attempt has been made on Hitler's life [...] by a German general' (*Definitive Edition*, p. 330). Frank's interpretation of the possible significance of the fact that a German soldier has threatened Hitler's life perhaps carries the echo of conversations among the adults. She suggests that this act of military rebellion indicates that the army officers are themselves tired of war and are unlikely to start another after Hitler's eventual downfall; underlying this suggestion is the theory that Germany was insufficiently de-militarized after the end of the First World War. Even here, however, Frank consciously attempts to rein in her optimism, noting, 'I'd hate to anticipate the glorious event [the end of the war]' (*Definitive Edition*, p. 331). Unfulfilled optimism is difficult to sustain in a situation in which one is powerless to act. Events happening outside are never merely contingent, but, as in this case, are too far removed for their true importance to be fully appreciable. Indeed, in the final entry of the diary, dated three days after the one just quoted, Frank returns to reflections of a much more introspective sort, identifying a split between her 'exuberant' (*Definitive Edition*, p. 332) outward self, and a more reflective, and, to her mind, preferable inner self, which has never been exposed to others. 'I [...] keep trying to find a way to become what I'd like to be and what I could be if... if only there were no other people in the world' (*Definitive*

Edition, p. 334). This irreconcilability of inner and outer self encapsulates the possible consequences of life in the Annexe as described in the diary. The question of how Frank can reconcile her two selves brings in its train the question of how the life lived in hiding could ever be reconciled with the life lived in the open.

These final two entries, with their juxtaposition of the optimism provoked by D-day and reflections on the problems of teenage subjectivity, exemplify the difficulties which interpreting the diary pose. These two topics appear to be related to each other by contingency – their appearance in consecutive entries – rather than by any other principle. This reflects the multi-functional nature of the diary as conceived by Frank. But to suggest that these two elements could exist independently of each other, to say that the diary could stand primarily as a record of a 'typical' adolescence (albeit gone through in hiding) is to exorcise what ultimately engenders the text: the Holocaust. To reassert this could be seen as rendering Frank a Holocaust victim over and above all else; it is perhaps preferable to believe that the wide circulation of the diary makes her a survivor of sorts, submitting to the logic that the author lives on through the text or can be reanimated through reading. In fact, as I have been attempting to show, this text is anything but a transparent window onto the soul of its author. Because of the status that Frank has attained, however, the danger remains that the apparent simplicity and straightforwardness of the text can somehow infect its context. Equally dangerous is the stress that has often been placed on the loss of Frank as an individual with particular talent and potential. Julia Neuberger describes Frank as 'a fine and substantial writer, who never reached her peak of expression' ('Why Anne Will Live', p. 1), whilst Cynthia Ozick believes that Frank was 'born to be a writer' (p. 74). But these were not the characteristics that marked her out for death; such comments seem to imply that the death in similar circumstances of someone with less apparent gifts would not have been quite so bad.

Conclusion: afterlives

After the Annexe was raided in August 1944, and the inhabitants arrested, Miep Gies, who worked as a secretary at 263 Prinsengracht and was one of those instrumental in enabling the Annexe dwellers to stay in hiding as long as they did, went in and collected as many of Frank's papers as she could find. She kept these locked in her office desk, and gave them to Otto Frank when he finally returned to Amsterdam after the liberation. He decided to type up edited selections from the diaries, translating them into German, so that he could send them to his mother in Switzerland; he then made a second, longer selection that was circulated among friends and which became the basis for the published text. Gerrold van der Stroom notes that '[f]or the sake of propriety, the good name of third parties, and in order to maintain interest, [Otto Frank] felt he had here and there to omit certain passages' (Frank, *Critical Edition*, p. 63). This selecting and editing process, together with the correction of grammatical errors, added fuel to Holocaust deniers' speculations about the authenticity of the diary; Otto Frank was not slow to have such accusations tested in the courts.[19] The Critical Edition of the diary was in part the academic response to such attacks, containing as it does an exhaustive account of the transformations which the text underwent from manuscript to published versions, as well as expert analysis of the diary's paper, ink and handwriting. However, even this edition retains at least one of the omissions made by Otto Frank in deference to his late wife, and the 'Definitive Edition', which reinstates much material absent from the published versions since the 1950s, is due to be revised further after other previously suppressed manuscript material came to light.[20] Given the circumstances of the text's production and survival, inconsistencies of this kind are unsurprising; in fact, in would be more surprising if the different manuscript versions had survived in their entirety. The instability of the text is itself testimony to the exigencies of its historical context, and so far as this is the case, the notion of a 'Definitive Edition' is a necessary fiction. Many gaps in the text can never be filled.

'Completing' the diary is, therefore, an unachievable task; completing Frank's story, through the use of biography, poses similar problems. Both Melissa Müller and Carol Ann Lee place Frank's story in the genealogical context of the story of her parents' courtship, and in the historical context the progress of the Holocaust in Holland, as indeed she does herself. Both also pay attention to the question of who betrayed the presence of the Annexe dwellers to the authorities, and gather what evidence is available about Frank's time in Auschwitz and Bergen-Belsen. But if such works might appear to satisfy the misgivings of those who believe that our knowledge about the Holocaust, and indeed about Frank, should go beyond the diary, biographies can only serve to renew our focus on the individual, whilst simultaneously detracting from the force of the diary as a Holocaust text. Biography becomes a means of reinforcing, rather than challenging, Frank's exemplary status, precisely because the existence of a biography is a means of guaranteeing the importance of an individual's life. Paradoxically, these biographers are forced to spend a disproportionate number of pages on Frank's forebears and her legacy, revealing both the paucity of available material for Frank's own life and the inadequacy of usual biographical protocol for such a subject.[21] Such genealogical material would more usually be used to establish the causes of particular personal characteristics or types of behaviour in adult life; in Frank's case, we have the causes, but only a partial sense of the effects. These biographies might oblige us to look the horrors of the Holocaust full in the face, but as Anne Karpf points out, this 'is not what we want Anne Frank for' ('Let's Pretend', p. 10), and neither Lee nor Müller breaks away in any fundamental sense from the portrayal of Frank as 'a symbol of beatified bravery' ('Let's Pretend', p. 10).

I have been arguing here that Frank's diary is still worth reading, but that it can benefit from being read differently. It is a fragile text to bear the weight of critical apparatus or critical interpretation; but looking beyond the commonly accepted images of Frank, as both writer and victim, can raise questions about why we needed the diary to perform the functions that it has performed over the years. It is important to acknowledge that the inconsistencies, uncertainties and disturbances to subjectivity that are explored in and displayed by the diary are as important than any message it might convey about the need for tolerance and hope. The apparent familiarity of Frank's musings and even of aspects of her daily life should not become a screen to mask the ultimate alterity of the Holocaust from the reader, not least because, as I have shown, they often appear to have failed to perform this role for the writer. Frank's diary is always complete in itself, as a piece of Holocaust testimony, and always partial and deficient as an historical document, but both these functions need acknowledging.

4
Charlotte Delbo: Writing and Survival

The first volume of Charlotte Delbo's autobiographical trilogy *Auschwitz and After* is called *None of Us Will Return*. Its final vignette, 'Springtime', ends with the juxtaposition of two blank statements: 'None of us will return. None of us was meant to return' (Delbo, *Auschwitz*, pp. 113–14)[1]. The narrator evokes, in the present tense, her belief, while she was in Auschwitz, that she would not survive, and then asserts not the positive fact of survival, but the sense that, as Primo Levi suggests, those who have survived are 'an anomalous minority' (Levi, p. 64). To survive is to defeat the destructive logic of the Holocaust but this is a bitter victory, not only because others have not been so fortunate, but also because of the impossibility of 'return'. Lawrence Langer has suggested that 'Delbo exposes the insufficiency of Freud's aphorism that to endure life one must be prepared for death, by modifying it in a way that Freud could not have anticipated: having survived death, how is one to return to life?' (*Age*, p. 203). More specifically, as the title of the trilogy indicates, Delbo asks whether it might be possible, through writing, to bridge the gap, both temporal and experiential, between before and after when after was not supposed to happen. As Michael Rothberg notes, Delbo is very much aware that the 'accidental release from the extreme [...] does not constitute a release from the demands of the extreme' (p. 162). Her project does not simply involve attempting to create an autobiographical narrative that can encompass the Holocaust and its impact on her as just another episode in her life. As the phrase, 'None of us will return' indicates, she is also concerned to express her experience as one of a group, whilst simultaneously displaying an awareness of the dangers of generalizing about Holocaust experience. This leads her to distinguish between the way in which she, as a female, French, non-Jewish political prisoner, is treated, and how other groups fare. It also results, in the final part of the trilogy in particular, in her combining her own first person account with accounts in other voices. Delbo is therefore alert both to the importance to her own survival of the altruism and assistance of others, and to the potential dangers of either universalizing such experiences or viewing them as an example of 'triumph over adversity'.

Rothberg characterizes the thee volumes of *Auschwitz and After* in the following way:

> *None of Us Will Return* [...] assembles micronarratives that in their isolation reveal the spatial closure and repetitive temporality of Auschwitz; *Useless Knowledge* renders narrative as a metonymic chain that both traces and transgresses the various internal and external borders of the concentrationary universe [...]; and *The Measure of Our Days* [...] presents a contradictory collective of individual voices that upsets the temporality of before/during/after. (p. 175)

This description conveys the changes in perspective which are perceptible in each successive volume. *None of Us Will Return* only gestures towards and does not describe the eventual end of the time in Auschwitz. We know that the narrator must have survived in order to be able to deliver the narrative, but what Delbo conveys strongly is the sense, then, that such survival was impossible. *Useless Knowledge* 'transgresses [...] borders' in its depiction of the liberation, but within this volume Delbo also describes her earlier imprisonment in France, and her move from Auschwitz to Ravensbrück. Rothberg identifies Delbo as a writer who challenges the notion of the 'concentrationary universe', and shows how its 'radical strangeness [...] opens onto the familiarity of the known world' (pp. 143–4).[2] This is one effect of the volume *The Measure of Our Days*, which contains a variety of responses to the aftermath of the Holocaust; the status of these, whether as Delbo's imaginative reconstructions of her former comrades' experiences, or as the transcription or reworking of interviews with them, is difficult to discern from internal evidence.[3]

However, although Rothberg's broad characterization of the different temporalities of these volumes is accurate, my concern here will be with the points at which they all, and not just *Useless Knowledge*, disturb usual notions of 'before/during/after'. As Rothberg notes, the very title of the trilogy, *Auschwitz and After*, asserts the necessity of confronting event and aftermath, not only on the part of survivors, and not only in a sequential, cause and effect manner.

Throughout the trilogy, as well as in later writings, Delbo attempts to anatomize how her memory functioned then, as well as how it functions at the moment of writing. One aspect of this is communicated by, 'None of us will return. None of us was meant to return'. Remembering from the vantage point of now what it felt like, then, to be living in a continuous present exposes the problems of creating continuity between now and then. It is not only the disjunctive nature of what she experienced at Auschwitz that makes it difficult, or even impossible, to incorporate into an autobiographical narrative in a straightforward fashion; memory and the perception of time are each shown to have been distorted and confused during her imprisonment also. If, while in Auschwitz, looking forward was barely possible, looking back, remembering life before, was also of little consolation. I will begin here by examining some of these different ways of conceptualizing memory, whilst acknowledging Delbo's concern with memory's deficiencies and failures and the concomitant problems with testimony. As Dori Laub points out, the therapeutic or personal functions of testimonial narrative do not always coincide with its historical functions (Felman and Laub, pp. 59–60). Delbo herself is very much aware of this, and thematizes the difficulties of bearing witness. At various points in *None of Us Will Return*, after describing episodes of murder or torture, Delbo comments 'Try to look. Just try and see' (*Auschwitz*, p. 84). This is an exhortation to herself as a witness to look and remember, even if these events seem unreal or incomprehensible, and a demand is simultaneously being made of the reader: do not turn away from these horrors.[4] Yet Delbo is too aware of the deficiencies of language to allow any simplistic or straightforward identification on the reader's part. The reader is both called upon to look and see, and, ultimately, made aware of the impossibility of ever really knowing what has been shown to them.

At the outbreak of war, Delbo was touring South America as assistant to the theatre director Louis Jouvet.[5] In late 1941 she travelled back to Paris to join her husband Georges Dudach, and became involved in the production of anti-German leaflets. Although never a member of the Communist Party, claiming her allegiance to communism to be philosophical rather than political, it was as a communist that she was arrested with Dudach in March 1942. He was executed by firing squad in May that year. Delbo remained in prisons in France until January 1943 and was then sent to Auschwitz-Birkenau, where she spent six months, before being moved to Raisko and finally on to Ravensbrück in January 1944. After each of these moves conditions for Delbo and her fellow prisoners improved, albeit marginally, and towards the end of the war, she and many of her compatriots in Ravensbrück were released into the hands of the Red Cross and sent to recuperate in Sweden. The time span over which Delbo initially produced her autobiographical writings is worth noting here. *None of Us Will Return* was written in 1946 but was not published until 1965. According to Lawrence Langer, Delbo put the text 'away in a drawer', wanting to ensure that it would stand 'the test of time' (Delbo, *Auschwitz*, p. x). *Useless Knowledge*, written in 1946–47, was first published in 1970, with *The Measure of Our Days*, written in the mid-1960s, appearing in 1971. Over the course of these volumes, Delbo manages to convey with precision the ways in which her experience, and her understanding of her experience, of the camps changed and developed.

Langer's comment implies a double function for the first two volumes: as attempts to capture the impact of the Holocaust in its immediate aftermath they are locked away; once published, they become interventions in a public debate about the memory, and indeed the history, of the Holocaust in France. Geoffrey Hartman, referring principally to the legacy of the Holocaust in America, suggests that although there were survivors telling their stories in the immediate aftermath of the Holocaust, the willingness to listen was displaced by a desire to look to the future. More problematically, 'the disbelief or guilt that cruel memories aroused isolated rather than integrated the survivor' ('Learning', p. 201). Otto Frank's first efforts to publish Anne Frank's diary in the late 1940s met with limited success,[6] and although as Thatcher notes, Primo Levi's *If This is a Man* first appeared in 1947, it was only on republication in 1958 that it received a wide readership (*Literary Analysis*, p. 25). Other memoirs published in the immediate aftermath of the war, such as Mary Berg's diary from the Warsaw ghetto, have never been republished. If the capture and trial of Eichmann in 1960 brought the Holocaust back into American public consciousness, as Hartman suggests, other events had relevance in the specifically French context. Henry Rousso has tracked the development of the 'myth of resistance' in France, which led to a focus on the fate of political prisoners rather than Jews in official and unofficial discourse on the Holocaust, as well as to a downplaying of the extent of French collaboration in the deportation of Jews and others. As Thatcher notes, 'The long delay in incorporating Jewish memory into national history has several causes [...] but bears witness above all to a reluctance to evoke the explicit anti-Semitism of the Vichy government' ('La Mémoire', p. 96).[7] Those returning from the camps at the end of the war, whatever the reasons for their imprisonment, did not fit the image of the heroic Resistance fighter, which became the most powerful and attractive element of the 'mythical' image of France at war.[8]

Although, according to Rousso, events in the mid- to late-1960s such as the interment of the remains of the Resistance leader Jean Moulin in the Panthéon in 1964, and the student protests of 1968, made this a propitious time for interventions into the debate on the legacy of the war, Delbo's memoir appears to refuse direct engagement with issues such as resistance and collaboration. Only infrequently, as in the chapter 'Jacques' in *The Measure of our Days*, is the tangled world of the Resistance portrayed directly. However, as Karein K. Goertz notes, 'Having been arrested by French police who then handed her over to the Gestapo, Delbo could personally testify against a myth that ignored widespread French collaboration with the Nazis. By foregrounding her concentration camp experiences rather than her activities in the resistance movement, she chose to oppose the national trend of evading unfavorable memories' ('Body, Trauma', p. 165). Issues of race and religion are introduced as factors affecting and limiting day-to-day interactions in the camps, and political critique remains implicit. Thatcher points out, for example, that patriotism is displaced for Delbo by solidarity with her compatriots, a bond based on linguistic expediency as much as common national roots ('La Mémoire', p. 100). Throughout the trilogy, however, identifying an otherwise anonymous individual as Jewish is a means by which Delbo acknowledges her own inevitable implication in the crude identity politics of the camp, and this is also how the broader historical and political context is incorporated into her autobiography. Delbo does not give a chronological, cause and effect account of how she came to be imprisoned, nor does she draw in the 'historical background' to her incarceration in a systematic fashion. But this does not de-historicize what happened to her. Rather, the gradual and indirect introduction of information about the reasons for her imprisonment indicates that the traumatic impact of her time in Auschwitz stemmed for Delbo from the manner in which the usual markers of individuality, and by extension, the historical, were apparently eroded. Delbo resists simply reinserting her experience into a context that seemed inaccessible or of little use to her then and instead attempts to replicate the emptying out and gradual recomposition of her subjectivity.

Traumatic memory

Delbo's most systematic and explicit attempt at exploring how her memories of Auschwitz affected her throughout the rest of her life is found in the first chapter of her final work, the posthumously published *Days and Memory* (1985). Beginning with a comparison between a snake shedding its skin and 'shedding' her Auschwitz self, she then comments that 'the skin of memory does not renew itself' (Delbo, *Days*, p. 2). The old self, and the old memories, cannot – even should not – be sloughed off, but have to be kept in some way sequestered. Developing this image, she suggests that 'an impermeable skin' (Delbo, *Days*, p. 2) keeps her former self separate from her present self:

> No doubt, I am very fortunate in not recognizing myself in the self that was in Auschwitz. To return from there was so improbable that it seems to me I was never there at all. [...] [E]verything that happened to that other, the Auschwitz one, now has no bearing upon me, does not concern me, so separate from one another are this deep-lying memory and ordinary memory. I live within a twofold being. The Auschwitz double doesn't bother me, doesn't interfere with my life. [...] Without this split I would not have been able to revive. (Delbo, *Days*, p. 3)

What is at stake here is not a denial of the importance or impact of the time in Auschwitz on who she now is. Rather, in writing of an

'Auschwitz self', Delbo is indicating the difficulty of remembering, and by extension, recording, that time, and the self she was then. The difference between 'deep-lying memory' and 'ordinary memory' is also important. Delbo refines this distinction, separating the 'deep memory' of Auschwitz from 'external' or 'intellectual' memory. Deep memory, normally kept apart from the everyday, can emerge unbidden in dreams, and has a visceral force: '[I]n those dreams [...] the suffering I feel is [...] unbearable [...] I feel death fasten on me, I feel that I am dying.' (Delbo, *Days*, p. 3) This type of uncontrollable remembering is contrasted with the type of memory of Auschwitz which arises from external memory, which is 'connected with thinking processes' (Delbo, *Days*, p. 3) and concerns itself with language rather than sensation, the latter being the realm of deep memory. This explains why Delbo can write or speak about Auschwitz in a measured, rational way. Words, she suggests, revert to their commonplace uses: 'Otherwise, someone who has been tortured by thirst for weeks on end could never again say "I'm thirsty. How about a cup of tea?"' (Delbo, *Days*, p. 4).

The distinction between these two types of memory works on two levels: external memory can be consciously engaged and works through language, whilst deep memory arises involuntarily and works through physicality.[9] Deep memory is excessive, assaulting the individual's subjectivity at a fundamental level: 'I feel that I am dying.' When Delbo comments: '[W]hile knowing perfectly well that it corresponds to the facts, I no longer know if it is real' (*Days*, p. 4), she is not merely indicating that memory can be unreliable. Factual, or external, memory has of necessity to leave the excessive reality conjured by deep memory unexpressed. This is a question not just of the difficulty of somehow integrating the two fields of memory with each other to produce a stable and unified self, but also of how this could possibly be communicated. As R.A. Kingcaid suggests, in Delbo's writing, 'it is not only the problem of the referent, that is, the experience of atrocity, of deeds too horrible to recount in words, that threatens the verbal representation of that experience; it is, rather, the loss of faith in the process of signification itself, begun and completed at Auschwitz' (p. 103). Deep memory does not completely defeat language, but it does appear to exceed it in fundamental ways. Lawrence Langer, applying these categories to other survivor testimonies, argues that external and deep memory perform different functions but are nevertheless interdependent:

> Deep memory tries to recall the Auschwitz self as it was then; common [or external] memory has a dual function: it restores the self to its normal pre- and post-camp routines but also offers detached portraits, from the vantage point of today, of what it must have been like then. Deep memory thus suspects *and* depends on common memory, knowing what common memory cannot know but tries nonetheless to express. [...] [W]itnesses [...] often appear troubled or exasperated [...] when the two types of memory intrude on each other, disrupting the smooth flow of their narratives. (*Holocaust*, p. 6, emphasis in original)

Langer here foregrounds the disruption of chronology which Delbo also identifies ('I feel I am dying'), and this notion of memory as defeating usual schemes of temporality or refusing assimilation into the flow of a narrative underlines the traumatic nature of both the events and the process of remembering and writing about them.

Perhaps unsurprisingly, the ways in which Delbo expresses her memories of her life in the camps develop as, temporally, she moves on. It could be suggested that by this point, more than thirty years after her release, she has developed a highly contrived mechanism for keeping certain events and associated emotions at bay. External memory appears to be both controlled and controlling, although it can nevertheless have no control over dreams. Delbo's description of the impact of her dreams about Auschwitz recalls Freud's description of traumatic dreams which 'repeatedly [bring] the patient back into the situation of his accident' (Freud, *Beyond*, p. 7), although her experience was not a single traumatic 'blow' or accident but a series of such blows, an encounter with death that was not momentary but sustained. Delbo brings into focus particular incidents such as her experience of extreme thirst, or the first time she witnesses the death of a fellow prisoner, incidents that are themselves traumatic 'blows', but these are embedded within an overarching situation that is itself traumatic. Kai Erikson has suggested that it is useful to think of trauma as a state that can arise 'from a period of severe attenuation and erosion as well as from a sudden flash of fear' (p. 185). Delbo's experience could be seen to have something in common with the other writers I have discussed here in that it appears to have combined both these aspects, the sudden flashes of fear embedded within a period of continual and sustained anxiety.

Ascertaining whether Delbo's writing displays evidence of neurosis or pathology, that is, whether these circumstances rendered her traumatized from a clinical point of view, is not my primary concern here, but it is worth briefly considering one reading of her work that does appear to attempt a 'diagnosis'. Bessel van der Kolk and Onno van der Hart cite Delbo's description of her 'double self' as an example of dissociation, in which two different internal worlds coexist but are not integrated with each other. Their primary focus is on how the theories of Pierre Janet might be used in the treatment of trauma, and specifically, how the process of the integration of painful memories might be eased. A key suggestion is the use of suggestive techniques in which the traumatic memory is, to some extent, neutralized: 'Memory is everything. Once flexibility is introduced, the traumatic memory starts losing its power over current experience. By imagining [...] alternative scenarios, many patients are able to soften the intrusive power of the original, unmitigated horror' (van der Kolk and van der Hart, p. 178). Ruth Leys explains that Janet viewed traumatic memory as simply repetitive, with the trauma constantly being re-experienced as happening in the present; he saw the task of therapy as the transformation of this into narrative memory, 'which *narrates the past as past*' (*Trauma*, p. 105, emphasis in original). However, as Leys points out, what is downplayed in an analysis such as van der Kolk and van der Hart's is 'that aspect of [Janet's] psychotherapy that seeks to make the patient *forget*' (*Trauma*, p. 106, emphasis in original). Introducing 'flexibility' ultimately meant, for Janet, the liquidation of the traumatic incident from the memory.

In van der Kolk and van der Hart's schema, Delbo, being '(partially) aware' of the nature of her experiences (rather than having completely dissociated them), would be likely to be able to tell her story 'with a mixture of past and present', but the past experiences might intrude in the form of 'guilt and shame' (van der Kolk and van der Hart, p. 178). In some respects, this is an accurate characterization of Delbo's writing. However, the disruption of memory is not simply a formal characteristic or narrative trope that could be stripped away in order to reveal the true nature of what happened. Delbo's description of living in symbiosis with her memories of the Holocaust evokes not the ossification of these memories but a constant process of reinterpretation and reassessment, reassessment that is traceable through the course of her writing on this subject. Deep memory is an inassimilable remainder of the Holocaust but, as I will show, throughout her work Delbo struggles to somehow convey its referential force whilst retaining the sense of its alterity and of her changing relationship to it. Even though she appears to experience deep memory in the present, implying that it is unassimilated, she nevertheless conveys the changing contexts in which it reimposes itself. This means that the disruption of chronology is not merely a narrative device but also a principle theme of Delbo's work.

Memory now

Given these disruptions of chronology, encapsulated by, 'None of us will return. None of us was meant to return', the trilogy as a whole is best described as episodic in structure. However, *None of Us Will Return* in particular is characterized by a repetitive temporality, conveyed largely through the descriptions of roll call that structure the text. Although by the end of the text, spring has arrived, for the most part, Delbo conveys a lack of differentiation between days, and the difficulty of measuring the passage of time. Chapter headings emphasize this: 'One Day', 'The Next Day', 'The Same Day', 'Roll Call', 'Daytime'. These markers attempt to anchor particular incidents but in fact serve to underline that the deadening – indeed deadly – routine is broken for the most part not by moments of respite (although these do occur) but by confrontation with horrors. Haft, discussing the attention given to roll call by writers including Delbo, notes, 'The normal ones, that is, the [roll calls] without incident, were in the minority' (p. 79). In 'One Day', for example, Delbo describes, initially in the past tense, standing at roll call and watching a woman who has broken ranks attempting to climb through a ditch, for no initially discernible reason. Averting her eyes from this sight, the narrator's gaze falls instead on a 'dancing female skeleton' (Delbo, *Auschwitz*, p. 26) outside Block 25, a transition point on the way to the gas chambers. At this point, however, a different time frame intrudes into the account: 'Presently I am writing this story in a café – it is turning into a story' (Delbo, *Auschwitz*, p. 26). This metanarrative intervention has several functions. The disjunction between the story being told and the setting in which it is being written could be seen as a way for Delbo to place the events being described at a safe distance: she saw these things, but she is not seeing them any more; she is writing them. Thatcher suggests that here Delbo also 'establishes a distance between the horror described and the reader' (*Literary Analysis*, p. 139), and that in exposing 'the fact that this is a retrospective reconstruction [she] allows herself and the reader to deal with the traumatic evocation' (*Literary Analysis*, p. 140). I would suggest that there is a potentially troubling aspect to this device, however. The reader is alerted to the fact that this account has taken on – is in the process of taking on – a literary form, but it is not clear whether 'turning into a story' is positive, in that it provides a means of working through and controlling these memories, or negative in that it detracts from their precision or initial impact.

Following this break, the story continues, in the present tense. The woman in the ditch has been trying, evidently, to reach a handful of snow to eat: 'Since the break of day she was fascinated by this clean snow she hoped to reach' (Delbo, *Auschwitz*, p. 27). The woman herself is not testifying to this fascination, and here, 'turning into a story' is evidenced in the narrator's focalization and explanation of the woman's sentiments. Perhaps more startlingly, at this point Delbo introduces a simile which further complicates the temporal and referential frame of the story:

> Her back hunches, shoulder blades protruding through the worn fabric of her coat. It's a yellow coat, like that of our dog Flac which had grown thin after being ill, and whose whole body curved, just before he died [...] She is huddling in the snow. His back-bone arched, Flac is going to die – the first creature I ever saw die. (*Auschwitz*, p. 27)

Delbo here remembers back to her childhood, and it is impossible to ascertain whether, sitting in the café, she is recalling that this parallel, between the woman and Flac, came to her at the time, or whether this is part of the process of turning the incident into a story. Using such an analogy, between a woman and a pet dog, might seem grotesque, or somehow unfitting. Berel Lang, discussing non-fictional representations of the Holocaust, argues that '[f]igurative discourse "estranges" the subject of representation [...] The effect of the addition [of the figurative] is then to misrepresent the subject and thus [...] to diminish it' (pp. 144–5). The ethical implications of such a misrepresentation are what exercises Lang; but this argument is based on limiting definitions of both Holocaust writing and figurative language. Addressing the apparent incompatibilities identified by Lang, Andrea Reiter suggests that in Holocaust memoirs what might be perceived as a 'metaphorical shortfall' or a clumsy use of figurative language can in fact be seen as 'reflecting the wish of former prisoners to keep at least linguistic sovereignty over the violent ending of life' (p. 42). Thus an apparently inappropriate metaphor can have a meaning beyond that which can be decoded from the words on the page. With specific reference to Delbo's use of the image of the dog, Nathan Bracher similarly suggests that this image, and its focalization from the point of view of a child, can be seen as symptomatic of the fact that Auschwitz has 'removed all purity of sentiment' (p. 257),[10] leaving the prisoners in a state of semi-articulacy and childlike helplessness. I would argue that Delbo is aware both of the potentially grotesque nature of this conjunction, but also of the reasons why it has come to mind. The death of the dog was her first experience of death, and her memories of it are vivid. The implication is twofold: not only are people allowed to die like dogs, here in Auschwitz, but this is a death for which there can be no explanation or consolation. Existing reference points – the death of a dog – reveal their own inadequacy.

The incident also has a coda in that the woman finally has an SS dog set on her. Again, the domestic or familial associations of the dog are shattered. It becomes instead an instrument of death. At this point, there is a second, more explicit, moment of identification with the dying woman: 'A wrenched-out scream. [...] We do not know if the scream has been uttered by her or by us, whether it has issued from her punctured throat, or from ours. I feel the dog's fangs in my throat' (Delbo, *Auschwitz*, p. 28). This not only conveys the visceral intensity of witnessing such an occurrence, but also underlines the sense that Delbo, at this point, knows that she could meet the same fate. I read this not as an appropriation of the anonymous woman's pain, or a diversion away from the other woman onto the feelings of the narrator; what is exposed is precisely the fragility, at this point, of Delbo's sense of herself as an individual. The final line of this chapter reinforces this: 'And now I am sitting in a café, writing this text' (Delbo, *Auschwitz*, p. 29). This blank statement communicates the author's own lack of belief in her own survival, that it seems incredible that she has survived where others did not, so incredible that it has to be repeatedly asserted. But it also re-emphasizes the difficulty of binding together then and now into a coherent whole. Writing seems to be the only means, however flawed, of attempting to forge such a connection.

The concluding chapter of this volume, 'Springtime' reinforces this difficulty, and not only through the conjunction of 'None of us will return' and 'None of us was meant to return'. Once again, memories of life before the camp are introduced. These are of a more general kind than the memory of Flac's death, but are no less painful. For most of *None of Us Will Return*, it is winter. The imminence of spring should at least provide the physical respite of warmth, but for Delbo it provokes memories that cannot be assimilated with her present situation:

> Far beyond the barbed wire, spring is flitting, spring is rustling, spring is singing. Within my memory. Why did I keep my memory?
>
> Why keep the remembrance of streets with echoing cobblestones, [...] the recollection of laughter, spring hats, bells ringing in the evening air [...] ?
>
> Here the sun is not the spring sun. It is the sun of eternity, a sun of the world before creation. And I have kept the memory of a sun shining on the earth of the living, a sun warming wheatfields. [...] Why did I keep my memory? (Delbo, *Auschwitz*, p. 112)

If, writing in the café, Delbo is unable to find a fit between her present situation and what she is remembering, in this passage a similar disjunction is shown to have been in operation then. Just as her existing understanding of death proves inadequate to death as she confronts it in Auschwitz, so existing associations of springtime are a burden rather than a means of sustenance. Effectively wishing away her earlier life through her dismissal of her memories, Delbo here also points to the impossibility of 'return'. Life afterwards cannot simply be stitched together with life before in some semblance of continuity, not least because of the assault on subjectivity with which Delbo finds herself wishing to collude at this point. It would be easier to give in and not have to think about before or after. Yet, if in suggesting that the sun here is 'not the spring sun' she remembers, Delbo seems to point to the notion of the camps as separate 'universe' with their own unique moral code and vocabulary, she simultaneously undercuts this suggestion when she switches back to the past tense: 'None of us was meant to return.' The suppression of memory, which might have served as a tactic for survival within the camps, cannot be reconciled with the need to continue afterwards. Indeed, afterwards, there is an imperative not to segregate, or indeed, forget, the disturbances which are being described here.

If in *None of Us Will Return* Delbo attempts to communicate the rawness of what would she would later label 'deep memory', in *Useless Knowledge*, a more systematized but no less complex representation of memory can be discerned. Parts of *Useless Knowledge* seem to overlap with the earlier volume; for example both contain descriptions of extreme thirst, but in *Useless Knowledge*, this thirst is finally satisfied, notably by the intervention of two other prisoners. *Useless Knowledge* does contain breaks in chronology similar to those found in *None of Us Will Return* but these tend not to be so jarring as, for example, the sudden switch to the author writing in the café discussed earlier. The problems posed by memory nevertheless remain. One important example is the chapter 'The Stream'. Here Delbo describes, paradoxically, an incident that she cannot remember. Indeed, there is doubt as to whether this incident happened at all:

> Strange, but I don't recall anything about that day. Nothing but the stream. [...]I was [...] with my small group: Viva, Carmen, Lulu, Mado. [...] [I]t is quite certain that on that day I must have been with them. Yet, though I see them clearly in all the places where we worked together, I find it impossible to envision them near me on the day of the stream. (Delbo, *Auschwitz*, pp. 147–8)

Delbo's recollection of being alone at the stream is contradicted by her knowledge of the lack of privacy that characterized life in the camp. She is able to calculate when the incident might have happened, mainly through her memory of when particular women died, but other details evade her and have to be supplied by inference: 'Perhaps we sat down, because the weather was fine. But sitting on what? [...] [W]as there any grass? Probably, since it was near the stream' (Delbo, *Auschwitz*, p. 148). The reader might ask why Delbo persists with the description of this incident given the paucity of verifiable detail. The reason is that she believes this to have been one of the few occasions to have provided respite during her imprisonment and it therefore has to be recuperated in some fashion:

> [A]ll my thoughts were focused on what I had to do to wash myself, to remove the dirt as fast and thoroughly as possible. [...] My hand full of wet earth, I started to rub the right thigh, directly above the knee. My skin was getting lighter, redder. Yes, it really looked lighter. [...] It must have happened like this, but I have no memory of it. I only recall the stream. (Delbo, *Auschwitz*, pp. 152–3)

It could be objected that Delbo here treads dangerous ground, blurring as she does the status of this incident, never making it clear whether it is a reconstructed memory, an hallucination or even wishful thinking. But it is important, I think, that she foregrounds her own uncertainty on this issue. She is not claiming to have complete recall of what happened, and does not lead the reader to believe that this would be possible. She cannot choose what she remembers, but she can exercise some choice over what she writes, and is careful to qualify any claim her account might have to accuracy.

This account could be interpreted as an example of the replacement of unpleasant with more bearable memories that van der Kolk and van der Hart prescribe: perhaps what is being veiled here is something deeply disturbing. Alternatively, the incident at the stream could be functioning as a 'screen' memory, which in Freud's definition involves the 'displacement' of 'really significant' impressions by 'indifferent ones' ('Childhood Memories', p. 43). However, Freud points out, comparing screen memories to another type of forgetting: 'With the forgetting of names we *know* that the substitute names are *false*: with screen memories we are *surprised* that we possess them at all' ('Childhood Memories', p. 45, emphasis in original). The screen memory is typically an apparently trivial one, which only yields the impressions it is masking in analysis. In Delbo's case, it is not so much that a 'trivial' memory has displaced a significant one, rather that only the bare fact of the existence of the stream itself can apparently be recalled: the rest has to be supposed or reconstructed in a conscious fashion. Indeed in a later example, 'The Funeral', from *The Measure of our Days*, Delbo seems almost to wish that some of the less significant events had left a greater impression. Delbo describes being reunited, some years later, with fellow survivors, on the occasion of the death of one of their number. When they reminisce, Delbo is unable to recall an incident, to which the others testify, when they managed, unusually, to obtain some tomatoes:

> "I know why she doesn't remember. It was the time she was in a daze. She was off her head".
> [...] Stupid to forget those tomatoes. Tomatoes don't constitute a weighty memory. Why not rather forget the smell and color of smoke, the red and sooty flames rising from the smokestacks, twisted by the wind, sending the stench in our direction? [...] Why not rather forget thirst, hunger, fatigue, since it does no good to remember all this, and since I'm unable to impart this knowledge? (Delbo, *Auschwitz*, p. 343)

The repeated, indeed continual, physical experiences of 'thirst, hunger, fatigue' persist in memory but are incommunicable. Delbo's vexation stems not only from her inability to share the memory of the tomatoes with her fellow survivors, and with the reader, but also from this difficulty of conveying what she can recall. Thus it is not simply a case of wanting to convey something 'good' that happened in the camps. What is recognized here, although not articulated explicitly, is the difference between deep and external memory. External memory fails, either because, as Delbo's friend suggests, the individual is in no physical state to register what is happening, or because, as in the incident of the stream, the event is overwhelmed by other contingencies. The deep memories of ongoing physical hardship persist, Delbo seems to indicate, because of their physical nature, their registration on the body.[11] In this sense, it is misleading to speak of 'remembering' in relation to deep memory, because, by Delbo's account, whilst they can be suppressed, these memories are never completely forgotten.

Literature and memory

In *Days and Memory*, Delbo describes an incident which occurred in Auschwitz, when she was on a work detail helping to move bricks:

> Those bricks were heavy, and got heavier as the day wore on. [...] Yvonne said to me: "Why can't I imagine I'm on the Boulevard Saint-Michel, walking to class with an armful of books?" and she propped the two bricks inside her forearm, holding them as students do books. "It's impossible. One can't imagine either being somebody else or being somewhere else." (p. 2)

This is one example of how memories of life before the camps failed to be of assistance in assuaging present pain. Rather than allowing Yvonne to imaginatively transport herself back to her earlier life as a student, imitating the gesture of carrying books serves only as a reminder of the disjunction between her earlier and her present circumstances. Particularly in *Useless Knowledge*, Delbo describes other attempts to bring earlier knowledge to bear on the present situation, as a means of meditating on the faculty of memory. The description of spring in *None of us Will Return* is an example of this, but in *Useless Knowledge*, Delbo also describes more formalized or even ritualistic uses of memory. She describes exercising her memory, while in Ravensbrück, by repeating telephone numbers or metro stations. Other exercises have a literary aspect; she manages 'at the price of infinite efforts' to remember fifty-seven poems: 'I was so afraid they might escape my mind that I recited them to myself every day, all of them' (Delbo, *Auschwitz*, p. 188). Then, she trades her bread ration for a copy of Molière's play *Le Misanthrope*: 'I had a whole book I could memorize [...] I learned *Le Misanthrope* by heart [...] [U]ntil departure, I kept the play within my throat' (Delbo, *Auschwitz*, p. 188). The desire to remember metro stops and telephone numbers might seem to contradict Delbo's earlier comment that 'one couldn't be sustained by one's past' (Delbo, *Auschwitz*, p. 168). However, what appears to be at stake here is not only the notion of memories of the past as an aspect of one's identity – attempting to summon, through a physical gesture, one's former status as a student, for instance – but also the very faculty, or structure, of memory. In the present circumstances, the telephone numbers are another form of 'useless knowledge'. Delbo is not simply reminding herself that she might one day need this knowledge again and should therefore cling to it. By setting herself the apparently random task of learning telephone numbers or *Le Misanthrope*, she is allowing herself some small degree of agency over what is entering her mind, using her memory in a way that is normally disallowed or unnecessary in the camps. She also uses this exercise as a means of distancing herself from present circumstances. So, for example, she notes that she would recite part of the play to herself during roll call each day. This is not simply memory being used as a form of escapism, something to take her mind off the present situation; Delbo does not, for example, suggest that the content of this play had any particular resonance for the situation in which she found herself, and keeps it in her 'throat', not her mind. Rather, to continue to use her memory in this way is a form of private resistance, a means of attempting to counterbalance the kinds of 'deep' memories that she is absorbing, involuntarily, throughout her imprisonment.

Perhaps unsurprisingly given Delbo's work in the theatre prior to her imprisonment, the incident with *Le Misanthrope* is not the only place where theatrical points of reference are introduced into the text. Noting that discussion of the life before was restricted, in the camp, to '[m]aterial, usable things' rather than anything that might 'awaken pain or regret' she maintains that, nevertheless, after the transfer to Ravensbrück, the women 'wished [they] could read, listen to music, go to the theater' (Delbo, *Auschwitz*, p. 168). Claudette takes it upon herself to 'reconstruct from memory [Molière's] *Le Malade Imaginaire*' (Delbo, *Auschwitz*, pp. 168–9). This act of reconstruction becomes a group effort and one which, like Delbo's later use of *Le Misanthrope*, serves as an intellectual exercise as much as a form of escape. Paradoxically, although the performed version has only four acts, as opposed to the five acts of the original, Delbo comments, '[A]s I recall, nothing had been left out' (*Auschwitz*, p. 169). She describes the actual performance of the play as having provided a reminder of the persistence of 'the imaginative faculty', noting that 'for the space of two hours, while the smokestacks never stopped belching their smoke of human flesh, for two whole hours we believed in what we were doing' (*Auschwitz*, p. 171). This is not a bland assertion of the power of art to somehow transcend human suffering, however. The two hours are, notably, contrasted with the five hundred days which will pass before freedom is attained: preparing and performing the play might allow a brief escape from the daily round of the camp but it is ultimately another form of 'useless knowledge'. Whilst reminding the women of common cultural reference points or indeed of their own humanity, it is not a gesture that can change, improve, or disguise their current situation.

Although Delbo does not use these dramatic texts as points of comparison for people or events in the camp, in *Useless Knowledge* she does refer to other literary representations of memory. Most notably, towards the end of the volume, recalling her superstitious assertion that the French women would be released on the twenty-third of the month, she recounts another event that took place on the twenty-third, her final meeting with her husband Georges Dudach before his execution. Delbo inserts a description of the final meeting as a means of allaying any sense of unalloyed hope at the forthcoming liberation. The description is split into two separate parts, the first in prose, the second in verse. In the first, she describes not what the pair said to each other but the parting itself, comparing this to the ending of Jean Giraudoux's play *Ondine* (1939). Ondine has to leave the mortal world when she has been called three times, and all recollection of her lover, the Chevalier, will be erased from her memory:

> A soldier called out, "Madame!" [...] He called me again, but I would not let go of Georges's hand. The third time he called, I had to go, just like Giraudoux's Ondine [...] After the third call, Ondine would forget her mortal existence and return to the underwater realm. I knew that, like Ondine, I would also forget, since to go on breathing is to forget, and to continue remembering is also to forget. The distance between life and death is far greater than the one between earth and the waters to which Ondine had to return in order to forget. (Delbo, *Auschwitz*, p. 207)

The use of this comparison has a number of effects. It allows Delbo to dilute the pain of the situation she is describing, by elaborating the literary metaphor. Describing the points of comparison between Giraudoux's play and this situation could be seen to function in the same way as reciting poetry or *Le Misanthrope* serves to distract her attention from roll call. However, here, too, literary points of reference are shown to be of limited use or comfort. Ondine's tragedy, at the end of the play, is precisely that she is rendered oblivious to the fact that she once shared the Chevalier's love and inhabited the world of human emotions. Like Ondine, Delbo has no choice but to leave her lover; unlike Ondine, Delbo will always know what it is she has to forget. She also seems to acknowledge that this process of forgetting is inevitable, simply because she will carry on living – 'to go on breathing is to forget'. Even the most conscious effort to recall would prove inadequate. The phrase 'remembering is also to forget' implies that memory, whilst able to preserve discrete images or emotions, ultimately voids them of their initial force. Repeatedly conjuring scenes in the memory not only reduces these scenes to ever-diminishing shadows of the original; there will always be more that is permanently lost. Retelling the final meeting with Georges in another, later piece of writing, Delbo elaborates: 'I call forgetting this faculty of rejecting into insensitivity the memory of a sensation, warm and alive, to transform into images which have lost their ecstatic or frightful power the memory of a living love, a love of flesh and warmth' ('Phantoms', pp. 20–1). The love affair, she seems to suggest, will be preserved only in external, rather than in deep memory; this forgetting is painful but inevitable and perhaps even necessary.

The second part of Delbo's account of this meeting introduces another aspect of her relationship with Dudach and its effect on her attitude towards her own imprisonment. Startlingly, Delbo writes: 'I said to him/ how handsome you are./ It was the beauty of his forthcoming death' (*Auschwitz*, p. 209). Such a comment, especially at this point in the trilogy, might seem simply obscene, or at best naïve. Towards the end of this section, however, Delbo elaborates: 'That's what made him so beautiful/ to have chosen/ chosen his life, chosen his death/ staring both in the face' (*Auschwitz*, p. 210). What is foregrounded here is the fact that, like Delbo, Dudach was a political prisoner, who had known, when undertaking his resistance activities, what the penalty could be. Delbo seems only to be able to make sense of his death by investing it with this element of agency, even if this means, incongruously, turning it into a thing of beauty. Delbo notes earlier: '[F]or my part, I chose the situation that turned me into a victim' (*Auschwitz*, p. 168). Here, she is comparing her fate with that of imprisoned army conscripts, but throughout this volume, Delbo is keen to differentiate between her own situation and that of other prisoners, particularly the Jews, in Auschwitz. Two important aspects of Delbo's autobiography are foregrounded here: the sense of belonging to a supportive group, and by extension, her attitudes towards those who are excluded from this group either by their sex or by their status in the camp.

Remembering the others

Although *None of Us Will Return* presents us with a narrator who often appears to be isolated and estranged from her surroundings, the opening part of the volume, 'Arrivals, Departures', creates a sense of the scope of the Holocaust by describing the diversity of arrivals at 'the largest station in the world' (Delbo, *Auschwitz*, p. 3). These include, 'some from Zagreb, [...] some from the Danube [...] some from Greece, [...] married couples who stepped out of the synagogue [...] boarding-school girls [...] intellectuals: doctors, architects, composers [...] the inexhaustible crowd of those who live in cities' (Delbo, *Auschwitz*, pp. 5–6). The fate of many of these individuals, however, is to be 'fuel' (Delbo, *Auschwitz*, p. 8) for smoking chimneys; this is one of the few but significant indications that Delbo is here focusing on the fate of the Jews. Thatcher suggests that beginning with an acknowledgement of the specific nature of the treatment of the Jews, and, by implication, what she escaped, was an important statement, given the predominant focus on the Resistance at the time the text was published (*Literary Analysis*, p. 114). In Delbo's account, those who do survive the initial selection are differentiated from each other in less nuanced ways. In 'Dialogue', Delbo shows such a system of differentiation in action:

> "You're French?"
> "Yes."
> "So am I."
> She has no F on her chest. A star. [...]
> "[Y]ou think we can survive this?"
> She is begging.
> "We've got to try."
> "For you perhaps there's hope, but for us ..."

She points to my striped jacket and then to her coat, a coat much too big, much too dirty, much too tattered. (Delbo, *Auschwitz*, p. 15)

The bond of nationality is not enough to counteract what both women recognize: that the Jewish woman is much less likely to survive. Throughout Delbo mentions different markers which distinguish the Jewish prisoners from the rest. Whilst all have their hair shorn on arrival, this procedure is repeated at intervals for the Jews, thus marking them out. The Jews, like the woman in 'Dialogue', do not, initially at least, wear striped uniforms, and are further differentiated by a red cross painted on the back of their clothes. Delbo does give one example, however, of a different form of allegiance. In *Useless Knowledge*, she describes being approached by Esther, a Jewish woman who works sorting through the belongings of prisoners who have just arrived. Esther approaches her because she knows Delbo is 'a comrade' (Delbo, *Auschwitz*, p. 139), a reference to Delbo's status as a political prisoner. However, when Esther brings her a toothbrush and toothpaste, Delbo is queasy about accepting such privileges. The toothpaste has Greek writing on it, a reminder that the latest group to arrive were Greek Jews, and that these items belonged to someone who has, in all probability, been gassed. It would be impossible to carry these things with her all the time but if she leaves them in the barracks they will be stolen, besides which, she and her friends have a policy of sharing any 'luxuries' they obtain; 'how does one share this?' (Delbo, *Auschwitz*, p. 141). Thus Delbo feels uneasy about exploiting the dubious advantage of having a 'comrade' who can obtain such goods.

Delbo's experience illustrates that the subdivision of prisoners into different categories served the purpose of dividing them against each other and creating a *de facto* hierarchy, if only between those more or less likely to survive. The corollary of this is that Delbo finds herself part of a group of women of her own nationality, who form altruistic bonds with each other. The beginnings of this, perhaps most strongly pronounced in *Useless Knowledge*, are discernible in *None of Us Will Return*, where Delbo seems to be aware of the fact that such bonds, necessary for survival, nevertheless involve the exclusion of others, or at least the disallowance of certain other empathic ties. As Anna Hardman suggests, 'the affirming memory of relationships coexists with the negation of women outside them.' (p. 61) On one occasion, for instance, during a work break, a woman is singled out when she approaches the stream to wash her cup and is shot by a guard. 'She had gone beyond the limit by less than twenty steps. We make a count of our group. Are we all here? [...] It was one of the Polish women' (Delbo, *Auschwitz*, p. 69). There is, albeit implicitly, relief here that it was not one of her group who was the victim, but in any case, no one could protest about this incident. Later, in *Useless Knowledge*, Delbo describes the disorientating effect of being separated from her group during a sweep of one of the streets in Ravensbrück. She finds herself suddenly 'in the midst of unknown faces. Russian women, Polish women, no one I recalled ever seeing before, no one who spoke French' (Delbo, *Auschwitz*, p. 193). This unfamiliarity, as much as her shadowy knowledge of what her fate might be now she has been gathered up in this way, is a cause of anxiety here. Fear of further transportation or even death is converted into a strong desire to get back to the (relative) safety of her group, away from these strangers. Such a separation might strengthen existing bonds, but it also underlines the fact that these bonds are fragile and can be broken at any moment, leaving Delbo stranded.

On other occasions, Delbo emphasizes the particular gendered qualities of these bonds, but as Hardman notes, the text exposes, 'a whole variety of contradictory, ambivalent and ambiguous memories of [...] relationships with other women' (p. 59). For example, Delbo describes Viva calling her name to bring her round after she faints at roll call: '[I]t is my mother's voice I hear. [...] I feel that I cling to Viva as a child to its mother' (*Auschwitz*, p. 65). While such a comment could be read as an affirmation of the strength of such a bond between women, with Viva powerfully evoking motherly authority in order to bring Delbo back to herself, it also has to be recognized that Delbo here portrays herself as infantilized. This tends to undercut any wholehearted endorsement of the type of 'female bonding' described here. Viva's behaviour is prompted by the circumstances rather than by any intrinsic mothering instinct, and indeed, Delbo also points out that Viva's adoption of the motherly role is a performance: having reproved Delbo for fainting, she switches to a more friendly tone of voice to ask if her friend has recovered. This ability to switch roles, to give reproof or support as necessary, is shown to be as important as any intrinsically female qualities that might be evidenced here.

Delbo describes having had only minimal contact with male prisoners during her imprisonment. Early on in *None of Us Will Return*, she recounts passing a column of men on the way to and from work. Some of the visual markers of identity are the same as for the women, with the Jews wearing civilian clothes, the rest in striped uniforms. Delbo's group whisper that they are French, hoping to find some compatriots, but receive no response. They decide to give the men the surplus of their bread ration, food that the women are too ill to eat: 'We stepped aside to make way for them. Poles? Russians? Pitiful men, oozing misery, like all men here' (Delbo, *Auschwitz*, p. 21). The men fight over the bread and do not thank the women for it and Delbo indicates that it was painful to see men reduced to this. 'We watched them fight, and wept' (Delbo, *Auschwitz*, p. 21). Such a comment might seem to rest, ultimately on a normative notion of proper masculine behaviour, but what is also brought to the fore is that the men's reaction to the gift of bread shows the extent to which their humanity itself, as much as any specifically gendered qualities of it, is being assaulted: they have 'wolves' eyes' (Delbo, *Auschwitz*, p. 21).[12]

The opening chapter of *Useless Knowledge*, 'The Men', explores more fully the extent to which normative gender roles retained a status as points of reference. Delbo suggests that, while imprisoned on the opposite side of the barbed wire, the female prisoners attempted to reassure the men who were unable to carry out their 'manly duty' (*Auschwitz*, p. 117) of protecting the women. On one level this involves falling back on 'resources [...] always possessed by women. They could do the wash, mend the only shirt' (Delbo, *Auschwitz*, p. 118). Carrying out such traditionally female tasks is not simply some spurious means of attempting to shore up the men's masculinity, but also provides a focal point, or distraction, for the women. They galvanize themselves into, for example, putting on a show for the men, in the process attempting to downplay the extent to which 'normal' relations have been suspended or eroded. Delbo's own sentiments towards the men are filtered through her own sense of loss, at this point only implied to the reader. She foreshadows her later description of visiting Dudach before his execution with the elliptical comment: 'I had no husband on the other side. I had been summoned at the Santé four months ago' (Delbo, *Auschwitz*, p. 120). Because of her own bereavement she feels an element of resentment towards the men for surviving at all and this is only eroded when some of her fellow prisoners, who have husbands on the other side of the wire, are summoned to bid them what seems likely to be a final farewell. Delbo feels ashamed of her own coldness towards the men, and, implicitly, for allowing her own sense of loss to prevent her from forming bonds with them. The removal of this group of men, 'indistinct and fraternal' (Delbo, *Auschwitz*, p. 122), is a loss which compounds her own individual loss, and it removes an opportunity for the women to cling onto some shadow of their previous life, even if this is comprised only of carrying out the menial tasks of 'looking after' the men.

In the course of this volume, Delbo describes being transferred to Ravensbrück, and the approach of liberation. Startlingly, for both Delbo and the reader, this transfer between camps involves a journey by civilian train and underground through the centre of Berlin. Delbo describes encounters en route which echo the process of group-formation characteristic of her description of the camp. Observing some workmen on a train station and hearing them speak French, the women try to attract their attention: ' "Hey, hey, over there! Hey, Frenchmen! You're French? We're Frenchwomen!" A man turns around, gives us an unpleasant look, muttering, "Merde!" then takes off at a run to jump into a train across from our track' (Delbo, *Auschwitz*, p. 181). This response is disappointing: 'We discovered an abyss between the world and us, and it made us very sad' (Delbo, *Auschwitz*, p. 181). This comment, with its embedded realization that their status as camp inmates overrides other markers of identification, foreshadows Delbo's later, more explicit expressions of the experiential gulf between those who have been in the camps and those who have not. More is at stake in this particular encounter: the women later realize that this Frenchman was probably part of a 'volunteer' labour corps, and as such unlikely to want to acknowledge his compatriots.[13] A little later in the journey, the women see a large group of men, also being transferred between camps, men in a much worse physical condition than they are: 'Among them there might be an acquaintance, who knows? [...] All of them were unrecognizable' (Delbo, *Auschwitz*, p. 182). They pass the men some bread, again implicitly acknowledging gradations in their status as prisoners. Noticing that passers-by on the station platform are avoiding moving near them, they mutter that they are political prisoners, rather than criminals. Whether such statements are liable to have any effect on the passers-by seems to be less important to the woman than being able to assert this particular marker of identity. Paradoxically, however, such assertions also help explain why the women are unable to take this opportunity to escape. Berlin might be 'full of French people' (Delbo, *Auschwitz*, p. 183) but they are not the right kind of French people – not the kind who would help.

Remembering afterwards

As I have indicated, this incident, in which Delbo and her companions enter the outside world as prisoners, can be seen to foreshadow the difficulties they later face when they have to re-enter the world as free women. Although Delbo retains contact with many of the women after liberation, their identity, as a group, which sustained them in the camps, is of limited use in the outside world. Indeed knowledge that was essential then is now seen as an impediment:

> I have returned
> from a world beyond knowledge
> and now must unlearn
> for otherwise I clearly see
> I can no longer live. (Delbo, *Auschwitz*, p. 230)

In the final volume of the trilogy, Delbo presents a number of different strategies by which she and her fellow prisoners coped after their release from the camps. In choosing to speak for these women – and indeed for two male prisoners – using first person narration, Delbo conveys the tenuous nature of the bonds which persist after liberation. The experiences, and coping strategies of these women are diverse, and some are evidently at odds with Delbo's own means of dealing with the past. In using a range of different first person voices, then, Delbo manages to show that the 'we' of earlier volumes has been fractured into multiple 'I's. As the incident with the forgotten tomatoes shows, these women both do, and do not, have a 'shared' history. This again serves to militate against any suggestion that there could have been anything positive about the women's camp experience, or that it could be something that continues to bind them together as a group. Delbo never loses sight of the adversity that ultimately necessitated these bonds. *The Measure of Our Days* can also be placed alongside the earlier, more concertedly documentary work, *The Convoy to Auschwitz*, first published in 1965, in which Delbo gives brief biographical sketches of all those who arrived in Auschwitz with her. This earlier volume, like a book of remembrance or roll of honour, preserves the bare details: for some prisoners, this is all that is available. There is no pretence that this is anything other than a partial record, however, and Delbo does not claim that she is telling the whole story of what happened at Auschwitz. Such limitations also inform the trilogy, as I have shown. Throughout, Delbo is wary of speaking beyond her own experience. This might seem at odds with the use of the 'I' of the others which occurs in *The Measure of Our Days*, and one might even question whether the use of such a tactic disqualifies this volume from being described as autobiography. But as I have already indicated, Delbo is here both continuing and problematizing the 'group' aspect of the earlier volumes, as well as indicating, at important points, her own attitudes towards the experiences of others. Attempting to write using the voice of the other is here not so much an appropriation as an attempt at 'trying out' these strategies. Delbo is thus not merely authorizing these other accounts through authoring them, but also using them as a means of elaborating or exploring her own experience of 'after'.

Two of the many different experiences described here can usefully be placed alongside each other. In the chapter entitled 'Mado', Delbo gives a first person account of Mado's experiences, expressing sentiments which echo those expressed in the earlier volumes. Despite having a husband and son, and taking an interest in the outside world, Mado has not assimilated or come to an understanding of her past experiences. Her husband expresses the view that not speaking of the past is the path to forgetting, but Mado asserts: 'Forgetting or remembering doesn't depend on our willing it, had we the right to do so. [...] I died in Auschwitz but no one knows it' (Delbo, *Auschwitz*, pp. 266–7). This sentiment echoes Delbo's later elaboration of the 'Auschwitz double': these women function in the 'outside' world but carry another world within them. This can be contrasted with the different tactics of Marie-Louise, in the chapter named for her. Here, Delbo describes, in the first person, her visit to the home of Marie-Louise and her husband Pierre, including large portions of direct speech in which Marie-Louise describes her happy home life. Her loquaciousness is presented as exhausting, and her praise for her husband unreserved: 'I can't tell you how he did it: he put me back in this life without my even noticing it' (Delbo, *Auschwitz*, p. 281). In direct contrast to Mado and her husband, Marie-Louise and Pierre have discussed her past experiences to the extent that Pierre prompts her when she cannot remember the name of the daughter of one of her fellow survivors, despite never having met these women. Delbo's own interventions in the conversation are brief and reserved and her attitude is difficult to discern. At the close of the chapter she refuses to stay the night with the couple: '"Charlotte, you know that this is your home, here with us, with your comrades," Pierre said. I left them standing on the threshold of their pretty house at the end of a cool, shady walk lined with pine trees' (Delbo, *Auschwitz*, p. 288).

Implicitly, such a continuing immersion in the past is something Delbo is not in sympathy with. She does not – could not – condemn the couple for the strategy they have formulated between them, but the brevity of her own interventions in this chapter and the almost comical effect of Pierre reeling off details of his wife's incarceration indicate the gulf between this and Delbo's own experience. However, Mado's relationship to her past is not presented as somehow more authentic simply because it is more obviously painful. What comes across most strongly in the juxtaposition of these survivor accounts is the very diversity of coping strategies that the women adopt, some successful, some much less so. One finds herself unable to leave the house, another finds herself compelled to move to the other side of the world. Some speak, either through choice or compulsion, others remain silent, for similarly diverse reasons. Even silence, or the inability to communicate is eloquent, however; testimony, Delbo implies, is not just about what is said, but about what cannot be said.

Conclusion

Delbo acknowledges the specific problems of writing autobiography about or after Auschwitz. Her own experience showed that to be part of a group was a necessary aspect of surviving there, but that such solidarity was tenuous and could not prevent the difficulties of afterwards. Having shared experiences with other people does not mean that one can necessarily share a history with them. Not only will one be subject to the exigencies of memory, but the group dissolves as quickly as it was formed, and indeed as Langer notes most of the members of that community 'did not return' ('Gendered Suffering?', p. 352). Delbo seems to imply that the notion of a community of survivors is a contradiction in terms, as any positive aspects of the notion of community are tainted by the guilt of having managed to survive at all, when others did not. Surviving an encounter with death, Delbo suggests, can have the paradoxical effect of undercutting the impact of any subsequent testimony: '[I]f what we say were true/ we wouldn't be here to say it' (*Auschwitz*, p. 276). Kingcaid has argued that Delbo seems to be pointing to the difficult conclusion that 'for the sake of coherence' (p. 108) it might have been better if no one came back. This analysis is a bleaker version of Primo Levi's argument that: '[W]e, the survivors, are not the true witnesses. [...] [T]hose who saw the Gorgon, have not returned to tell about it or have returned mute' (pp. 63–4). However, I would suggest, contrary to Kingcaid, that although Delbo acknowledges that the Holocaust was intended to defy witnessing ('None of us was meant to return'), to refuse to testify would be to submit to this logic. Survival is no triumph, and Delbo has no ready formula for how life and indeed writing can continue to be meaningful in the aftermath of destruction, but there was Auschwitz, and there is 'after' and the two have somehow to be encompassed, both autobiographically and historically.

5
Memory in a Foreign Language: Texts by Daughters of Holocaust Survivors

Throughout this study I have examined texts in which the writer concerned describes not only her own experiences but also those of her family, friends or immediate circle. I have suggested that this tactic, not uncommon in autobiography, takes on a special interest when the events concerned are traumatic. A writer such as Delbo, for example, describes sharing particular experiences with her fellow prisoners, but in such a way as to emphasize her isolation at other times. In a different context, Brittain's description of the aftermath of the war focuses on the losses she suffered, but the experiences of the men she mourns remain more or less opaque, both to her and to us. The texts that I will be discussing in this chapter focus on the experiences of others in a rather different way. At the core of Lisa Appignanesi's *Losing the Dead: A Family Memoir* (1999) and Anne Karpf's *The War After: Living with the Holocaust* (1996) are events that occurred not only at a spatial distance but also at a generational one. The subtitles are helpful here. Appignanesi makes a generic claim, foregrounding the fact that she is writing not simply her own autobiography but a life-story which encompasses other members of her family, and not only those who are still living. Karpf uses a different tactic, stressing the continuity of the past into the present. Her focus is the war at one remove; the emphasis is not on living during the Holocaust, but living *with* it, not as a completed past event but as one that has ongoing consequences for both her parents and herself. Appignanesi introduces 'the dead' in the very title of her book, reflecting the importance to her of the retrieving of family history, and attempting to put the dead finally to rest. Karpf might focus to a greater extent than Appignanesi on her own childhood and youth, but she shares this concern with the dead, and both texts also encompass the death of the writer's father. The third text under discussion here, Eva Hoffman's *Lost in Translation: A Life in a New Language* (1989), although also by the daughter of Holocaust survivors, has most usually been discussed in the light of its representation of the difficulties of integrating into a new culture.[1] Nevertheless the Holocaust surfaces in Hoffman's text in ways that make it a useful point of comparison with *Losing the Dead* and *The War After*.

At the outbreak of the war Hoffman's parents, who were already married, left Zalosce, their hometown near Lvov, and travelled to Cracow before going into hiding, initially in a 'branch-covered forest bunker' (Hoffman, *Lost*, p. 4), later in the attic of a peasant farmer's house. A different tactic was used by Appignanesi's parents, who went into 'open' hiding to evade the Warsaw ghetto, passing themselves off as non-Jews. Karpf's parents, who met after the war, both experienced incarceration of different kinds. Karpf's mother, having escaped from Cracow and Tarnów as ghettos were established, was finally captured in Warsaw and sent to P aszów, before being moved to Auschwitz and finally Lichtwerden in the Sudetenland. Karpf's father, meanwhile, was captured by the Soviets during the invasion of Poland at the start of the war and was sent to a Russian labour camp, later working on a collective farm before ending the war in hiding in Warsaw. Despite the differences in these family histories, these authors share a desire to either form or retain a relationship with Poland, as well as to establish a subject position in relation to the events of the immediate past, through the use of autobiography. Hoffman's text in particular exposes the difficulties that arise from being deprived of the 'mother tongue', and similar expressions of linguistic displacement in Karpf and Appignanesi's texts provoke a consideration of wider questions of exile and identity. Although Karpf was born in England, she, like the Polish-born Appignanesi and Hoffman, describes a sense of being insufficiently rooted in British culture to completely 'pass' as a native. It will be necessary then to consider the literal and metaphorical uses to which the term 'exile' has been put in order to consider whether this is an appropriate term for the particular type of displaced, and indeed Jewish, subjectivity that these writers describe. The journeys (back) to Poland undertaken by each writer are also important. These journeys have particular personal, memorial functions, but also provide Appignanesi and Karpf in particular with the opportunity to reflect on the collective means by which the Holocaust has been memorialized or forgotten. I will consider the roles these journeys have as acts of mourning, and what it means to mourn for people one never actually knew.

Storytelling and childhood

Many of the texts I have considered so far contain a representation of the moment when the author undertook the decision to write or rewrite her life story. In the cases of Appignanesi and Karpf, the fact that the autobiographical text is structured round a quest for knowledge means that it becomes self-reflexive. Rather than writing from a fixed narratorial perspective at a point in time after the 'end' of the events depicted, as Brittain does, these two writers, through the use of a mixture of tenses and structural techniques, create the illusion that we as readers are sharing the process of discovery with them. In both these examples, however, a further aspect of the completed text is a display on the author's part of a particular kind of 'expertise', in the form of the knowledge which has been acquired during the journey. So for example, the second part of Karpf's book contains a description of the treatment of post-war Jewish immigrants to Britain as well as a digest of research on the psychological consequences of the Holocaust for children of survivors. It is evident that this research was undertaken by Karpf not simply as a means of providing the reader with some kind of historical context for her experiences and those of her parents but also as a way of providing context for the author herself. This is reflected in the fact that *The War After* traces not only the journeys undertaken by Karpf's parents from Poland to England, but also shows Karpf exploring her own childhood and upbringing.

Although Karpf's researches do lead her to a greater awareness of the broader community to which she might belong, both as a child of survivors and as a Jew, her decision to segregate the socio-historical portion of her research in the centre of the book is emblematic of a continuing sense of uncertainty about relying on supposedly affirmative commonalities. This uncertainty is shared by

Appignanesi, who takes a different approach to the combination of autobiographical and biographical; her description of her journey to investigate places in Poland that have resonance for her family is told in chapters which alternate with descriptions of what actually happened to her parents in wartime. Thus the process of discovery – or at least one aspect of it, the journey – is intercut with the end result, a narrative of her parents' war. However, in both cases, the apparently seamless fit between the present and the bedrock of the past on which it rests is belied by uncertainties, gaps and unanswered questions.

Although Hoffman's text does not have such unusual structural characteristics, her focus on her attempt to become integrated into North American life whilst still holding onto an awareness of herself as Polish displays a similar rift between past and present self, enacted this time on a personal as much as on an inter-generational level. The three parts of *Lost in Translation* are called 'Paradise', 'Exile' and 'The New World', reflecting Hoffman's progress from Poland, to Canada and on to university in America. If in Karpf's and Appignanesi's texts, we as readers follow the authors as they collect and assimilate the information which will become an integral part of their story, Hoffman might appear, in contrast, to have embarked on a journey which takes her only inwards. When she decides to undergo psychoanalysis, she does so in English rather than in Polish, her mother tongue, describing the process as 'translation therapy, the talking cure a second-language cure' (Hoffman, *Lost*, p. 271). The account of her childhood is delivered in the medium of a tongue in which it was not experienced, and her comments about her analysis could equally apply to the book itself, which is as the subtitle tells us, a 'life [story] in a new language': 'It's only when I retell my whole story, back to the beginning, and from the beginning onward, in one language, that I can reconcile the voices within me with each other' (Hoffman, *Lost*, p. 272). However, as Susan Ingram notes, this use of language has to negotiate 'the losses inherent in the translating process' (p. 273). Any translation will be pieced together from fragments.[2] In a sense then, Hoffman does share the self-reflexivity of the other two, as she displays not only the fruits of her research and reflection but also the (apparent) success of the process of assimilation which she is describing.

Hoffman writes from a position of being settled, if not assimilated, in North America, whilst Appignanesi and Karpf are spurred on to write not only by the fact that their parents are getting older, but also by an awareness that they themselves are. This not only means that they have reached a stage of independence from their parents, and, in this respect, have 'lives' worth writing, but they are also starting families of their own. Having children adds an extra dimension to the inter-generational project which each has undertaken. Yet this sense of continuity, or of a legacy being handed on to a third generation is held in tension with a need for the past to be done with, and for the dead to be definitively buried. Karpf expresses a caveat which is relevant here:

> It would be dreadful if being a child of survivors became, in some perverse way, a desirable badge of victimhood. It seems to be difficult for us to maintain the distinctiveness of different historical experiences without ranking them in order of importance and grading their suffering, but [...] there were real similarities and real differences in the experiences of refugees and survivors and their children, and both need acknowledging. The Nazis saw the Jews as a homogenous group, defined only by ethnicity; it behoves us to be able to examine our differences. (*War*, pp. 240–1)

Karpf is here pointing both to the differences between survivors as individuals, and to the differences between being a survivor and being the child of one. In *The War After*, she shows that for many years she had difficulty retaining such distinctions: 'It was as if my parents' experience had become my own; I'd soaked up their fear of loss' (Karpf, *War*, p. 44). The kinds of self-defensive behaviour appropriate to wartime prove inappropriate to the postwar period; Karpf takes on the fears and anxieties projected by her parents but these are excessive in the face of the mundane difficulties she confronts. As Karpf notes, it seems impossible to imagine that the experiences which her parents went through would not have had an effect on their behaviour *as* parents, but this is not intended as a condemnation of them. There is after all no way of assessing what course their lives would have taken in other circumstances, and there is a danger of judging 'Holocaust survivor parents [...] against some ideal of parenting rather than the norm' (Karpf, *War*, p. 234).

144 Women's Autobiography

Interestingly, each of these writers uses a similar analogy to describe how their parents' stories impacted on them when they were children. Taking the fairy tale as the normative type of story told to children, they defamiliarize this narrative form. This is not to say that fairy tales are usually unthreatening or straightforwardly comforting for children; comparing Holocaust narratives to fairy tales foregrounds the fact that both forms of narrative can be simultaneously domestic and estranging.[3] The Holocaust narratives which these women learn as children involve apparently familiar people in circumstances which are beyond immediate comprehension. Hoffman, who writes *Lost in Translation* in the present tense in an attempt to capture the sense of her growing consciousness and self-consciousness, recalls her mother weeping on the anniversary of her younger sister's death:

> The man who saw her go into the gas chamber said that she was among those who had to dig their own graves, and that her hair turned gray the day before her death. That strikes me as a fairy tale more cruel, more magical than anything in the Brothers Grimm. Except that this is real. But is it? It doesn't have the same palpable reality as the Cracow tramway. (pp. 6–7)

Attempting to recreate the perspective of her childhood self, Hoffman shows here that for the child reality is measured in terms of the empirical and experiential; everything else is relegated to the realms of the fairy tale. Later, she describes her father breaking his silence in this way: '[I]t is not until the events have receded into the past that he recounts a few stories from those years – by that time so far removed that they seem like fables again, James Bond adventures' (Hoffman, *Lost*, p. 23). For the teenage Hoffman, in contrast to Karpf, it is easier to simply move on from these stories which seem to contain 'no useful lessons' (*Lost*, p. 25) for her own life. It is only when, some years later in New York, she meets a woman who knew her parents during the war, and hears a new, terrible story about what happened to them, that she can acknowledge that 'this – the pain of this' (Hoffman, *Lost*, p. 25) is where she is from. She has a responsibility to listen again, as an adult, and make a renewed attempt at understanding.

Appignanesi similarly uses the fairy tale as a means of describing her childhood perception of her parents' experiences. She recalls listening to her parents and their friends reminiscing about their earlier lives, at a time when the concept of the 'Holocaust survivor' had yet to be formulated:

> In a sense, these were my childhood fairytales – hideous trajectories, skilfully navigated towards some kind of happy ever after. No one bothered with Grimm. But at the age when I had grown out of fairytales, they persisted. Bored with the repetition, I would go off and lie on the sofa and read the less loaded adventures of the Bobbsy twins or Nancy Drew. I didn't realise then that the repetition was necessary. (Appignanesi, *Losing*, p. 22)

Like Hoffman, however, the grown-up Appignanesi later regrets her inability to appreciate the significance of these narratives, not only for her parents but also for herself. Observing her widowed mother's 'gradual and growing dotage' (Appignanesi, *Losing*, p. 77) she attempts to 'elicit her stories from her in a systematic way' only to discover that '[h]er memories, of course, elude system' (Appignanesi, *Losing*, pp. 80–1). Appignanesi understands her sudden desire for knowledge as a reaction against the valorization of youth which characterized the 1960s, when she was growing up. However, she also has to acknowledge that this desire is belated. By the time she has reached an age at which she wishes to know, her mother's memories have 'already congealed into a series of tableaux' which, in Appignanesi's view, paint over 'the horrors of the War from which they [...] emerged' (*Losing*, p. 81). Appignanesi acknowledges that in order to construct the fullest version of what occurred during the war, she must supplement this 'congealed' version, which doubtless serves particular purposes for her mother at this point of her life, with what she can remember herself of the earlier versions. Like Hoffman, she also sees that third parties (such as acquaintances of her parents) may be of assistance. Thus Appignanesi takes the view that her own task is to discover what underpins the 'fairytale', even if this proves to be devoid of comfort or reassurance. She recognizes that her mother's narratives, while not 'inaccurate' or 'incorrect', are in need of supplementation if their import for her, the daughter, is to be grasped.

Interestingly, Appignanesi's mother also gives a video testimony to a university research team. This too has 'fairy tale' qualities in that, in Appignanesi's view, it draws on particular stereotypical situations. 'There are good people everywhere, good Germans and brave Poles' (*Losing*, p. 82). Although it seems coherent when she views it, when Appignanesi examines a transcript of the testimony, this too is fragmentary and she concludes that it is 'as if the only point of cohesion were her [mother's] own speaking body' (*Losing*, p. 82). Geoffrey Hartman, in his discussion of the Yale video testimony project, expresses a similar point: '[I]n video testimonies [...] there is nothing between us and the survivor; nor, when the interview really gets going, between the survivor and his recollections' ('Learning', p. 198). Hartman believes that the immediacy of testimony makes it more readily comprehensible and in fact induces a greater degree of empathy than 'archive footage depicting [...] anonymous victims' ('Learning', p. 198); Appignanesi's familiarity with her mother as an individual, above and beyond the experience of viewing the video, proves to be a drawback. Indeed Appignanesi finds the roots of her frustration in her feeling that her mother's testimony is 'devoid of history' (*Losing*, p. 83). That her mother, like the witness of the Auschwitz uprising discussed by Laub, cannot provide this context for her own experiences is for Appignanesi a stumbling block. But turning to historical texts leads her to a realization that the post hoc rationalization which the structures of history provide belies the distinguishing qualities of her parents' stories. '[W]hile my parents lived the War, it was a frenzied rush of days and nights [...] Confusion ruled' (Appignanesi, *Losing*, p. 83). It is the desire to ground this rush of events, preserving its immediacy whilst also bridging the gap between the 'fairy tales' and history, that provokes Appignanesi's project. What she also notes at this stage is the fact that in Britain, where she is at this point resident, the cultural mythologies of war are vastly different from those she wishes to understand. Not least, Jewishness is absent, a point which is also made by Karpf. Thus, for Appignanesi, the process of 'grounding' requires, perforce, a journey to Poland.

Anne Karpf takes the decision to systematically tape-record interviews with her parents about their experiences. Prior to this, she, like Hoffman and Appignanesi, has less formal means of assimilating stories about her parents' past. 'The Holocaust was our fairy-tale,' she recalls. 'Other children were presumably told stories about goblins, monsters, and wicked witches; we learned about the Nazis'

(Karpf, *War*, p. 94). Karpf also describes the process by which she developed her own version of their story, and notes a similar effect to the congealing which Appignanesi identifies.

> Through constant recounting, my mother's story also acquired a kind of mythical quality. It was as if the narrative had taken on a life of its own, detached from the original events to which it referred. I found, curiously, that I could never remember those details of either of my parents' wartime experiences which fell outside my usual account. (*War*, p. 95)

Karpf's version takes on a life and truth of its own which is subsidiary to any external points of reference. What she describes here resembles the process which the psychologist Judith S. Kestenberg calls transposition. This is 'an intrinsic factor in the transmission of cultural heritage' and occurs when 'the parent's culture is elaborated by the children and modified' (Kestenberg, p. 70). *The War After* describes Karpf's attempts to unfreeze this narrative and create a version which gains its force from more than just repetition. Whilst Appignanesi creates a freestanding narrative of her parents' past, supplementing what she has learned from them with what she discovers during her journey, Karpf transcribes her interviews with her parents, so that what she, as the author, might have treated as source material to be absorbed and reworked is presented in a relatively unmediated fashion to the reader. This means that Karpf exploits the advantages which Hartman attributes to testimony – such as its directness – and also that, concerned as she is for the most part with the effects of these stories on her own psychological development, she nevertheless allows her parents to speak for themselves. Karpf in this way avoids the danger she identifies of becoming fixated on her own victimhood.

For these writers, then, autobiographical writing involves far more than a simple act of recall and transcription. Each acknowledges the ways in which her own memories, and indeed her own interest in remembering, change over time. One might, as an adult, be able to decode the ideological content of a fairy tale in order to reveal a meaning which was opaque when the story was first told, but the story will nevertheless retain some of its uncanny qualities. When the Holocaust is part of the writer's childhood mythology, this double weight of the comprehensible and the obscure is amplified, not least because ultimately, Holocaust stories are not merely fables or a means of encoding proper behaviour but events with historical causes and effects. Through the use of the fairy tale analogy these writers pose the question of what, if anything, of this should be passed on to the next generation. But each also acknowledges a need to address the question of what would have happened if their parents had not felt the need to leave Poland. For Hoffman, who has memories of her life before emigration, this is a question with concrete implications: throughout the text she reflects on what she would be doing and who she would be with if she were in Poland, at one point suggesting that 'the strange tribe of adolescents' among whom she finds herself in Canada are a 'relatively unidentified species' (*Lost*, p. 131) back there. For Karpf, the question of what might have been has a much hazier answer. During her visit to Poland, she goes to a café and reflects that 'had it not been for the war, this would have been one of my cafés and this my life (My life had always seemed full of the subjunctive.)' (Karpf, *War*, p. 294). But this perhaps perverse nostalgia for what she has never actually known is soon undercut by her acknowledgement that 'had the war not occurred, I probably wouldn't have existed at all: my mother would have remained married to Julius Hubler [her first husband, who died in the war] and given birth to a different set of children' (Karpf, *War*, p. 295). As we shall see, Appignanesi's hope that her visit to Poland will awake childhood memories is dashed in a way which also appears to disallow nostalgia. Thus the search for cultural and indeed linguistic origins is never revelatory of some earlier state of unity, not least because of the fact that these journeys are made in the shadow of death. Hoffman comments that her parents' desire to emigrate in the 1950s was fuelled in part by a fear of events repeating themselves. 'Poland is home, in a way, but it is also hostile territory' (*Lost*, p. 84). This doubling of home and hostile territory is echoed in the relationships which these authors have with their mother tongue.

Mother tongues and naming

The facility to communicate in different languages might be considered an advantage for a writer but the immigrant has in the first instance more mundane reasons for supplementing his or her mother tongue with a second language. Although it is a truism that younger children have a greater facility than adults for acquiring new languages, this does not necessarily make attaining cultural competence any more straightforward.[4] Lisa Appignanesi's experience is a useful example here. Her parents move with her and her older brother from Poland to Paris, but the French which Appignanesi acquires there, at the age of three or four, proves less useful than her parents anticipated when they arrive in Québec. 'French was then not a language for Jews. [...] French schools were for Catholics only. [...] French was battered out of me by a succession of English-speaking teachers of Québecois who didn't like my Parisian' (Appignanesi, *Losing*, pp. 13, 27). Appignanesi's family has unwittingly landed in a country riven by linguistic and religious differences, where anti-Semitism is also prevalent. This means that, 'the duplicities learned in war persisted. [...] [A]t home we were Jewish and in the town we weren't' (Appignanesi, *Losing*, p. 30). This comment echoes Zygmunt Bauman's succinct summation of the late nineteenth- and early twentieth-century assimilationist philosophy: 'Be a Jew at home but a man in the street' (Bauman, p. 86), but Appignanesi also notes that her parents are able to become part of what is essentially an expatriate community of European Jews, which has its own 'lingua franca': Yiddish. The use of Yiddish effaces any prior national identities because it is 'a truly democractic language which [pays] no attention to national borders' and can be 'spoken with any variation of accents or vowels with no stigma of class attached' (Appignanesi, *Losing*, p. 15). If a language can be used in this way, without specific reference to a single national affiliation, it is perhaps not surprising that, conversely, knowledge of a language can also exist aside from an immersion in its cultural context. Appignanesi realizes when she returns to Poland as an adult that she still has a passive knowledge of the language, but this does not help to make Poland any more homely. Karpf shares this ambivalence. Having acquired Polish as a small child despite not being born in Poland, she begins to learn English at the age of two when her older sister starts school. '[O]ur parents continued to talk Polish between themselves and to address us in it, though we replied in English. Polish, therefore, became for me almost entirely a passive language' (Karpf, *War*, p. 294). Realizing on arriving in Poland that she can read

Polish signs and adverts, she feels phrases 'suddenly emerging from the deep sediment of childhood' (Karpf, *War*, p. 294).

However this is not to imply that Karpf, resident in her birth country, necessary feels more 'at home' there than Appignanesi or Hoffman. Karpf notes the role reversal that at times characterizes her relationship with her parents, citing in particular a visit to a supermarket with her father, when she, despite being only two and a half, is able to help him orientate himself. 'I took him by the hand and led him to the right [shelf]. [...] This story said that I was [my parents'] guide, mediating an alien culture to them. This story said I already knew my way around' (Karpf, *War*, p. 17). Yet Karpf also sees a negative aspect of this reversal, in that she, the child, fears for her parents health and safety to an unwonted degree. There are also limits to 'knowing her way around'. She and her sister are 'linguistically more competent' (Karpf, *War*, p. 17) than her parents, but she later cites her inability to acquire 'countless English idioms' which are just one aspect of the 'arcane cultural code' she 'haplessly' fails to grasp. (Karpf, *War*, p. 287) The point Karpf makes here is partly about the type of knowledge one might ordinarily acquire from one's parents, but it is also about the place of the Second World War in British culture; the war of D-day and the Blitz is not the war lived by her parents, and another aspect of Karpf's project is to highlight the relative lack of understanding and knowledge of the events of the Holocaust in Britain throughout the 1950s, 1960s and 1970s, and the concomitant suspicion, often amounting to anti-Semitism, directed towards post-war immigrants. She also has to acknowledge, 'I've always automatically said "they" about the English' (Karpf, *War*, p. 51).

Karpf describes a means by which she communicated some of these dislocations which, while not strictly speaking a language, appears to have functioned as such. Having had eczema as a baby, she later suffers a resurgence of her skin-disorder during a tense period when her parents express disapproval about her non-Jewish boyfriend: '[E]ventually, it all extruded through my hands, unerring somatic proof (the body being an incorrigible punster) that I couldn't in fact handle it' (Karpf, *War*, p. 98). Scratching herself, a form of relief that is simultaneously self-harming, becomes a substitute for linguistic communication: 'But if my unconscious self was trying to articulate its distress, it spoke in a language my conscious self couldn't comprehend, much less converse in. [...] [M]y body [was] the site of war and my skin its front line' (Karpf, *War*, pp. 103, 140). She makes a difficult admission: 'I'd always envied my parents their suffering. [...] In its drama, enormity, and significance, their war could never be matched' (Karpf, *War*, pp. 125–6). Through her autobiography, Karpf comes to incorporate and better understand such feelings, by both considering the experiences of other children of survivors, but also, as I have noted, listening to (and transcribing) her parents' own stories. In this way she can acknowledge the root causes of her parents' behaviour, as well as tracing the genealogy of her own feelings. For Karpf, psychic and cultural history are closely entwined.

It is in *Lost in Translation* that the process of emigration and the switching between languages which this necessitates is most explicitly portrayed as traumatic. Marianne Hirsch has criticized Hoffman for her 'Edenic construction of Cracow' (Hirsch, p. 224), the plausibility of which is severely undermined, for Hirsch, by the stories of Hoffman's parents' wartime experiences. However any nostalgia in the first section of the book, entitled 'Paradise', is effectively undercut by the time Hoffman describes her journey back to Poland. Although she might not feel completely at home in North America, it becomes clear to Hoffman that Poland is no longer home either. Hirsch downplays the fact that Hoffman's description of her 'Edenic' childhood is focalized from a child's point of view: Hoffman does not display nostalgia but rather critiques it. Not least, she comes to the realization that her parent's stories are indeed more than fairy tales. Hoffman's description of her induction into Canadian society on her arrival emphasizes the violence with which earlier attachments are broken. This is particularly apparent in the often-cited incident of Hoffman and her sister's 're-naming' on their first day at school:[5]

> All it takes is a brief conference between Mr. Rosenberg and the teacher [...] Mine – "Ewa" – is easy to change into its near equivalent in English, "Eva." My sister's name – "Alina" – poses more of a problem, but after a moment's thought, Mr. Rosenberg and the teacher decide that "Elaine" is close enough. My sister and I hang our heads wordlessly under this careless baptism. (Hoffman, *Lost*, p. 105)

Ewa and Alina have a complete lack of agency in this process, and for Hoffman the new name has no organic connection to herself in the way the old one seemed to. The names are hung on the sisters as artificially as 'identification tags' (Hoffman, *Lost*, p. 105). Hoffman's sense of revolt against this 'careless baptism' can be contrasted with Marianne Hirsch's experience of a similar process. Hirsch's is a story of multiple displacements, from Timisoara to Bucharest and on to Vienna before a final departure for the United States when Hirsch is a teenager. Not only does Hirsch, like Appignanesi, acquire a version of a language (in her case German) which turns out not to be the 'real thing', but the multiple re-locations which she experiences mean that the issue of naming is 'never resolved' (Hirsch, p. 239). 'Marianne' is pronounced differently is French, German and Rumanian and is simplified and broken down into Mary Anne or Mary Anna or Marian in English. However, Hirsch is able to conceptualize this flexibility as something pleasurable or even playful, perhaps because what is at stake for her is not the absolute split between one name and another which Hoffman describes, but a layering of names which may all be in use by different individuals at a given point in time.[6]

A further aspect of the relationship between names and identities is relevant here. Names can be used as a means of remembering one's forebears. Hoffman notes that her sister Alina is named after her mother's sister who was killed in the Holocaust. '[M]y mother often feels a strange compassion for her younger daughter, as if with the name, she bestowed on her some of fate's terrible burden' (Hoffman, *Lost*, p. 7). The switch to Elaine puts an end to this act of remembrance, at least until Hoffman's sister decides, as an adult, to change her name back to its original Polish form. Visiting Warsaw, Appignanesi notes that the monument at the site of the ghetto is engraved not with family names but first names, 'the names mothers use, the first names European Jews give to their offspring, in that traditional commemoration of the dead which is the act of naming' (*Losing*, p. 149). Karpf, who is determined to retain her 'apparently intractable surname' (*War*, p. 217) also notes the use of names as a means of memorialization in the manner described by Hoffman, and points in particular to the psychological problems which can result from a child becoming in this way 'a substitute for a dead predecessor' (*War*, p. 231).[7] This use of naming is essentially melancholic, a means of retaining a reminder or remainder of past experience. Lawrence Langer, citing examples from video testimony, notes in particular the distressing predicament of those who lose their 'first' family in the Holocaust and fashion a second in its image. In one case the continuing tie to the past is evidenced through accidental rather than actual naming; a male survivor absent-mindedly refers to the children of his second marriage by the names of those from his first, who died with their mother in the war.[8] For Langer such a slip, as much as a conscious and deliberate naming, is evidence of 'the literal existence of the divided self' and powerfully illustrates how the 'totally innocent' (*Holocaust*, p. 74) can be drawn into the events of the past.[9] The concern about names in these texts has a number of aspects, then. The name roots the individual in a particular culture but it can also function as a connection to the past. As in the case of language in general, there is a tension between the desire to assert difference (that one comes from elsewhere) and a desire to assimilate (because it seems impossible to do otherwise). This mirrors an ambivalence towards (family) history which the name also implies: how can one remember enough without remaining trapped in the past?

The complexities of this issue of naming therefore reflect many of the concerns these women have about the losses which might result from assimilation. Difference is very much a double-edged sword. A writer such as Hirsch is able, as her more playful attitude towards names suggests, to realize the advantages of '[t]he marginalized position of the exile [which] at the very least, provides the exile with the perspectives of an outsider, kinds of perspective that enable one to see the loopholes and flaws of the system in ways that those inside the system cannot' (Grosz, p. 69). For the writers under discussion here, however, and particularly for Hoffman, the supposed advantages of this perspective shift are by no means immediately apparent. In Hoffman's analysis the loss of the mother tongue compounds exile because the new country and culture are only accessible via a new idiom. Steven G. Kellman has suggested that Hoffman at times endorses the Sapir–Whorf hypothesis, 'the doctrine of linguistic determinism by which each language is unique in the way that it governs a speaker's apprehension of experience' (pp. 155–6). The effects of this are complicated by the fact that the first language atrophies over time like an unused muscle; as Kristeva puts it, 'that language of the past […] withers, without ever leaving you' (*Strangers*, p. 15). As she becomes an adult, Hoffman realizes that just as Polish points of reference were useless for the navigation of North American culture when she was a child, she would equally be at a loss if forced to express her adult perceptions in her childhood language. One example she gives is that she does not know the Polish for 'pathetic fallacy', a term she encounters when studying literature at university.[10] Paradoxically, Hoffman's time as a student coincides with the rise of structuralism, which means she is able, by her own account, to dissect literary texts without feeling the lack of a cultural context for them. '[W]hether I'm reading Chaucer, or Jacobean tragedy, or *The Sound and the Fury*, I'm asked to parse pieces of text as if they were grammatical constructions. [...] Luckily for me, there is no world outside the text' (Hoffman, *Lost*, p. 182). Yet this rather sterile relationship with literary language is not enough; Hoffman later describes what amounts to an epiphany which occurs when she is teaching the poetry of T.S. Eliot and finally feels she has achieved an understanding of the way English is 'crosshatched with a complexity of meaning, with the sonorities of felt, sensuous thought' (Hoffman, *Lost*, p. 186). This notion of language as a guarantor of unity, or at least of successful communication, could itself be felt to have problems but it is symptomatic of the bewilderment which Hoffman feels when she looks at her fellow university students: 'I want to live within language and to be held within the frame of culture; they want to break out of the constraints of both language and culture' (*Lost*, p. 194). A similar sentiment is expressed by Anne Karpf who reflects that, as a teenager in the sixties, she 'couldn't countenance the idea of rebelling, and was sure it would devastate [her] parents' (*War*, p. 43). Difference and unity are again held in tension. In Karpf's case, unity with her parents has to take precedence over any act of rebellion whilst for Hoffman, the notion of breaking out of a culture presupposes that one feels at home there in the first place.

Exile and assimilation

The concept of exile is related to both language and culture. Marianne Hirsch makes a connection between her status as an exile and her commitment to feminism, which, for her, takes the form of 'an enlarged borderland space' (p. 238). This reflects the fact that, unlike Hoffman, Hirsch is sustained throughout her various relocations by female friends, all of whom are similarly displaced. She therefore views her feminism as an extension of these childhood friendships, providing, like them, 'a home on the border' (Hirsch, p. 238). Two factors are important here: one is that Hirsch, throughout her essay, distinguishes her own position from Hoffman's by asserting that, whereas Hoffman feels at home in Poland, and in Polish, she, Hirsch, has no home as such from which to plot the trajectory of her exile. Her 'cultural home' (Hirsch, p. 226), Czernowitz, from whence her parents were forced to migrate, is a place she has never visited. Therefore whilst Hirsch sees Hoffman's text as describing placement, displacement and replacement, she views her own progress as perpetual displacement. Gender is also important for Hirsch. She argues that the pains of adolescence, which Hoffman believes are exacerbated by her ignorance of North American social mores, are no less estranging for the native. However, Hirsch asserts:

> [M]y own and Hoffman's process of unlearning and learning, of resisting and assimilating, was a double one which must have been doubly difficult to negotiate. [...] If most girls leave their "home" as they move into adolescence, Hoffman and I left two homes – our girlhood and our Europe. (p. 222)

Taken together with Hirsch's description of feminism as a home on the border, these comments imply that the entry into womanhood is itself a form of exile. Hirsch's use of 'exile' in relation to an experience which involves a psychic as much as physical displacement begs a similar question to the use of the word trauma to describe both structurally and historically provoked events. Where do the limits of this experience lie? Is it appropriate to use the terminology of exile to discuss, for example, gender?

The notion of a lost or buried childhood language, which Appignanesi, Karpf and Hoffman each discuss, could be read through a parallel with the entry (or exile) into language, itself a process involving loss, and, particularly, loss of unity with the mother. In Kristevan terms, the transition from the semiotic into the symbolic is an originary, constitutive trauma. Gill Plain sums up the gendered trajectory of this transition:

> [T]wo options for women are discerned: to identify with the mother, remaining true to the pre-Oedipal semiotic elements of

the self, a course which can ultimately only confirm her margin-ality; or to identify with the father and thereby be implicated in the very symbolic order that oppresses her ('From War Time', p. 345).

Susannah Radstone argues that this split will necessarily have an effect on what happens when women look back, suggesting that 'from *this* side [within the symbolic], the mythical object of nostalgic desire emerges [...] as phallic' ('Remembering', p. 176). The challenge for female writers is to work-through, rather than repeat, this nostalgia and avoid falling back into a sexually undifferentiated position. In Radstone's analysis, Hoffman succeeds in this respect because she 'remembers that her memories of Poland have been formed retrospectively, in the new language, in the new country' (Radstone, 'Remembering', p. 178). This means that any nostalgia in *Lost in Translation* is 'self-reflexive and critical' and contains a recognition that 'while the lure of nostalgia continues, the object of its desire is a myth' (Radstone, 'Autobiographical', p. 216). In Hirsch's reading, however, Hoffman's exile from Europe figures principally as a repetition of the earlier psycholinguistic event, and this working-through is never achieved. I have already noted that Hirsch views the usual rituals of femininity as themselves a form of self-estrangement or exile and that her feminism develops at least in part as a response to this. It is important that her feminism develops out of a positive sense identification with other women rather than as a reaction against victimization;[11] but it is also difficult to blame Hoffman, as Hirsch seems to, for not recognizing that this aspect of estrangement might actually be the source of a bond with other adolescents and indeed women

Julia Borossa notes that Hoffman herself seems to view her rela-tionship with language, particularly her feeling of being 'the sum of [her] languages' (Hoffman, *Lost*, p. 273), as a compounded version of an experience common to all. In Borossa's summation, 'we are subjects in/of history who live through a series of displacements away from a lost origin. We all mourn the mother we never really possessed [...] We all long for a mother tongue we can never speak' (p. 400). But importantly, we don't all mourn a country from which we have been politically exiled. Although the linguistic experiences of exiles such as Hoffman or indeed Appignanesi could be seen to display, in an extreme form, a repetition or reiteration of stages through which we all pass, it is dangerous to then presume that their particular historically and politically determined experiences can necessarily mirror our own in a parallel fashion. Michael André Bernstein's comments are relevant here:

> Eva Hoffman's *Lost in Translation* [...]was praised by Eva Figes in the *New York Times* as being "not just about emigrants and refugees. It is about us all." But that is just what *Lost in Translation* is not about. Instead, and in strict accord with the paradoxical law of literary imagination, which holds that what is most personal and distinct will touch readers most deeply, it is the very narrowness and exclusivity of Hoffman's self-absorbed curiosity that gives her writing its distinctive tone. (p. 183)

The comments which Borossa quotes, in which Hoffman herself seems to open the door for a parallel between her experience and ours, need then to be placed back into their broader context, as part of a painful and very personal struggle. Perhaps Hoffman's assertion that we are all 'the sum of our languages' is not so much a confirmation that we are like her, but rather expresses a hope that she might, after all, be like us.

Approaching the joint issues of exile and assimilation from a sociological perspective, Zygmunt Bauman describes the law of diminishing returns by which assimilation is governed. The 'Others' or the 'strangers' are necessary for defining the boundaries of any particular culture. Even in an apparently liberal society which appears to provide cultural rewards for those willing to assimilate, 'the finishing-line [always] seems to be receding' (Bauman, *Modernity*, p. 71). Complete assimilation is a contradiction in terms. Accepting the offer of cultural rewards inevitably requires the down-grading of one's origins, and Bauman goes so far as to suggest that the old identity must even appear '*never to exist in the past*' (*Modernity*, p. 72, emphasis in original). Historically, suspicion has been directed against those who 'pass' too proficiently and overcompensating for one's difference by adopting an exaggerated version of the 'native' characteristics simply deepens this suspicion. Bauman identifies the Jews as having been 'the prototypical strangers in Europe [...] They were the ultimate incongruity – a *non-national nation*' (*Modernity*,

p. 85, emphasis in original). This is one aspect, of course, of the crude logic of Nazi anti-Semitism, in which the Jew was envisioned as an enemy within, and the gloomy conclusion would therefore be that, like the Franks' sense of being at home in Holland, any belief that Hoffman's, Karpf's or Appignanesi's family had of being at home in Poland was illusory in the first place.

Appignanesi's description of the assimilatory performance undertaken by her parents in wartime illustrates many of these paradoxes of the assimilatory project. Their decision to go into 'open hiding' is taken partly because Appignanesi's mother Hena is blonde, and, it is felt, can pass as Polish (Aron, Appignanesi's father does not have this natural advantage, but grows 'a Hitler moustache' [Appignanesi, *Losing*, p. 154]). Attempting this disguise required, as Appignanesi points out, a degree of brazen self-confidence and an ability to deal with the necessary bureaucracy and bribes to obtain false identities. A genuine birth certificate, providing one with the identity of a child who died young, and which could be used as evidence to obtain other necessary documents, was safer than, for example, a forged work or residency permit based on a completely fake identity. But as Appignanesi shows, having the right papers was only helpful if one was prepared to inhabit the role completely. 'A slip of the Aryan mask to reveal the Jew beneath would mean death' (Appignanesi, *Losing*, p. 137). Aron, like other Jewish men, has an additional problem; evidence that a man had been circumcised was considered a failsafe way of identifying him as a Jew. On one occasion, it is only with the unexpected help of a police doctor, who backs up his ad hoc explanation of his circumcision, that Aron manages to escape from the Gestapo. This particular danger, coupled with the fact that a man of Aron's age would normally be expected to have a job, means that his 'hiding' is a degree less open than his wife's. He leaves their lodgings each morning as though to go to work but has to kill time in other ways, spending some of it sitting in church. In contrast, some of Hena's spur-of-the-moment decisions to trust particular individuals involve an almost incredible 'careless bravura' (Appignanesi, *Losing*, p. 157). Although the sections of Appignanesi's text which describe her parents' wartime experiences are sometimes written in novelistic form, including for example 'transcriptions' of conversations, she does acknowledge that, aside from the contextual detail she has been able to glean from historical sources, she is dependent on what they have told her. Thus for example after recording how Hena throws down the gauntlet to one official with the challenge, 'You can kill me. Or you can help me' (Appignanesi, *Losing*, p. 158), Appignanesi admits that this incident might appear incredible to the reader. 'This is how my mother recounts the episode. When pressed on why she confided in this particular man, she always responds that he had a good face' (Appignanesi, *Losing*, p. 158). Thus a successful performance seems to require that the mask does, occasionally slip and that one's Otherness is acknowledged.

After the war is over, however, there can be no simple reversion to the previous identity. The family continue to live a clandestine existence. The final decision to emigrate is taken after an incident involving Appignanesi's brother, who, schooled throughout the war to cope with 'forbidding knocks on the door', has now to deal not with SS men but with 'Russian and latterly Polish secret service men' (Appignanesi, *Losing*, p. 212) in search of black market goods. On this occasion: 'When the three policemen asked him whether his father's name was Zablocki or Borensztejn, Staszek found himself replying, "Both"' (Appignanesi, *Losing*, p. 212). Even with the war over, the full truth cannot be told. Although the revelation of black market trading is the main immediate danger here, Appignanesi notes that 'it was still safer not to be Jewish' (*Losing*, p. 212). For Appignanesi, her parents' masquerade is precipitated not only by the Nazi invasion of Poland but also by existing Polish anti-Semitism. In this respect, her parents' disguise foregrounds the illusory nature of their earlier assimilation. Once the war is over, it is impossible to return to the earlier way of life, not only because of changed political circumstances but because taking on or indeed removing an adopted name and identity can never leave the 'original' identity unmarked. The parallel with wearing a mask is in this sense misleading, not only because it implies a straightforward process of reversion or removal but also because it suggests that the necessary changes are principally external, signalled by false papers or cosmetic alterations of one's appearance, when in fact they have to emerge from within. Reflecting on her parents' behaviour when crossing the border from America to Canada after family holidays, her father silent, pale and sweating, her mother keeping up 'an inane patter about anything and everything but the matter in hand', Appignanesi realizes that this dynamic 'was, in miniature, a reliving of their wartime experience' (*Losing*, pp. 50–1) and that this repetition was involuntary. The habits of behaviour necessitated by the performance of open hiding are here adapted in an attempt to facilitate actual assimilation. In this respect Appignanesi's parents never completely emerge from hiding.

The journey back

Appignanesi's trip to Poland is not simply a means of giving the stories of her parents' wartime experiences a topographical foothold; as in Karpf's case the process of extracting information from official archives and locating the graves of relatives gives the visit a practical intent which distinguishes it from a mere sentimental journey. Searching for documentation can be a means of rooting individual memory within the official archive; Appignanesi also hopes to find some trace of her Uncle Adek, a figure who has mythical proportions in her narrative, having defiantly passed as Aryan and performed Schindler-esque acts of salvation. She hopes that the official record will be able to provide information which her mother was never able to discover. Karpf and Appignanesi both intend to report back to their mothers with the information they have discovered, but they also go to perform acts of mourning. It is here that the biographical and the autobiographical feed into each other. These writers have to attempt to complete one story – their parents' – before they can continue with their own. The journey is a means of repairing the breach which emigration caused, but it becomes apparent that just as one cannot revert to one's usual way of life after a period in hiding, there is no easy way to forge a new attachment to the old culture. It will be necessary to consider the specific details of the journeys described in *Losing the Dead* and *The War After*, as the broad similarities between them mask some important differences.

The section of Appignanesi's memoir dealing with her journey to Poland alternates between chapters dealing with wartime and chapters headed 'On Site' which describe Appignanesi's investigations. This whole section of the text is called 'Excavations', but although Appignanesi seems here to be gesturing towards the Freudian idea of memory work as akin to archaeology, she is soon relieved of any delusion that gathering the fragments will result in the reconstruction of an unblemished whole. The supplementation of her parents' recollections with historical contextualization in the 'Wartime' narrative belies the fact that many gaps and uncertainties remain, and the very fact that Appignanesi includes the record of her often frustrating attempts to find out more illustrates her fallibility. Appignanesi is always aware of room for doubt. She notes early on that one legacy of her parents' wartime subterfuge was that her 'mother was [a] liar' (Appignanesi, *Losing*, p. 30). In many respects these are the 'inevitable white lies all grown-ups engage in' (Appignanesi, *Losing*, p. 32), but they are underlain with an urgency which for Appignanesi points to their initial function. Her mother depended on lies to survive. However, even more disconcertingly, Appignanesi's own birth becomes enmeshed in untruths. Although she was born in Poland it is not difficult for her mother to pass her off as having been born in Paris, because of her proficiency in French. This leads to actual uncertainty on Appignanesi's part: '[O]ne isn't after all really present at one's own birth' (Appignanesi, *Losing*, p. 33) and therefore other sources of evidence have to be relied on. Locating a birth certificate for herself is one of the tasks Appignanesi wishes to fulfill during her trip, but even this apparently simple piece of evidence is denied her. Having hoped to find material means of guaranteeing her childhood memories from Poland, Appignanesi is disappointed in this task also.

Appignanesi, like Karpf, visits both official and unofficial monuments during her travels in Poland. However, the split between, for example, the monument to the Warsaw Ghetto Uprising and the police building in Aleje Szuhca where her father was for a time imprisoned, is not an absolute one. As James E. Young has suggested, official monuments become meaningless if they are absorbed into their surroundings and function only as abstract landmarks. It is necessary to 'make visible the activity of memory in monuments' (p. 14), for it is the individual act of remembering which gives the monument its meaning. Whilst memorials and monuments could be distinguished from each other on the basis that memorials are personal and tragic, whilst monuments are public and triumphant, Young suggests instead that monuments can in fact take on memorial functions, especially insofar as their meanings are not permanent but evolving. Similarly, Appignanesi's act of remembering her father's imprisonment at its original site can be seen as making that site, albeit temporarily, a memorial to what happened there.

For Appignanesi, this will never simply be another building, as it is freighted with the stories she has been told about it. Not least, she recalls her father 'returning' here during his final illness.

> This was once the inner sanctum of Nazi power, the headquarters of the Gestapo, the building euphemistically known by the name of the street on which it stands, Aleje Szucha – as if the function it contained was too terrible to speak. [...] I touch the ridge of the columns, feel the coldness of stone. Here is the original site of my father's recurring nightmares, the location of his final delirium. Do I want to will this mute stone into speech? (Appignanesi, *Losing*, p. 171)

This rhetorical question is placed at the end of a chapter, preceding Appignanesi's description of her father's incarceration in this place 'from which it is known few ever return alive' (Appignanesi, *Losing*, p. 177). The fact that the reader is presented with a description of what happened to her father there seems to indicate that Appignanesi does in fact will the stones to speech, simply by uniting the physical presence of the building with the act of recalling her father's story. The question is whether this is desirable, or even moral: is it her place to appropriate her father's 'recurring nightmares' in this fashion? In calling the stones to speak, Appignanesi evokes the figure of prosopopeia, in which an inanimate object is hailed in the expectation that it will reply, a figure which De Man employs to signal the self-contradictions of autobiographical writing (De Man, 'Autobiography', pp. 75–81). She expresses a radical doubt which applies to the whole intention of her journey. Re-locating her father's story at its original scene not only necessitates telling of the encounter with death which happened there but is also a reminder of his actual death, when he revisited this place in his delirium. Towards the end of her memoir, Appignanesi imagines that her parents communicated their past troubles in a 'ghost language [...] beside it, around it, there was the language of everyday practicalities' (*Losing*, p. 221). It is this type of language which Appignanesi seems to expect to summon from the Aleje Szucha, but she also knows that she will not necessarily be able to understand it.

Locating this 'counter-monument'[12] is in many respects, then, a pyrrhic victory, which can be compared with Appignanesi's disappointment when she tries to locate buildings which have resonances of a domestic kind. Her parents' former home 'has been torn down and replaced by a public library' (Appignanesi, *Losing*, p. 109). She attempts to console herself for the disappointment of not being able to enter rooms familiar 'from family story' (Appignanesi, *Losing*, p. 109), deciding that her father would have liked the idea of a library being built there. No such consolation seems available when she goes to revisit her own childhood home, the place where she locates her earliest memories. This, it transpires, has been levelled to make way for a car-park. The irony here, that those places associated with positive memories should have gone, whilst the Aleje Szuhca still remains, is not lost on Appignanesi, and is compounded by the impossibility of retrieving either a birth certificate for herself, or any evidence of the eventual fate of her Uncle Adek. These failures, however, lead to a recognition on Appignanesi's part that such absences do not fundamentally alter either the terms of reference of her parents' stories or her own understanding of it. When she comments that 'Official history refuses to coincide with family memory. Everything is open to invention' (Appignanesi, *Losing*, p. 231), she is not licensing counter-factual leaps of imagination, rather acknowledging that without external evidence the work of memory, and a task such as her own, take on a greater urgency. During her visit Appignanesi also tries, and fails, to locate the grave of her grandmother, who died after the war in Lódź. This is a disappointment, but it later leads Appignanesi to reflect on the importance of at least being able to visit her father's grave in London and compounds her recognition of the limits of her memorial journey. She could never really recuperate her parents' past for them, nor would it be proper to do so. What Appignanesi comes to understand more fully are some of the reasons why the events of the war were such a persistent albeit shadowy presence in her own childhood. In failing to find the markers which she believed would allow her to find a new way of relating to that past, she is forced to face anew the impossibility of understanding the traumatic dislocation with which her parents have lived.

Anne Karpf too eventually realizes that making the journey to Poland with the conscious intention of developing some greater understanding, or at least knowledge, of what happened to her parents there is ultimately a category error:

> I've confused time and place, history and geography, as if coming in person to the site of terrible events which occurred fifty years

ago could somehow yield them up for us to transform them – they might actually extrude through the stones and earth and be mitigated by modern sorrow. But it's time which has enfolded and buried those events, not place, and it was their contemporaries on different continents who had the possibility of intervening, not those of us standing here now. (*War*, p. 300)

There is an echo here of Appignanesi wondering if she can, or should, make stones speak; Karpf, who at this point in her narrative is visiting Auschwitz, is also questioning her own motives. Feeling disturbed and upset by what she sees there is perhaps inevitable, but it makes no difference to what happened. Karpf realizes that taking on the task of mourning for all those killed at Auschwitz becomes meaningless, not least because, as she points out, what marks the place most are not the million dead but 'the millions of tourists [who] have visited subsequently' (*War*, p. 300). For Karpf then, despite the part it plays in her family story as the place where her mother and aunt were imprisoned, Auschwitz is, in Young's terminology, a monument rather than a memorial. The very fact that it has become a metonym for the Holocaust reduces its communicative power.[13]

This can be contrasted with a different act of remembrance which Karpf carries out when, like Appignanesi, she is unable to locate a particular family grave. Visiting Cracow, she tries to find the grave of her mother's nanny who died during the war, but she knows that some stones were in any case uprooted and destroyed in the conflict. Eventually Karpf says a prayer at 'a random unmarked grave' (Karpf, *War*, p. 309) instead. The symbolism of the act is here seen to be as meaningful as Karpf wants it to be. Although in all likelihood detached from its intended referent (the actual grave), saying a prayer in any case gives Karpf the sense of having completed, on her mother's behalf, an act of memorialization. Indeed this act could be classed as postmemorial, in Hirsch's terms, in that Karpf prays for an individual she never knew. However Karpf herself is wary of the potentially appropriative nature of her journey. She is suspicious of the reduction of the memory of pre-war Polish Jewry to 'mementoes and trinkets' (Karpf, *War*, p. 303) on sale to tourists, and, in particular, is not slow to decode the nostalgia into which she retreats on her return to London. Although she admits to initially feeling 'like a visitor from another planet' and listens 'endlessly to lachrymose Yiddish melodies' (Karpf, *War*, p. 310), the limit is soon reached. When she decides she would like to visit the hospital where she was born, she is brought up short on discovering that it has closed down. 'I'd gone too far: I was now dusting everything in the past with dolour' (Karpf, *War*, p. 310). Karpf acknowledges the ridiculousness of wanting to return to the place of her birth, an event of which she can have no real memory or ownership; but there is a certain rationality to this limit case. Having (apparently) located a cultural origin for herself in Poland, Karpf feels the urge to return to her *actual* origin, her birth. She is perhaps more self-deprecating about this incident than the logic of its trajectory would necessarily require. Instead, Karpf shares the many photographs, documents and mementoes she has acquired on her visit with her mother. The task of supplementing her mother's memories in this way is part of the pretext for Karpf's journey throughout, but in the light of the distress which her mother feels, and which is only compounded by the fact that Karpf's father has recently died, Karpf begins to doubt her own motives. For a time, her mother becomes 'exclusively a Holocaust survivor' (Karpf, *War*, p. 312) and Karpf reflects that, given her own preoccupation with the unspoken residue of her parents' war throughout her childhood, her actions could be seen as forcing her mother to take back this burden. However it is also important that at this point in the text Karpf does explicitly state that it is her mother who is the survivor. The distinction between her own nostalgia and her mother's memories is one which it is essential to uphold.

Both Karpf and Appignanesi are attuned to the particular dislocations which follow from visiting Poland as a Jew. Appignanesi in particular records a lack of understanding which is shocking to her, and describes a number of occasions when she is subject to anti-Semitic comments or even simply suspicion. Thus the neighbours living opposite the site of her childhood home are reluctant to speak to her in case she has come to claim property rights. Similarly, despite acknowledging that 'Holocaust tourism' is unlikely to reduce anti-Polish prejudice on the part of visiting Jews, Karpf nevertheless admits: 'I found myself surprised by the anti-Semitic attitudes I found in present-day Poland' (*War*, p. 302). Given that the families of both women left Poland at least partly because of a fear of renewed anti-Semitism in the post-war, such sentiments are unsurprising.

Eva Hoffman's view is necessarily rather different, not least because she continually identifies herself as Jewish *and* Polish to an extent that the other two do not, but she is very much aware of the changes in Polish society in the late 1950s which provoked her parents to leave. '[I]t begins to seem less and less possible to be Jewish and of our class – that is, definitely Jewish, non-Communist, without a particular stake or significance in the society – and to remain' (Hoffman, *Lost*, p. 83). On her return to Poland as an adult she admits that her '*recherche du temps perdu*' has had 'mixed results' (Hoffman, *Lost*, p. 237). Not only does she admit that even if her parents had not left, she herself would most likely have been forced to at some later date, but she also notes: 'The Jews have become exotic in Poland, an almost extinct species' (Hoffman, *Lost*, p. 239). Polish-Jewish culture appear to have vanished, and Hoffman is confined to her bed for part of her visit, unable to cope with the atmosphere of heavily industrialized Cracow.

All three writers I have been considering here make journeys, of different kinds, in search of answers. Both Karpf and Appignanesi hope to supplement the stories their parents have told them, but if they initially hope to make these stories their own, they are instead faced with the impossibility of this. Visiting places which should have resonance all too often proves a disappointment, and the hope that their detective work will produce official evidence to fill the gaps is frequently ill-founded. Producing autobiographical narratives in these circumstances becomes a process of retrieving fragments. This could too easily lead to a portrayal of the irretrievable past as the lost key to the author's identity. However, I believe that these writers ultimately avoid fetishizing the past in this manner. As Radstone suggests of Hoffman, working-through ultimately takes priority over repetition. Evidently, foregrounding the process of the creation of a narrative has a role here. In refusing to adopt the position of a controlling narrator, these writers acknowledge from the outset that they will not necessarily be able to produce all the answers.

Conclusion

In their discussion of the different suggestions which were made for the future of the camp at Auschwitz, Dwork and van Pelt describe a controversial design entailing the construction of a raised walkway over the remains of the camp, which would then have been left to disintegrate. '[E]ventually nature would regain possession of the site, leaving the layers of history below to be excavated by archaeologists in the distant future' (Dwork and van Pelt, p. 376). This notion of 'organic' forgetting, or layering over, of the past is an inviting one although as Dwork and van Pelt point out, the design was rejected because it did not take account of the needs of survivors. Texts such as those I have been considering in this chapter seem to imply that, potentially, there will always be 'survivors', and that the inter-generational project of remembrance could carry on ad infinitum. However, I would suggest that these autobiographies go some way towards demarcating the limits of such a project. Already, as these texts evidence, individual memories fade and archives disintegrate. Although Karpf and Appignanesi might have set out with the intention of creating narratives which would militate against this disinte-gration, this ultimately proves unfeasible. At the end of her book, Appignanesi is glad to be sure, at least, of where her father's grave lies, despite having been unable to locate the other 'lost' dead. Being able to thus foreclose the act of mourning for those others is not an admission of defeat or a betrayal of their memory; the narrative of the journey back is itself a testimony to this loss. Autobiography is still possible in the face of absences and unanswered questions. In fact, for these writers, the articulation of these questions in an auto-biographical framework is the means, ultimately, of letting them lie.

Afterword

The writers whose work I have considered here all chose to explore, through the medium of autobiographical writing, events of a difficult and often painful nature. Not all of them wrote with the supposed benefit of hindsight; for diarists such as Woolf and Frank, however, the very act of writing can be considered a means of creating a perspective on their present experiences and, to some extent, exercising control over them. Yet even in the case of those writers who consider events that are at a temporal distance, the notion of completion, or of writing as a means of ordering and incorporating events into an individual life-story, is placed in question. The act of writing itself disallows any absolute separation between 'then' and 'now', or even between cause and effect. This is not to say that these writers must remain slaves to their pasts (or indeed their family histories) in perpetuity, or that traumatic events must remain incommunicable in order to warrant the name; rather I would suggest that works such as those considered here expose the extent to which traditional styles and genres fall short.

Each of these writers uses the literary techniques familiar to her, but what becomes clear in considering these diverse texts is that a critique of these techniques often becomes an integral, if submerged, aspect of the work as a whole. Writing is both the medium through which experiences are communicated but also a topic which is itself critiqued. This is not to suggest that the shortcomings of language must lead us to the conclusion that silence is the only adequate response to terrible events; nor, conversely, that writing must always cynically parade its own flaws and failures. In attempting to encompass traumatic events within narrative, and revealing, in the process, that traditional forms of expression and structures are not necessarily of assistance, these writers, in their different ways, underline the disjunctive nature of their experiences. These experiences, clearly, do not defeat the power of language to express them, but none of these texts provides evidence that the writing can have a straightforwardly cathartic or palliative effect. The attempts by these writers to assimilate source material – whether in the form of their own earlier writings, news reports, or historical texts – often emphasize the impossibility of narrative completion, but this lack of unequivocal closure is not a signal of the failure of the autobiographical project, rather of a refusal to allow traditional narrative trajectories to smooth over the exigencies of individual experience.

It is also apparent from these narratives that the notion of a complete and harmonious self being disturbed by external events and then reconstructed through writing is not necessarily adequate. Such a model suggests both that a coherent subjectivity exists prior to the traumatic rupture, but also that this rupture can remain ring-fenced from other types of experience. The types of war-associated trauma I have been examining are both disjunctive from the everyday, and in important ways continuous with it. This is a paradox that becomes particularly apparent for Delbo; reference points from before are inadequate, but to abandon them completely would be to surrender crucial aspects of her personality, if not, indeed, her humanity. If anything, writings such as Delbo's expose the problems with conceptions of subjectivity, and indeed narrative forms, which presume that the retrieval of an earlier 'wholeness' is either plausible or desirable. Subjectivity is inevitably a series of improvisations in the face of changing circumstances. When these circumstances are traumatic, and change occurs in a shocking, unpredictable and frightening way, the fallible and fragile nature of these improvisations is forcefully brought home. For none of these writers does writing appear to be straightforwardly restorative or compensatory; if anything, an attempt to coerce writing into this function proves only to foreground its inadequacies in this regard. At best, writing provides a means of attempting to bridge the gaps which the traumatic event opens up between then and now, history and memory, the self and the other. Encountering these texts will not necessarily lead the reader into any greater understanding of what is being described; nor is the reader necessarily liable to identify with the events these writers explore. We can, however, be led to question the efficacy of both traditional literary modes, and socially and culturally established forms of mourning and memorialization.

Notes

Introduction: Trauma and the Autobiographical

1. A more recent collection of essays shows even in its very title the continuing, albeit contested, influence of Fussell's work: Patrick J. Quinn and Steven Trout eds. *The Literature of the Great War Reconsidered: Beyond Modern Memory*.
2. Indeed, as Tylee notes, 'Bergonzi's book managed without any reference to a woman writer whatsoever, even in the chapter entitled "Civilian Responses"', whereas Fussell 'did mention the names of some dozen women within lists, or as the recipients of letters, or where they corroborated points made by one of his *500* literary sources' (p. 7, emphasis in original).
3. See for example, Maroula Joannou, 'Vera Brittain's *Testament of Youth* Revisited', which suggests that although Brittain was herself a feminist by the time the text was published, *Testament of Youth*'s status as a feminist work is debatable.
4. See especially studies by Zwerdling, Ouditt, Lee, *Virginia Woolf*, Levenback, and Snaith.
5. For example, a recent collection of essays on this subject foregrounds this issue in its title: Andrew Leak and George Paizis, eds. *The Holocaust and the Text: Speaking the Unspeakable*. Saul Friedlander's influential collection *Probing the Limits of Representation: Nazism and the 'Final Solution'*, expresses a similar idea.
6. See for example studies by Felman and Laub, Hermann and Caruth. Critical engagements with the models established by Caruth can be found in Radstone, 'Screening Trauma', Leys, *Trauma*, and Gilmore, *Limits*.
7. Kirby Farrell, discussing contemporary American culture in particular, characterizes it this way: '[T]rauma is both a clinical syndrome and a trope something like the Renaissance figure of the world as a stage: a strategic fiction that a complex, stressful society is using to account for a world that seems threateningly out of control' (p. 2).
8. See Masson, Malcolm and Crews, *et al.*
9. Linda Ruth Williams points out the distinction made by Laplanche between a trauma caused by a childhood event (or fantasy) and one caused by a more recent or indeed contemporary event. See Williams, p. 56, n. 39.
10. For a discussion of the British official inquiry into shell shock, see Bogacz. Stone discusses how the effects of the diagnosis of shell shock on British psychology more generally. For a wide ranging discussion of the treatment of war neurosis, see Shepard.

11. For a detailed exploration of the physical and psychic effects of railway travel, see Schivelbusch. The 'shock of the new' is also discussed in Benjamin, 'Some Motifs'.

12. In 'Inhibitions, Symptoms and Anxiety', Freud expresses the view that this type of separation, rather than birth itself, is a primary traumatic scene.

13. For an exploration of the fact that Freud is actually both the grandparent and the analyst in the *fort-da* scenario, see Jacques Derrida, 'To Speculate – on "Freud"'.

14. It is also worth noting here the distinction which LaCapra makes between 'structural' trauma and 'historical trauma'. He defines structural trauma as, for example, separation from the mother, a type of trauma that anyone could experience. Historical trauma, on the other hand, 'is specific and not everyone is subject to it or entitled to a subject position associated with it' (LaCapra, *Writing History*, p. 78). See also Radstone, 'Autobiographical Times'. Radstone notes the effects of gender on the trajectory of nostalgia.

15. This can be contrasted with models of dissociated memory, often drawn from Pierre Janet, which underlie what has come to be referred to as the recovered memory movement and which imply the recovery of events which have been completely effaced from consciousness. In this model, memories of a happy childhood may suddenly be revealed to have a dark supplement in memories of abuse. This is rather different to the railway accident model; there is no suggestion in Freud that the fact of the accident itself will be effaced.

16. Leigh Gilmore makes a similar point: 'Language is asserted as that which can realize trauma even as it is theorized as that which fails in the face of trauma' (*Limits*, p. 7).

17. See van der Kolk and van der Hart, p. 178.

18. Donald Spence objects to Freud's use of this image because of its focus on form prior to content, and because of a lack of clear differentiation between construction and reconstruction. See Spence, pp. 175–6.

19. This incident is also discussed by LaCapra, *Writing History*, pp. 87–9, and critiqued by Kali Tal, pp. 56–7.

20. In 'Learning from the Survivors', Hartman also gives an example in which a mistake (in his case, apparent self-contradiction on the part of the survivor) in fact serves to underline the impact of the event on the survivor. See pp. 198–9.

21. In fact it can mean either depending on the context but this distinction is not always sufficiently clear, especially when 'witnessing' is used intransitively. In a legal context, an individual can bear witness to his or her own presence at, for example, the scene of a crime, but can also bear witness on behalf of another who was (or was not) present. See also Derrida, 'A Self-Unsealing Poetic Text', especially pp. 198–202.

22. From this period see especially Jelinek ed.

23. A number of critics have suggested that this is one of the shortcomings of Jelinek's work. See Smith and Watson eds. In relation to this particular

example of the diary, Nussbaum, in an essay which defines the diary as distinct from other forms of autobiography, makes the following observations which are relevant here: 'Much of eighteenth century writing – journal, diary, letter, epistolary novel – rests uneasily on the perplexing boundary edge between the private and public worlds [...] Among those who were the most prolific diarists were individuals with secrets to tell, especially women and dissenters' (p. 134). Here marginality by reason of gender is placed alongside marginality by reason of faith.

24. See Graver for a discussion of the background to this adaptation and Roth for a fictional portrayal of the Holocaust, and especially Anne Frank, in American Jewish culture of the 1960s.

1 Vera Brittain and the 'Lost Generation'

1. It is worth noting, however, that in *Thrice a Stranger*, the record of her travels to the United States, Brittain describes her pride at having sections of *Testament of Youth* included in an American Armistice Day broadcast in 1934. She also takes the opportunity to stress the importance of American intervention to the outcome of the war (pp. 191–8).

2. The diaries contained in *Chronicle of Youth* cover the period 1913–17 and were first published in 1981, eleven years after Brittain's death.

3. In her book *Women's Work in Modern England*, Brittain also notes the changes which wartime recruits made to the culture of the nursing profession: 'the war-time [...] V.A.D. nurses [...] were less inclined than the pre-war probationer to submit meekly to authority and to keep their ideas of progress to themselves [and this] has had its effect upon a long-established and somewhat conservative profession' (pp. 80–1).

4. Similar sentiments are apparent in the estrangement, described by both Robert Graves and Erich Maria Remarque, which was experienced by men going home on leave. See, for example, Graves, *Goodbye*, p. 188, Remarque, pp. 128–32.

5. It should be noted that Brittain's and Mrs Leighton's descriptions of this incident do not quite tally with each other. Brittain does mention meeting Mrs Leighton after the purchase of the dagger but Mrs Leighton doesn't mention Brittain being present when her son shows it to her.

6. Hilary Bailey has pointed out that there are discrepancies between Brittain's account of this incident and that provided by Claire Leighton, Roland's sister, who does not mention Brittain being present when the uniform was returned. Without wishing to dismiss the issue of the factuality or otherwise of Brittain's account, it is important that she feels the need to describe Leighton's belongings in such detail, and that her brother Edward is the recipient. See Bailey, pp. 31–3.

7. Susan Leonardi, in 'Brittain's Beard', suggests a repressed lesbian attraction between the two women, but Marion Shaw advises caution in the use of such labels. See Shaw, *Clear Stream*, pp. 289–91.

8. This dream contains an interesting echo of the plot of Rebecca West's *Return of the Soldier*, in which the hero returns unable to remember his marriage and believes he is still involved in an earlier affair.
9. See Berry and Bostridge, pp. 182–5 and p. 39. Kennard also explores in detail the biographical basis of Brittain and Holtby's works.
10. Brittain is here alluding to an incident that is not treated in her autobiographical writing. In the early 1930s she discovered that her brother Edward was to have faced court martial after a letter from him to a junior officer was found by the censor to contain evidence of a sexual relationship between the two men. This awoke the possibility that he had deliberately set out to be killed in battle. See Berry and Bostridge, pp. 129–35.
11. Robert Carbury's career (although not his marriage) is based on that of Dick Sheppard, founder of the Peace Pledge Union.

2   Virginia Woolf between the Wars

1. See Shaw, *Clear Stream*, pp. 246–52 for a discussion of the development of this project.
2. See for example Bertrand Russell's *Which Way to Peace?* and Aldous Huxley's *What are you Going to do About it?*, both published in 1936, and both of which Woolf is known to have read. These texts focus in particular on the likelihood of an increased use of airpower in a renewed conflict, and the potential impact of this on the civilian population. Ceadel, 'Popular Fiction', gives a fascinating analysis of a range of fictional representations of the 'next war' from the 1920s and 1930s.
3. Karen Levenback suggests, however, that, 'Finally, Woolf denied seeing much connection between the Great War and World War II. The reality of the first year, 1939–40, seemed in prospect more like what Woolf herself called a "non-war" than a renewal of the Great War' (p. 154).
4. This is not to ignore the fact that Woolf experienced both the anticipation, and the effects, of aerial bombardment during the First World War. These were recorded in both her letters and diaries: '16 German aeroplanes have just passed over Richmond [...] We went and sat in the cellar and listened to them' (Woolf, *Question*, p. 185); 'We saw the [bomb] hole in Piccadilly this afternoon' (Woolf, *Diary I*, p. 65).
5. See for example a letter to Katherine Cox from June 1916: 'Leonard has been completely exempted from serving the Country in any capacity [...] It's a great mercy for us. But the whole of our world does nothing but talk about conscription, and their chances of getting off' (*Question*, p. 102).
6. Although it has to be acknowledged that the portrayal of Septimus's madness was also informed by Woolf's own experience of illness, it is nevertheless important that, within the narrative, his disorder is clearly connected to his time in combat.
7. For a detailed and fascinating discussion of Woolf's use of narrative voice in this novel see Daniel Ferrer, pp. 8–39.

8. For a description of the Spanish Medical Aid Committee, which Bell was attached to, see Buchanan, pp. 101–6. Attempts were made after Bell returned from China to find a political post for him in Britain, in order to prevent him going to Spain. Woolf writes to Ethel Smyth in March 1937, 'We've been bothered about Julian [...] wanting to fight in Spain: and have to stop him, which means seeing people – politicians' (*Leave*, p. 113).

9. In an exchange of letters from September 1939, Woolf is inclined to agree with Vita Sackville-West's suggestion that it was probably better for Bell to die for his beliefs in Spain than to be conscripted to participate in the Second World War, which Sackville-West describes as 'a general holocaust' (qtd in Woolf, *Leave*, p. 357).

10. There is also a connection to be made, both here and in *Three Guineas*, to Woolf's eventual realization of the gulf between herself and her brother Thoby's Cambridge friends as described in the essay 'Old Bloomsbury', in *Moments of Being*, pp. 159–79.

11. In a diary entry from April 1935 Woolf describes a discussion with Alix Strachey and Julian Bell on the subject of 'whether one can give people a substitute for war. Must have the danger emotion: must climb mountains, fight bulls; but this emotion mixed, I say, with philosophy, doesn't last more than a few months in the case of war' (*Diary IV*, p. 307). With regard to the counterpointing of the destructive and maternal instincts, Elshtain points to the dangers of using maternity as a 'weapon' (pp. 238–9).

12. The review, by Howard Spring, included the comment: 'I do not often feel about a book that it has in it the stuff of immortality, and when you do feel like that about a book it's as well to shut up about it in this cynical world; but that is how I feel about *The Years*' (Majumdar and McLaurin, p. 376). Spring went on to praise Woolf's representation of the passing of time and her handling of a large cast of characters.

13. Bell's volume of poems, *Work for the Winter*, was published by the Hogarth Press in March 1936, but as Lee notes, Woolf, 'at the worst point of her struggle with *The Years*' (p. 612) advised Bell against writing a novel. Lee also points out that when, later in 1936, Woolf rejected Bell's essay on Roger Fry, which Bell had hoped the Hogarth Press would publish, 'Julian was mortified, and Vanessa was furious' (p. 672).

14. Woolf of course might have realized that, as was indeed the case, any photographs might have been omitted from later editions of the text and could not therefore be referenced directly. However, the decision to describe but not include the Spanish photographs is nevertheless an interesting one.

15. The particular dangers to which Jews would be subject in the event of an invasion were another crucial difference of which the Woolfs were aware.

16. Susan Sellars suggests: 'The most consistent use Woolf appeared to anticipate for her diaries was as a record for her memoirs [...] there is evidence in the diaries that she was writing with a reader in view [...] while she

stated categorically that she did not intend full publication, she did
consider that Leonard might make "a little book" from them' (p. 115).

17. For a discussion of the Stephen family tradition of autobiography and
Woolf's place within it see Dahl.

18. Woolf had been reading F.L. [Peter] Lucas's *Journal Under the Terror, 1938*
and *André Gide's Journal 1885–1939*, both published in 1939.

19. Hermione Lee points out that Leonard Woolf stressed that his wife's suicide was caused by her fear of an approaching nervous breakdown, rather
than the war, but 'the story of the feeble, delicate lady authoress giving
up on the war-effort began to be built into the posthumous myths of
Virginia Woolf' (*Virginia Woolf*, p. 766).

3   Anne Frank: The War from the Annexe

1. Bob Moore estimates that of over 120,000 Jews registered in the
Netherlands in 1940, 16,000 survived the war in hiding (pp. 259–60).

2. As an interpretative category, the uncanny has not only been taken up by
literary critics. Martin Jay, citing a renewed interest in the work of Walter
Benjamin and the application of the uncanny to the analysis of city life,
notes that it can be extracted from 'its purely psychological or aesthetic
context' and can be shown to have 'larger social and cultural implications' (p. 22).

3. The controversy that was sparked by accusations from the author Meyer
Levin that his own adaptation of the diary had been rejected for foregrounding the Jewish aspects of the text is detailed by Graver.

4. *Dear Anne Frank*, a collection of letters written to Frank by school-
children, in response to the diary, promotes a similar type of identification.

5. I am quoting here from the *Definitive Edition* of the diary, as it is now
most readily available version. The *Critical Edition*, published in 1989,
reproduces as parallel texts the different versions of the diary and I refer
to this when Frank's rewriting affects my interpretation. The *Critical
Edition* was in part a response to attacks on the diary's authenticity. It
contains details of analyses carried out on the handwriting of the manuscript, and other background material on the diary's publication history.
The *Definitive Edition*, which appeared in 1997, draws on the *Critical
Edition* and reinstates passages omitted by Otto Frank when the diary
was first published, but distinctions between earlier and later drafts are
elided.

6. The *Critical Edition* of the diary shows that, in the first instance, Frank
addressed letters to a number of girls besides Kitty. These are characters
from Cissy van Marxveldt's popular series of children's books *Joop ter
Heul*. See Pressler, pp. 31–4, Waaldijk, pp. 115–18 and de Costa, *Anne
Frank*, pp. 33–8 for an exploration of the influence these texts may have
had on Frank's writing. Dalsimer sees 'Kitty' as functioning in a similar
way to the 'imaginary friend' of childhood; see pp. 71–6.

7. Denise De Costa provides a useful physical description and analysis of all the material by Frank, including stories, notes and a commonplace book, recovered from the Annexe. See De Costa, *Anne Frank*, pp. 27–61.

8. In the diary, Frank disguises the names of the other inhabitants of the Annexe. The family referred to as the van Daans were in fact called van Pels, and the dentist Dussel, who arrived later, was really called Pfeffer. I will here refer to these individuals by their textual names.

9. Despite Frank's foregrounding of these linguistic distinctions, in the context of a discussion of the authentication of the diary, Harry Muslich suggests that in the Annexe 'a kind of Germanic Dutch was being spoken' (p. 98) and that this accounts for Frank's occasional use of German rather than Dutch syntax.

10. In the first draft these comments appear only after the Franks have gone into hiding, whilst in the rewritten version they are moved to an earlier, more strictly chronological position. In the original entry, Frank continues, 'But life went on in spite of it all' (Frank, *Critical Edition*, p. 226) a comment implying her sense that whereas before she was deprived of certain freedoms, she is now deprived of freedom *per se*.

11. Zygmunt Bauman also discusses the ambivalent position of the assimilated Jew; I return to his arguments in Chapter 5.

12. In 'Sublimity in the Home: Overcoming Uncanniness', in *Caught by History* (pp. 193–205) Ernst van Alphen uses the concepts of the uncanny and the sublime to discuss his experience of living in an Amsterdam house designed, and once occupied by, architect Harry Elte, who died in Theresienstadt. Other discussions of how the Holocaust distorts notions of the home and the un/homely, include Michael Mazor's *The Vanished City*, an account of life in the Warsaw Ghetto: 'I know of many cases where a man who had gone out for a short time, on coming home, found neither his wife, nor his children, nor his aged parents. The man came home: Everything was in its place in his apartment – the table with the leavings of an interrupted meal, the notebook in which his child was leaning to write its first letters, toys… Only the human beings who animated these poignant, henceforth useless objects, did not answer to any call – having ceased to exist' (pp. 149–50).

13. Notably, several of the short stories that Frank wrote deal with the notion of contact with nature and the outdoors as a means of renewal and hope. See for example 'Jackie': 'Anyone who looks at nature, which is the same as looking into oneself, long and deeply enough, will, like Jackie, be cured of all despair' (*Tales from the Secret Annexe*, p. 69).

14. This danger is exemplified for me by Katherine Viner's article, 'Dear Diary', in which Viner compares her own teenage diary with Frank's: 'It may sound glib to compare the diary of a girl hidden away in German-occupied Holland during world war two [sic] with the ramblings of a 1980s teenager in North Yorkshire. But so much of what she wrote in her diary is what I wrote in mine, which is precisely why the book was so important' (p. 7).

15. Karein Goertz suggests that, more generally, Frank's transformation of 'the privations of everyday life into amusing anecdotes' and 'longing and

loneliness into a romance plot' are a means of distancing herself from the present situation, and points to similar tactics in other accounts by or about children in hiding ('Writing', p. 650, 659, n. 2).

16. See Dalsimer, p. 62 ff. for another interpretation of the different Peters.

17. Edith Velman's autobiography serves this purpose to some extent, but for accounts by historians of the fate of the Jews of the Netherlands, see Hilberg, pp. 570–97, and Moore.

18. Noting that Frank also turns to reading after the cooling of the affair with Peter, Dalsimer suggests that immersing herself in work is a means of 'reasserting control' (p. 69) over her situation.

19. See David Barnouw, 'Attacks on the Authenticity of the Diary' in Frank, *Critical Edition*, pp. 84–101.

20. See Jay Rayner, p. 5.

21. After a flash-forward to the raid on the Annexe, Müller describes Frank's birth but pp. 14–76 of her book (which runs to just over 260 pages, excluding an epilogue), taking Frank to the age of nine, are principally concerned with her parents rather than herself. A similar proportion of Lee's biography also focuses on Frank's forebears.

4   Charlotte Delbo: Writing and Survival

1. In the English translation, which I quote throughout this chapter, the reader is required to turn the page before being confronted by the second of these sentences. In the French original, the second sentence is isolated on a facing page, but the two sentences are laid out typographically at the same level, so that the eye moves straight across from one to the other (see Delbo, *Aucun de nous ne reviendra*, pp. 182–3). In both cases, the fractional pause or gap before the second sentence is read facilitates the kind of interpretations suggested here.

2. Rothberg is here citing the title of David Rousset's influential 1946 study, *L'Univers Concentrationnaire*.

3. Rothberg describes *The Measure of our Days* as being comprised in part of ' "transcripts" of survivor (and occasionally bystander) interviews done years after the fact' (p. 163) but the cautious quotation marks here indicate that it is not possible to verify this suggestion.

4. In the original, the use of the plural or formal 'vous' form – 'Essayez de regarder. Essayez pour voir' (*Aucun*, p. 137) – might be interpreted as being solely addressed to the reader (or readers) but the indeterminate temporality of the imperative means that it could be understood as being addressed to those with her in the camp.

5. For more detailed biographical information on Delbo, see Langer's introduction to *Auschwitz and After* and Thatcher's *Literary Analysis*.

6. Kushner details Otto Frank's difficulties in this respect as well as describing the marketing and the reception of the diary across Europe.

7. All translations from this article are my own.

8. Caroline Wiedmer details how changing attitudes towards and understanding of the deportation of Jews and political prisoners can be traced through the establishment of memorials and remembrance days.

9 There is a parallel here with Proust's distinction between voluntary and involuntary memory, especially insofar as involuntary memory is associated with events that have not been absorbed into consciousness. See Beckett, pp. 29–35.

10. Translations from this article are my own.

11. In his discussion of writers testifying to illness, Arthur Frank argues: 'The stories that ill people tell come out of their bodies. The body sets in motion the need for new stories when its disease disrupts the old stories' (p. 2). Although Frank principally focuses on those describing current or ongoing conditions of an organic nature, this notion of being forced to rethink the way in which one's body either facilitates or disrupts particular narratives also seems relevant here.

12. Cynthia Haft compares this incident with an account by André Verdet that 'describes this same scene from the male point of view. The men are ashamed when they take the bread, he tells us, and most do not want it; they want the women to keep it for themselves' (p. 135).

13. After the occupation, some French citizens volunteered to go to work in Germany, 'motivated less by politics than the prospect of higher wages and reports of good working conditions' (Jackson, p. 298). In 1943, however, the conscription of French workers, the Service de Travail Obligataire (STO), began and many individuals evaded this by fleeing to join resistance groups. This meant that after the war, little distinction was made between those who had volunteered in the early 1940s and those who, for whatever reason, could not or did not resist conscription after 1943. 'Over those who had worked in Nazi Germany floats the suspicion that they could – or should – have avoided STO and joined the Resistance' (Jackson, p. 611). Delbo's description of the man's reaction here imputes guilt, and in this regard is echoed by Marguerite Duras's description of the arrival of STO workers back in Paris at the end of the war. See Duras, pp. 17–19.

5 Memory in a Foreign Language: Texts by Daughters of Holocaust Survivors

1. See for example essays by William A. Proefriedt, Steven G. Kellman and Danuta Z. Fjellestad.

2. Ingram cites Walter Benjamin's comparison of a translated text to a broken vessel which has been pieced together but is nevertheless a conglomeration of fragments. See Benjamin, 'The Task of the Translator'.

3. Andrea Reiter suggests that the fairytale might seem an appropriate point of reference for Holocaust narrative because it 'shows the child by example how to behave in certain situations (mostly ones of mortal danger) in order to come out of them unscathed' (p. 186).

4. Although a writer such as Steven Pinker, who takes an evolutionary and genetic view of language ability, suggests that there are biological reasons why children learn languages, including second languages, with greater competence than adults, this holistic view, based on an analysis of the functioning of the 'language-learning circuitry of the brain' (Pinker, p. 291) downplays the fact that in specific aspects of second language acquisition, adults can be equally competent. Susan M.Gass and Larry Selinker note, for instance, that the main advantage to children seems to be in the area of phonology, so that a child will be less likely than an adult to speak the second language with a 'foreign' accent. This difference could have cultural and psychological rather than biological causes. See Pinker, and Gass and Selinker, pp. 239–46.

5. For other discussions of this passage, see Suzanne Stern-Gillet, p. 103, Ada Savin, pp. 59–60 and Frances Bartowski, pp. 112–13.

6. This experience of renaming is found in numerous immigrant memoirs and is of course not exclusive to female immigrants. Another example worth noting here is that of the historian Saul Friedlander who describes a series of culturally dictated name changes which foregrounds the issue of Jewishness:

> At home I had been called Pavel, or rather Pavlicek, the usual Czech diminutive [...] then from Paris to Neris I had become Paul which for a child was something quite different. As Paul I didn't feel like Pavlicek any more, but Paul-Henri was worse still, [...] Paul could have been Czech and Jewish; Paul-Henri could but nothing but French and res-olutely Catholic [...] I subsequently became Shaul on disembarking in Israel, then Saul, a compromise between the Saul that French requires and the Paul that I had been. In short it is impossible to know which name I am and that in the final analysis seems to me sufficient expres-sion of a real and profound confusion. (qtd in Melton, pp. 183–4)

The turn-of-the-century immigrant Mary Antin, on the other hand, with her characteristic assimilatory fervour, is disappointed that her name change is not as radical as those of her siblings:

> Fetchke, Joseph and Deborah issued as Frieda, Joseph and Dora. As for poor me, I was simply cheated. [...] My Hebrew name being Maryashe [...] my friends said it would hold good in English as *Mary*; which was very disappointing, as I longed to possess a strange-sounding American name like the others. (Antin, p. 188, emphasis in original)

7. Karpf is here referring to an idea developed in Dina Wardi's study *Memorial Candles: Children of the Holocaust*.

8. Art Spiegelman's *Maus II* culminates in a similar incident, when the aged and confused Vladek calls his son Art by the name of his dead child Richieu.

9. Such a melancholic use of naming can be contrasted with Maurice Halbwachs' suggestion that naming a child after a forebear can in fact

assist the process of mourning by giving the name a completely new set of associations and connections. Halbwachs thus sees the name as secondary to the network of associations and memories within which the individual is situated and in which s/he participates. See Halbwachs, *On Collective Memory*, pp. 72–4.

10. An interesting counter example to this is that of Janina Bauman, who, arriving in Britain from Poland as an adult in the 1960s, learns English by surreptitiously attending literature lectures at the University of Leeds: 'After a year of this work my knowledge of English would have been good enough to write a major dissertation on Tobias Smollett or Thomas Peacock, neither of whom I had ever heard of before, but was still not sufficient to talk about daily matters' (*Dream*, p. 159).

11. In 'Women's Time' Kristeva notes that 'women [...] seem to feel they are the casualties, that they have been left out of the socio-symbolic contract of language as the fundamental social bond'(p. 199), and that this can lead to an identity formed only through rejection.

12. 'Counter-monument' (*Gegen-Denkmal*) is the term which, as James Young notes, was used by Joachen and Esther Gerz, the designers of the Hamburg Monument against Fascism, War and Violence – and for peace and Human Rights. This monument, which takes the form of a tall black pillar, is gradually being sunk into the ground and will eventually vanish from sight completely. In Young's words, '[O]ne day, the one thing left standing here will be the memory-tourist, forced to rise and to remember for himself' (p. 30). I think this is an appropriate term to apply to the Aleje Szuhca because its meaning too is necessarily 'activated' only by the individual act of memory. It is only in this that its resonance persists.

13. For discussions of the 'monumentalisation' of Auschwitz in the post-war period see Gillian Rose, pp. 15–39, Dwork and van Pelt, pp. 354–78 and Cole, pp. 97–120.

Bibliography

Published Sources

Aldington, Richard. *Death of a Hero* (London: Sphere, 1968 [1929])

Anderson, Linda. *Autobiography* (London: Routledge, 2001)

——. *Women and Autobiography in the Twentieth Century: Remembered Futures* (London: Prentice Hall/Harvester Wheatsheaf, 1997)

Anonymous [Marie Leighton]. *Boy of My Heart* (London: Hodder and Stoughton, 1916)

Antin, Mary. *The Promised Land* (London: William Heinemann, 1912)

Antze, Paul and Michael Lambek eds. *Tense Past: Cultural Essays in Trauma and Memory* (New York and London: Routledge, 1996)

Appignanesi, Lisa. *Losing the Dead: A Family Memoir* (London: Vintage, 2000 [1999])

——. *Memory and Desire* (London: HarperCollins, 1997 [1991])

——. *Sanctuary* (London: Bantam Books, 2001 [2000])

——. *The Things We Do For Love* (London: HarperCollins, 1997)

Bailey, Hilary. *Vera Brittain* (Harmondsworth: Penguin, 1987)

Barrett, Michele. 'Introduction', in Virginia Woolf. *A Room of One's Own / Three Guineas* (Harmondsworth: Penguin, 1993) pp. ix–liii

Bartov, Omer. *Mirrors of Destruction: War, Genocide and Modern Identity* (Oxford: Oxford University Press, 2000)

Bartowski, Frances. 'Careless Baptisms: Eva Hoffman's *Lost in Translation*', in *Travelers, Immigrants, Inmates: Essays in Estrangement* (Minneapolis: University of Minnesota Press, 1995) pp. 109–17

Baruch, Gracie K. 'Anne Frank on Adolescence', *Adolescence* 3 (1968) 425–34

Bauman, Janina. *A Dream of Belonging: My Years in Post-war Poland* (London: Virago, 1988)

——. *Winter in the Morning: A Young Girl's Life in the Warsaw Ghetto and Beyond 1939–1945* (London: Virago, 1986)

Bauman, Zygmunt. *Modernity and Ambivalence* (Oxford: Polity Press, 1993 [1991])

Bazin, Nancy Topping and Jane Hamovit Lauter. 'Virginia Woolf's Keen Sensitivity to War: Its Roots and its Impact on her Novels', in Mark Hussey ed. *Virginia Woolf and War: Fiction, Reality and Myth* (New York: Syracuse University Press, 1991) pp. 14–39

Beckett, Samuel. *Proust* (London: John Calder, 1965 [1931])

Begley, Louis. *Wartime Lies* (London: Picador, 1992)

Bell, Julian. 'War and Peace: A Letter to E. M. Forster', in Quentin Bell ed. *Julian Bell: Essays, Poems and Letters* (London: Hogarth Press, 1938) pp. 335–90

——. ed. *We Did Not Fight 1914–18: Experiences of War Resisters* (London: Cobden Sanderson, 1935)

Benjamin, Walter. 'The Task of the Translator', (1923) in *Illuminations* trans. Harry Zohn (London: Fontana, 1992) pp. 70–82

——. 'Some Motifs in Baudelaire', (1939) in *Charles Baudelaire: A Lyric Poet in the Era of High Capitalism* trans. Harry Zohn (London: Verso, 1997) pp. 107–54

Berg, Mary. *Warsaw Ghetto: A Diary* ed. S.L. Schneiderman (New York: L.B. Fischer, 1945)

Berger, James. *After the End: Representations of Post-Apocalypse* (Minneapolis: University of Minnesota Press, 1999)

Bergonzi, Bernard. *Heroes Twilight: A Study of the Literature of the Great War* (3rd ed. [rev] London: Carcanet, 1996)

Berlant, Lauren. 'Trauma and Ineloquence', *Cultural Values*, 5.1 (2001) 41–58

Bernheimer, Charles. 'A Shattered Globe: Narcissism and Masochism in Virginia Woolf's Life-writing', in *Psychoanalysis And ...* eds. Richard Feldstein and Henry Sussman (London: Routledge, 1990) pp. 187–206

Bernstein, Michael André. 'Exile, Cunning and Loquaciousness', *Salmagundi*, Summer (1996) 182–94

Berry, Paul and Mark Bostridge. *Vera Brittain: A Life* (London: Pimlico, 1996)

Berryman, John. 'The Development of Anne Frank', in *The Freedom of the Poet* (New York: Farrar, Straus and Giroux, 1976) pp. 91–106

Bettelheim, Bruno. 'The Ignored Lesson of Anne Frank', in *Surviving and Other Essays* (New York: Alfred Knopf, 1979) pp. 246–57

Bishop, Alan and Mark Bostridge eds. *Letters from a Lost Generation: First World War Letters of Vera Brittain and Four Friends* (London: Little, Brown and Company, 1998)

Blunden, Edmund. *Undertones of War* (Harmondsworth: Penguin, 1982 [1928])

Bogacz, Ted. 'War Neurosis and Cultural Change in England 1914–1922: The Work of the War Office Committee of Enquiry into "Shell-shock." ', *Journal of Contemporary History*, 24 (1989) 227–56.

Borossa, Julia. 'Identity, Loss and the Mother Tongue', *Paragraph* 21.3 (1998) 391–402

Bracher, Nathan. 'Faces d'histoire, figures de violence: métaphore et métonymie chez Charlotte Delbo', *Zeitschrift für Französische Sprache und Literatur* 102.3 (1992) 252–62

Bradshaw, David. 'British Writers and Anti-Fascism in the 1930s Part Two: Under the Hawk's Wings', *Woolf Studies Annual* (1998) 41–66

Brenner, Rachel Feldhay. *Writing as Resistance: Four Women Confronting the Holocaust* (Pennsylvania: University of Pennsylvania Press, 1997)

Brittain, Vera. *Account Rendered* (London: Virago, 1982 [1944])

——. *Born 1925: A Novel of Youth* (Basingstoke: Macmillan, 1948)

——. *Chronicle of Youth: Great War Diary 1913–1917* ed. Alan Bishop (London: Phoenix, 2000 [1981])

——. *The Dark Tide* (London: Virago, 1999 [1923])

——. *Honourable Estate: A Novel of Transition* (London: Virago, 2000 [1936])

——. *Lady into Woman: A History of Women from Victoria to Elizabeth II* (London: Andrew Dakars, 1953)

Brittain, Vera. *Not Without Honour* (London: Grant Richards, 1925)
——. *On Becoming a Writer* (London: Hutchinson, 1947)
——. *Testament of a Peace Lover: Letters from Vera Brittain* eds Winifred and Alan Eden-Green (London: Virago, 1988)
——. *Testament of Experience: An Autobiographical Study of the Years 1925–1950* (London: Virago, 1979 [1957])
——. *Testament of Youth: An Autobiographical Study of the Years 1900–1925* (London: Virago, 1978 [1933])
——. *Thrice a Stranger: New Chapters of Autobiography* (London: Victor Gollancz, 1938)
——. *Women's Work in Modern England* (London: Noel Douglas, 1928)
—— and Geoffrey Handley-Taylor eds. *Selected Letters of Winifred Holtby and Vera Brittain (1920–1935)* (Bath: Cedric Chivers, 1970 [1960])
Broe, Mary Lynn and Angela Ingram eds. *Women's Writing in Exile* (Chapel Hill: University of North Carolina Press, 1989)
Bronfen, Elisabeth. 'Risky Resemblances: On Repetition, Mourning and Representation', in Sarah Webster Goodwin and Elisabeth Bronfen eds. *Death and Representation* (Baltimore: Johns Hopkins University Press, 1993) pp. 103–29
Brooks, Peter. 'Freud's Masterplot', *Yale French Studies* 55–56 (1977) 280–300
Broughton, Trev Lynn. *Men of Letters, Writing Lives* (London: Routledge, 1999)
Buchanan, Tom. *Britain and the Spanish Civil War* (Cambridge: Cambridge University Press, 1997)
Cannadine, David. 'War and Death, Grief and Mourning in Modern Britain', in Joachim Whaley ed. *Mirrors of Mortality: Studies in the Social History of Death* (London: Europa, 1981) pp. 187–242
Caruth, Cathy. 'An Interview with Geoffrey Hartman', *Studies in Romanticism* 35 (1996) 631–52
——. 'An Interview with Robert J. Lifton', in Cathy Caruth, ed. *Trauma: Explorations in Memory* (Baltimore and London: Johns Hopkins University Press, 1995) pp. 128–47
——. *Unclaimed Experience: Trauma, Narrative and History* (Baltimore: Johns Hopkins University Press, 1996)
——. ed. *Trauma: Explorations in Memory.* (Baltimore and London: Johns Hopkins University Press, 1995)
Ceadel, Martin. *Pacifism in Britain 1914–1945: The Defining of a Faith* (Clarendon: Oxford, 1980)
——. 'Popular Fiction and the Next War 1918–1939', in Frank Glover Smith ed. *Class, Culture and Social Change* (Sussex: Harvester Press, 1986) pp. 161–84
Chiarello, Barbara. 'The Utopian Space of a Nightmare: The Diary of Anne Frank', *Utopian Studies* 5.1 (1994) 128–40
Cole, Tim. *Images of the Holocaust: The Myth of the 'Shoah Business'* (London: Duckworth, 1999)
Cooke, Miriam and Angela Woollacott eds. *Gendering War Talk* (Princeton: Princeton University Press, 1993)

Crews, Frederick ed. *The Memory Wars: Freud's Legacy in Dispute* (London: Granta, 1997 [1995])

Cunningham, Valentine ed. *Spanish Front: Writers on the Civil War* (Oxford: Oxford University Press, 1986)

Dahl, Christopher. 'Virginia Woolf's *Moments of Being* and the Autobiographical Tradition in the Stephen Family', *Journal of Modern Literature* 10 (1983) 175–96

Dear Anne Frank: A Selection of Letters to Anne Frank Written by Children Today (Harmondsworth: Penguin, 1995)

——. 'Anne Frank and Etty Hillesum: Diarists', in Hyman Aaron Enzer and Sandra Solotaroff Enzer eds. *Anne Frank: Reflections on Her Life and Legacy* (Urbana and Chicago: University of Illinois Press, 2000) pp. 214–22

De Costa, Denise. *Anne Frank and Etty Hillesum: Inscribing Spirituality and Sexuality* trans. Mischa F.C. Hoynick and Robert E. Chesal (New Brunswick: Rutgers University Press, 1998)

Delbo, Charlotte. *Aucun de Nous Ne Reviendra* (Paris: Les Editions de Minuit, 1970 [1965])

——. *Auschwitz and After* trans. Rosette C. Lamont (New Haven: Yale University Press, 1995)

——. *Une Connaissance Inutile* (Paris: Les Editions de Minuit, 1970)

——. *Convoy to Auschwitz: Women of the French Resistance* trans. Carol Cosman (Boston: Northeastern University Press, 1997)

——. *Days and Memory* trans. Rosette C. Lamont (Vermont: Malboro Press, 1990)

——. *La Mesure de Nos Jours* (Paris: Les Editions de Minuit, 1971)

——. 'Phantoms, My Companions' trans. Rosette C. Lamont *Massachusetts Review* 12.1 (1971) 10–31

——. *Who Will Carry the Word?* trans. Cynthia Haft, in Robert Skloot ed. *The Theatre of the Holocaust* (Madison and London: University of Wisconsin Press, 1982) pp. 267–325

De Man, Paul. 'Autobiography as De-Facement', in *The Rhetoric of Romanticism* (New Haven: Yale University Press, 1984) pp. 67–81

——. ' "Conclusions": Walter Benjamin's "The Task of the Translator" ', *Yale French Studies* 69 (1985) 25–46

De Meester, Karen. 'Trauma and Recovery in Virginia Woolf's *Mrs Dalloway*', *Modern Fiction Studies* 44.3 (1998) 649–73

Derrida, Jacques. 'To Speculate – On "Freud" ' in *The Post Card: From Socrates to Freud and Beyond* trans. Alan Bass (Chicago: University of Chicago Press, 1987) pp. 257–410

——. ' "A Self-Unsealing Poetic Text": Poetics and Politics of Witnessing', trans. Rachel Bowlby, in Michael P. Clark ed. *Revenge of the Aesthetic: The Place of Literature in Theory Today* (Berkley: University of California Press, 2000) pp. 180–207

Diski, Jenny. 'The Girl in the Attic', *London Review of Books*, 6 March 1997, p. 11

Douglas, Lawrence. 'Wartime Lies: Securing the Holocaust in Law and Literature', *Yale Journal of Law & the Humanities* 7.2 (1995) 367–96

Dunn, Jane. *A Very Close Conspiracy: Vanessa Bell and Virginia Woolf* (Boston: Little, Brown and Company, 1990)

Duras, Marguerite. *The War: A Memoir* trans. Barbara Bray (New York: New Press, 1990)

Dwork, Deborah and Robert Jan van Pelt. *Auschwitz 1270 to the Present* (New York: W.W. Norton, 1996)

Elshtain, Jean Bethke. *Women and War* (Chicago and London: University of Chicago Press, 1995)

Engel, Susan. *Context is Everything: The Nature of Memory* (New York: W.H. Freeman, 1999)

Epstein, Helen. *Children of the Holocaust: Conversations with Sons and Daughters of Survivors* (New York: G.P. Putnam's Sons, 1979)

Ergas, Yasmine. 'Growing up Banished: A Reading of Anne Frank and Etty Hillesum', in M. Randolph Higonnet *et al* eds. *Behind the Lines: Gender and the Two World Wars* (New Haven and London: Yale University Press, 1987) pp. 84–95

Erikson, Kai. 'Notes on Trauma and Community', in Cathy Caruth ed. *Trauma: Explorations in Memory* (Baltimore and London: John Hopkins University Press, 1995) pp. 183–99

Farrell, Kirby. *Post-traumatic Culture: Injury and Interpretation in the Nineties* (Baltimore: Johns Hopkins University Press, 1998)

Felman, Shoshana. *What Does a Woman Want? Reading Sexual Difference* (Baltimore: Johns Hopkins University Press, 1993)

—— and Dori Laub. *Testimony: Crises of Witnessing in Literature, Psychoanalysis and History* (London: Routledge, 1992)

Ferrer, Daniel. *Virginia Woolf and the Madness of Language* trans. Geoffrey Bennington and Rachel Bowlby (London: Routledge, 1990)

Fjellestad, Danuta Z. 'The Insertion of the Self into the Space of Borderless Possibility: Eva Hoffman's Exiled Body', *MELUS*, 20.2 (1995) 132–47

Foley, Barbara. 'Fact, Fiction, Fascism: Testimony and Mimesis in Holocaust Narratives', *Comparative Literature* 34.4 (1982) 330–60

Forster, E. M. 'Notes for a Reply', in Quentin Bell ed. *Julian Bell: Essays, Poems and Letters* (London: Hogarth Press, 1938) pp. 391–2

Frank, Anne. *The Diary of Anne Frank: The Critical Edition* eds David Barnouw and Gerrold van der Stroom trans. Arnold J. Pomerans and B.M. Mooyaart-Doubleday (New York: Doubleday, 1989)

——. *Tales from the Secret Annexe* (Harmondsworth: Penguin, 1986)

——. *The Diary of a Young Girl* eds Otto H. Frank and Mirjam Pressler trans. Susan Massotty (Harmondsworth: Viking, 1997)

Frank, Arthur. *The Wounded Storyteller: Body, Illness and Ethics* (Chicago: University of Chicago Press, 1995)

Freud, Sigmund. *Beyond the Pleasure Principle* (1920) in *The Standard Edition of the Complete Works of Sigmund Freud Volume XVIII* trans. and ed. James Strachey with Anna Freud, Alix Strachey and Alan Tyson (London: Hogarth Press and the Institute of Psycho-analysis, 1955) pp. 1–64

——. 'Childhood Memories and Screen Memories' (1901) in *The Standard Edition of the Complete Works of Sigmund Freud Volume VI* trans. and ed.

James Strachey with Anna Freud, Alix Strachey and Alan Tyson (London: Hogarth Press in association with Ernest Benn, 1960) pp. 43–52

——. 'Civilisation and its Discontents' (1930) in *The Standard Edition of the Complete Works of Sigmund Freud Volume XXI* trans. and ed. James Strachey with Anna Freud, Alix Strachey and Alan Tyson (London: Hogarth Press and the Institute of Psycho-analysis, 1961) pp. 57–146

——. 'Constructions in Analysis' (1937) in *The Standard Edition of the Complete Works of Sigmund Freud Volume XXIII* trans. and ed. James Strachey with Anna Freud, Alix Strachey and Alan Tyson (London: Hogarth Press and the Institute of Psycho-analysis, 1964) pp. 255–71

——. 'Inhibitions, Symptoms and Anxiety' (1926) in *The Standard Edition of the Complete Works of Sigmund Freud Volume XX* trans. and ed. James Strachey with Anna Freud, Alix Strachey and Alan Tyson (London: Hogarth Press and the Institute of Psycho-analysis, 1959) pp. 75–172

——. 'Mourning and Melancholia' (1917) in *The Standard Edition of the Complete Works of Sigmund Freud Volume XIV* trans. and ed. James Strachey with Anna Freud, Alix Strachey and Alan Tyson (London: Hogarth Press and the Institute of Psycho-analysis, 1957) pp. 237–59

——. 'On Transience' (1917) in *The Standard Edition of the Complete Works of Sigmund Freud Volume XIV* trans. and ed. James Strachey with Anna Freud, Alix Strachey and Alan Tyson (London: Hogarth Press and the Institute of Psycho-analysis, 1957) pp. 303–8

——. 'Thoughts for the Times on War and Death' (1917) in *The Standard Edition of the Complete Works of Sigmund Freud Volume XIV* trans. and ed. James Strachey with Anna Freud, Alix Strachey and Alan Tyson (London: Hogarth Press and the Institute of Psycho-analysis, 1957) pp. 273–300

——. 'The "Uncanny"' (1919) in *The Standard Edition of the Complete Works of Sigmund Freud Volume XVII* trans. and ed. James Strachey with Anna Freud, Alix Strachey and Alan Tyson (London: Hogarth Press and the Institute of Psycho-analysis, 1957) pp. 217–56

Fry, Roger. *The Artist and Psycho-analysis* (London: Hogarth Press, 1924)

Furst, Desider and Lilian R. *Home is Somewhere Else* (Albany: SUNY, 1994)

Fuss, Diana. *Identification Papers* (London: Routledge, 1995)

Fussell, Paul. *The Great War and Modern Memory* (Oxford: Oxford University Press, 1975)

Gass, Susan and Larry Selinker. *Second Language Acquisition: An Introductory Course* (Hillsdale: Laurence Erlbaum, 1994)

Gerrard, Nicci. 'Our Fathers, Who Art in Heaven', *Observer*, 7 July 1996

Gilbert, Sandra M. and Susan Gubar. *No Man's Land: The Place of the Woman Writer in the Twentieth Century Volume 2: Sexchanges* (New Haven and London: Yale University Press, 1989)

Gilman, Sander L. *Jewish Self-Hatred: Anti-Semitism and the Hidden Language of the Jews* (Baltimore: Johns Hopkins University Press, 1986)

Gilmore, Leigh. *Autobiographics: A Feminist Theory of Women's Self Representation* (Ithaca: Cornell University Press, 1994)

——. *The Limits of Autobiography: Trauma and Testimony* (Ithaca: Cornell University Press, 2001)

Giraudoux, Jean. *Ondine* in *Plays: Volume II* trans. Roger Gellert (London: Methuen, 1967) pp. 177–273

Goertz, Karein K. 'Body, Trauma and the Rituals of Memory: Charlotte Delbo and Ruth Klüger', in Julia Epstein and Lori Hope Lefkovitz eds *Shaping Losses: Cultural Memory and the Holocaust* (Urbana and Chicago: University of Illinois Press, 2001) pp. 161–85

——. 'Writing from the Secret Annex: The Case of Anne Frank', *Michigan Quarterly Review* (Summer 2000) 647–60

Gorham, Deborah. *Vera Brittain: A Feminist Life* (Oxford: Blackwell, 1996)

Graver, Lawrence. *An Obsession with Anne Frank: Meyer Levin and the Diary* (Berkeley: University of California Press, 1995)

Graves, Robert. *But it Still Goes On* (London: Jonathan Cape, 1930)

——. *Goodbye to All That* (Harmondsworth: Penguin, 1960 [1929; rev ed. 1957])

Gregory, Adrian. *The Silence of Memory: Armistice Day 1919–1946* (Oxford and Providence: Berg, 1994)

Grosz, Elizabeth. 'Judaism and Exile: The Ethics of Otherness', in Erica Carter, James Donald and Judith Squires eds. *Space and Place: Theories of Identity & Location* (London: Lawrence Wishart, 1993) pp. 57–71

Gualtieri, Elena. '*Three Guineas* and the Photograph: The Art of Propaganda', in Maroula Joannou ed. *Women Writers of the 1930s: Gender, Politics and History* (Edinburgh: Edinburgh University Press, 1999) pp. 165–78

——. *Virginia Woolf's Essays: Sketching the Past* (Basingstoke: Macmillan, 2000)

Haaken, Janice. *Pillar of Salt: Gender, Memory and the Perils of Looking Back* (New Brunswick and London: Rutgers University Press, 1998)

Haft, Cynthia. *The Theme of the Nazi Concentration Camps in French Literature* (The Hague: Mouton, 1973)

Halbwachs, Maurice. *The Collective Memory* trans. Francis J. Ditter Jr and Vida Yazdi Ditter (New York: Harper Colophon, 1981[1950])

——. *On Collective Memory* trans. and ed. Lewis Coser (Chicago: University of Chicago Press, 1992)

Hamacher, Werner. 'Journals, Politics' trans. Peter Burgard *et al.* in Werner Hamacher, Neil Hertz and Thomas Keenan eds. *Responses: On Paul de Man's Wartime Journalism* (Lincoln and London: University of Nebraska Press, 1989)

Hanley, Lynne. *Writing War: Fiction, Gender and Memory* (Amherst: University of Massachusetts Press, 1991)

Hardman, Anna. 'Representations of the Holocaust in Women's Testimony', in Andrew Leak and George Paizis eds. *The Holocaust and the Text: Speaking the Unspeakable* (Basingstoke: Macmillan, 2000) pp. 51–66

Hartley, Jenny. *Millions Like Us: British Women's Fiction of the Second World War* (London: Virago, 1997)

Hartman, Geoffrey H. 'Darkness Visible', in *The Longest Shadow: In the Aftermath of the Holocaust* (Bloomington: Indiana University Press, 1996) pp. 35–59

——. 'Learning from the Survivors: The Yale Testimony Project', *Holocaust and Genocide Studies*, 9.2 (1995) 192–220

——. 'On Traumatic Knowledge and Literary Studies'. *New Literary History* 26 (1995) 537–63

——. ed. *Holocaust Remembrance: The Shapes of Memory* (Oxford: Blackwell, 1994)

Haste, Cate. *Rules of Desire: Sex in Britain World War I to the Present* (London: Chatto and Windus, 1992)

Heinemann, Margot. *Gender and Destiny: Women Writers and the Holocaust* (New York and London: Greenwood Press, 1996)

Henke, Suzette A. *Shattered Subjects: Trauma and Testimony in Women's Life Writing* (New York: St Martin's Press, 1998)

——. 'Virginia Woolf and Post-traumatic Subjectivity', in Ann Ardis and Bonnie Kime Scott eds. *Virginia Woolf: Turning the Centuries* (New York: Pace University Press, 2000) pp. 147–52

Hermann, Judith. *Trauma and Recovery* (New York: Basic Books, 1992)

Higonnet, Margaret R. and Patrice L-R Higonnet, 'The Double Helix', in Margaret R. Higonnet *et al.* eds. *Behind the Lines: Gender and the Two World Wars* (New Haven and London: Yale University Press, 1987) pp. 31–47

Hilberg, Raul. *The Destruction of the European Jews Volumes I–III* (rev. ed. New York and London: Holmes and Meier, 1985)

Hirsch, Marianne. *Family Frames: Photography, Narrative and Memory* (Cambridge, Mass.: Harvard University Press, 1997)

Hoffman, Eva. *Exit into History: A Journey Through the New Eastern Europe* (London: William Heinemann, 1993)

——. *Lost in Translation: A Life in a New Language* (London: Vintage, 1998 [1989])

——. *Shtetl: The Life and Death of A Small Town and the World of Polish Jews* (London: Secker and Warburg, 1998)

Holtby, Winifred. *Virginia Woolf* (London: Lawrence & Wishart, 1932)

Horowitz, Sara R. 'Women in Holocaust Literature: Engendering Trauma Memory', in Dalia Ofer and Leonore Weitzman eds. *Women in the Holocaust* (New Haven: Yale University Press, 1998) pp. 364–77

Hungerford, Amy. 'Memorizing Memory', *Yale Journal of Criticism* 14.1 (2001) 67–92

Huxley, Aldous. *What are you Going to do About it? The Case for Constructive Peace* (London: Chatto & Windus, 1936)

Ingram, Susan. 'When Memory is Cross-Cultural Translation: Eva Hoffman's Schizophrenic Autobiography', *TTR: Traduction, Terminologie, Redaction* 9.1 (1996) 259–76

Jackson, Julian. *France: The Dark Years 1940–1944* (Oxford: Oxford University Press, 2001)

Jay, Martin. 'The Uncanny Nineties', *Salmagundi* 108 (1995) 20–9

Jay, Paul. *Being in the Text: Self-Representation from Wordsworth to Roland Barthes* (Ithaca: Cornell University Press, 1984)

Jelinek, Estelle C. 'Introduction: Women's Autobiography and the Male Tradition', in Estelle C Jelinek ed. *Women's Autobiography: Essays in Criticism* (Bloomington: Indiana University Press, 1980) pp. 1–20

Joannou, Maroula. 'Vera Brittain's *Testament of Youth* Revisited', *Literature and History* 2.2 (1993) 46–72

Kaplan, Ann E. 'Shattered Subjects: Trauma and Testimony in Women's Life-Writing', *Biography* 23.1 (2000) 223–31

Karpf, Anne. Let's Pretend Life is Beautiful', *Guardian*, 3 April 1999

——. 'The War After: Living with the Holocaust (London: Minerva, 1997 [1996])

Kellman, Steven G. 'Lost in the Promised Land: Eva Hoffman revises Mary Antin', *Prooftexts*, 18.2 (1998) 149–59

Kennard, Jean E. *Vera Brittain and Winifred Holtby: A Working Partnership* (Hanover and London: University Press of New England, 1989)

Kestenberg, Judith. 'Transposition Revisited: Clinical, Therapeutic and Developmental Considerations', in Paul Marcus and Alan Rosenberg eds. *Healing Their Wounds: Psychotherapy with Holocaust Survivors and Their Families* (New York: Praeger, 1989) pp. 67–82

King, Nicola. *Memory, Narrative, Identity: Remembering the Self* (Edinburgh: Edinburgh University Press, 2000)

Kingcaid, R.A. 'Charlotte Delbo's Auschwitz et Après: The Struggle for Signification', *French Forum* 9.1 (1984) 98–109

Kirmayer, Lawrence J. 'Landscapes of Memory: Trauma, Narrative and Dissociation', in Paul Antze and Michael Lambek eds. *Tense Past: Cultural Essays in Trauma and Memory* (New York and London: Routledge, 1996) pp. 173–98

Klein, Kerwin Lee. 'On the Emergence of Memory in Historical Discourse', *Representations* 69 (2000) 127–50

Kristeva, Julia. 'A New Type of Intellectual: The Dissident' (1977), trans. Sean Hand in Toril Moi ed. *The Kristeva Reader* (Oxford: Basil Blackwell, 1986) pp. 292–300

——. 'Women's Time.' (1979) trans. Alice Jardine and Harry Blake in Toril Moi ed. *The Kristeva Reader* (Oxford: Basil Blackwell, 1986) pp. 187–213

——. *Strangers to Ourselves* trans. Leon S. Roudiez (London: Harvester Wheatsheaf, 1991 [1988])

——. *Nations without Nationalism* trans. Leon S. Roudiez (New York: Columbia University Press, 1993)

Krupnik, Mark. 'Assimilation in Recent American Jewish Autobiographies', *Contemporary Literature* XXXIV.3 (1993) 451–74

Kuhn, Annette. *Family Secrets* (London: Verso, 1995)

Kushner, Tony. ' "I Want to go on Living After my Death": The Memory of Anne Frank', in Martin Evans and Ken Lunn eds. *War and Memory in the Twentieth Century* (Oxford: Berg, 1997) pp. 3–25

LaCapra, Dominick. *History and Memory After Auschwitz* (Ithaca and London: Cornell University Press, 1998)

——. *Writing History, Writing Trauma* (Baltimore: Johns Hopkins University Press, 2001)

Lang, Berel. 'Holocaust Genres and the Turn to History', in Andrew Leak and George Paizis eds. *The Holocaust and the Text: Speaking the Unspeakable* (Basingstoke: Macmillan, 2000) pp. 17–31

——. 'The Representation of Evil: Ethical Content as Literary Form' in *Act and Idea in the Nazi Genocide* (Chicago and London: University of Chicago Press, 1990) pp. 117–61

Langer, Lawrence. *The Age of Atrocity: Death in Modern Literature* (Boston: Beacon Press, 1978)

——. 'Gendered Suffering? Women in Holocaust Testimonies' in Dalia Ofer and Leonore J. Weitzmann eds. *Women in the Holocaust* (New Haven and London: Yale University Press, 1998) pp. 351–63

——. *Holocaust Testimony: The Ruins of Memory* (New Haven: Yale University Press, 1991)

Lassner, Phyllis. *British Women Writers of World War II: Battlegrounds of their Own* (London: Macmillan, 1997)

Laurence, Patricia. 'The Facts and Fugue of War: From *Three Guineas* to *Between the Acts*', in Mark Hussey ed. *Virginia Woolf and War* (New York: Syracuse University Press, 1991) pp. 225–45

Leak, Andrew and George Paizis, eds. *The Holocaust and the Text: Speaking the Unspeakable* (Basingstoke: Macmillan, 2000)

Lee, Carol Ann. *Roses from the Earth: The Biography of Anne Frank* (London: Viking, 1999)

Lee, Hermione. *Virginia Woolf: A Biography* (London: Vintage, 1997 [1996])

——. 'Virginia Woolf and the Essay', in Sue Roe and Susan Sellers eds. *The Cambridge Companion to Virginia Woolf* (Cambridge: Cambridge University Press, 2000) pp. 91–108

Leed, Eric J. *No Man's Land: Combat and Identity in World War I* (Cambridge: Cambridge University Press, 1979)

Lejeune, Philippe. *On Autobiography* trans. Katherine Leary (Minneapolis: University of Minnesota Press, 1989)

Leonardi, Susan. 'Brittain's Beard: Transsexual Panic in *Testament of Youth*' LIT 2 (1990) 77–84

——. *Dangerous by Degrees: Women at Oxford and the Somerville College Novelists* (New Brunswick and London: Rutgers University Press, 1989)

Levenback, Karen L. *Virginia Woolf and the Great War* (Syracuse: Syracuse University Press, 1999)

Levi, Primo. *The Drowned and the Saved*, trans. Raymond Rosenthal (London: Abacus, 1989)

Leys, Ruth. *Trauma: A Genealogy* (Chicago and London: University of Chicago Press, 2000)

——. 'Traumatic Cures: Shell Shock, Janet and the Question of Memory', in Paul Antze and Michael Lambek eds. *Tense Past: Cultural Essays in Trauma and Memory* (New York and London: Routledge, 1996) pp. 103–45

Lichenstein, Rachel and Iain Sinclair. *Rodinsky's Room* (London: Granta, 1999)

Littlewood, Jane. *Aspects of Grief: Bereavement in Adult Life* (London: Tavistock/Routledge, 1992)

Llewelyn Davies, Margaret ed. *Life as We Have Known It by Co-operative Working Women* (London: Virago, 1977 [1931])

Lucas, F. L. *Journal Under the Terror, 1938* (London: Cassell, 1939)

Majumdar, Robin and Allen McLaurin eds. *Virginia Woolf: The Critical Heritage* (London: Routledge and Kegan Paul, 1975)

Malcolm, Janet. *In the Freud Archives* (London: Jonathan Cape, 1984)

Marcus, Laura. *Auto/biographical Discourses* (Manchester: Manchester University Press, 1995)

——. ' "Enough About You, Let's Talk About Me": Recent Autobiographical Writing'. *New Formations* 1 (Spring 1987) 77–93

——. 'Oedipus Express: Trains, Trauma and Detective Fiction'. *New Formations* 41 (Autumn 2000) 173–88

——. *Virginia Woolf* (Plymouth: Northcote House, 1997)

Marin, Louis. 'Montaigne's Tomb, or Autobiographical Discourse', trans. Geoff Bennington. *Oxford Literary Review* 4.3 (1981) 43–58

Masson, Jeffrey Moussaieff. *The Assault on Truth: Freud's Suppression of the Seduction Theory* (London: Faber & Faber, 1984)

Mazor, Michael, *The Vanished City: Everyday Life in the Warsaw Ghetto* trans. David Jacobson (New York: Marsilio Publishers, 1993 [1955])

Melton, Judith M. *The Face of Exile: Autobiographical Journeys* (Iowa City: University of Iowa Press, 1998)

Mesher, D. 'The Recovered Self: Auschwitz and Autobiography', *Judaism* 45.2 (1996) 237–46

Michaels, Walter Benn. ' "You Who Was Never There": Slavery, and the New Historicism, Deconstruction and the Holocaust', *Narrative* 4.1 (1996) 1–16

Miller, J. Hillis. *Fiction and Repetition: Seven English Novels* (Cambridge: Harvard University Press, 1982)

Mitchell, Juliet. *Madmen and Medusas: Reclaiming Hysteria and the Effects of Sibling Relations on the Human Condition* (Harmondsworth: Penguin, 2000)

Molière, Jean-Baptiste Pocquelin de. *The Hypochondriac*, trans. Alan Dury, in *Molière: Five Plays* (London: Methuen, 2000) pp. 347–431

——. *The Misanthrope*, trans. Richard Wilbur, in *Molière: Five Plays* (London: Methuen, 2000) pp. 201–68

Moore, Bob. *Victims and Survivors: The Nazi Persecution of the Jews in the Netherlands 1940–1945* (London: Arnold, 1997)

Mosse, George L. *Fallen Soldiers: Reshaping the Memory of the World Wars* (New York: Oxford University Press, 1990)

Müller, Melissa. *Anne Frank: The Biography* trans. Rita and Robert Kimber (London: Bloomsbury, 1999)

Muslich, Henry. 'Death and the Maiden', in Hyman Aaron Enzer and Sandra Solotaroff Enzer eds. *Anne Frank: Reflections on Her Life and Legacy* (Urbana and Chicago: University of Illinois Press, 2000) pp. 94–9

Neuberger, Julia. 'The Storyteller's Hard-won Victory', *The Times*, 18 July 1996

——. 'Why Anne Will Live for Ever', *The Times: Weekend*, 11 January 1997

Neverow, Vara. 'Thinking Back Through Our Mothers, Thinking in Common: Virginia Woolf's Photographic Imagination and the Community of Narrators in *Jacob's Room, A Room of One's Own*, and *Three Guineas*', in Jeanette McVicar and Laura Davis eds. *Virginia Woolf and Communities* (New York: Pace University Press, 1999) pp. 65–87

Nora, Pierre. 'Between Memory and History: *Les Lieux de Memoire'*, trans. Marc Roudebush *Representations* 26 (1989) 7–25

Nussbaum, Felicity. 'Toward Conceptualizing Diary', in James Olney ed. *Studies in Autobiography* (Oxford: Oxford University Press, 1988) pp. 128–40

Ofer, Dalia and Leonore J. Weitzman. 'Introduction: The Role of Gender in the Holocaust', in Dalia Ofer and Leonore J. Weitzman eds. *Women in the Holocaust* (New Haven: Yale University Press, 1998) pp. 1–18

Ouditt, Sharon. *Fighting Forces, Writing Women: Identity and Ideology in the First World War* (London: Routledge, 1994)

Ozick, Cynthia. 'Who Owns Anne Frank?', in *Quarrel and Quandary* (New York: Vintage, 2000) pp. 74–102

Parkes, Colin Murray. *Bereavement: Studies of Grief in Adult Life* (Harmondsworth: Penguin, 1986)

Pawlowski, Merry M. ed. *Virginia Woolf and Fascism: Resisting the Dictator's Seduction* (Basingstoke: Palgrave, 2001)

Pinker, Steven. *The Language Instinct: The New Science of Language and Mind* (Harmondsworth: Penguin, 1994)

Plain, Gill. *Fiction of the Second World War: Gender, Power and Resistance* (Edinburgh: Edinburgh University Press, 1996)

——. 'From War Time to Women's Time: Coping with Conflict in Women's Fiction of the 1940s', *Time & Society* 3.3 (1994) 341–64

Pressler, Mirjam. *The Story of Anne Frank* (Basingstoke: Macmillan, 1999)

Proefriedt, William A. 'The Immigrant or "Outsider" Experience as a Metaphor for Becoming an Educated Person in the Modern World: Mary Antin, Richard Wright and Eva Hoffman', *MELUS* 16.2 (1989–90) 77–89

Quinn, Patrick J. and Steven Trout eds. *The Literature of the Great War Reconsidered: Beyond Modern Memory* (Basingstoke: Palgrave, 2001)

Raczymow, Henri. 'Memory Shot Through with Holes' trans. Alan Astro, *Yale French Studies* 85 (1994) 98–105

Radstone, Susannah. 'Autobiographical Times', in Tess Cosslett, Celia Lury and Penny Summerfield eds. *Feminism and Autobiography: Texts, Theories and Methods* (London: Routledge, 2000) pp. 201–19

——. 'Remembering Ourselves: Memory, Writing and the Female Self', in Penny Florence and Dee Reynolds eds. *Feminist Subjects, Multi-media: Cultural Methodologies* (Manchester: Manchester University Press, 1995) pp. 171–82

——. 'Screening Trauma: *Forrest Gump*, Film and Memory', in Susannah Radstone ed. *Memory and Methodology* (Oxford and New York: Berg, 2000) pp. 79–107

——. 'Social Bonds and Psychical Order: Testimonies', *Cultural Values* 5.1 (2001) 59–78

Rawlinson, Mark. *British Writing of the Second World War* (Oxford: Clarendon Press, 2000)

Rayner, Jay. 'Anne Frank's Father Censored Her Diaries...' *Observer* 23 August 1998

Reiter, Andrea. *Narrating the Holocaust* trans. Patrick Camiller (London and New York: Continuum, 2000 [1995])

Remarque, Erich Maria. *All Quiet on the Western Front* trans. Brian Murdoch (London: Vintage, 1996 [1929])

Ringelheim, Joan. 'The Split Between Gender and the Holocaust', in Dalia Ofer and Leonore J. Weitzmann eds. *Women in the Holocaust* (New Haven: Yale University Press, 1999) pp. 340–50

Rittner, Carol and John K. Roth eds. *Different Voices: Women and the Holocaust* (New York: Paragon Press, 1993)

Roe, Sue. *Writing and Gender: Virginia Woolf's Writing Practice* (Sussex: Harvester Wheatsheaf, 1990)

——. Susan Sellers, Nicole Ward Jouve and Michele Roberts. *The Semi-Transparent Envelope: Women Writing – Feminism and Fiction* (London: Marion Boyars, 1994)

Rogers, Kim Lacy, and Selma Leydesdorff with Graham Dawson eds. *Trauma and Life Stories: International Perspectives* (London and New York: Routledge, 1999)

Rose, Gillian. *Mourning Becomes the Law: Philosophy and Representation* (Cambridge: Cambridge University Press, 1996)

Rose, Jacqueline. 'Virginia Woolf and the Death of Modernism' *Raritan* 18.2 (1998) 1–18

——. *Why War? Psychoanalysis, Politics and the Return to Melanie Klein* (Oxford: Blackwell, 1993)

Rosen, Norma. 'The Fate of Anne Frank's Diary', in *Accidents of Influence* (Albany: SUNY, 1992) pp. 81–6

Rosenfeld, Alvin H. 'Popularization and Memory: The Case of Anne Frank', in Peter Hayes ed. *Lessons and Legacies: The Meaning of the Holocaust in a Changing World* (Evanston: Northwestern University Press, 1991) pp. 243–78

Rothberg, Michael. *Traumatic Realism: The Demands of Holocaust Representation* (Minneapolis and London: University of Minnesota Press, 2000)

Rousso, Henry. *The Vichy Syndrome: History and Memory in France Since 1944* trans. Arthur Goldhammer (Cambridge and London: Harvard University Press, 1991)

Russell, Bertrand. *Which Way to Peace?* (London: Michael Joseph, 1936)

Santner, Eric. 'History Beyond the Pleasure Principle: Some Thoughts on the Representation of Trauma', in Saul Friedlander ed. *Probing the Limits of Representation: Nazism and the Final Solution* (Cambridge, Mass.: Harvard University Press, 1992) pp. 143–54

——. *Stranded Objects: Mourning, Memory and Film in Post-war Germany* (Ithaca: Cornell University Press, 1990)

Sarup, Madan. 'Home and Identity', in George Robertson *et al* eds. *Travellers Tales: Narratives of Home and Displacement* (London: Routledge, 1994) pp. 93–104

Sassoon, Siegfried. *Memoirs of a Fox-Hunting Man* (London: Faber & Faber, 1928)

Savin, Ada. 'Passage to America or When East Meets West – Eva Hoffman's *Lost in Translation: A Life in a New Language*', *Caliban* 31 (1994) 57–63

Schivelbusch, Wolfgang. *The Railway Journey: The Industrialisation of Time and Space in the Nineteenth Century* (Berkley: University of California Press, 1986)

Schneider, Karen. *Loving Arms: British Women Writing the Second World War* (Lexington: University Press of Kentucky, 1997)

Schreiner, Olive. *The Story of an African Farm* (Harmondsworth, Penguin, 1982 [1883])

——. *Women and Labour* (London: Virago, 1978 [1911])

Sellers, Susan. 'Virginia Woolf's Diaries and Letters', in Sue Roe and Susan Sellers eds. *The Cambridge Companion to Virginia Woolf* (Cambridge: Cambridge University Press, 2000) pp. 109–26

Shapiro, Susan. 'The Uncanny Jew: A Brief History of an Image', *Judaism* 46.1 (1997) 63–78

Shaw, Marion. ' "Alien Experiences:" Virginia Woolf, Winifred Holtby and the Thirties', in Keith Williams and Steven Matthews eds. *Rewriting the Thirties: Modernism and After* (London: Longman, 1997) pp. 37–52

——. *The Clear Stream: A Life of Winifred Holtby* (London: Virago, 1999)

Shepard, Ben. *War of Nerves: Soldiers and Psychiatrists 1914–1994* (London: Jonathan Cape, 1994)

Silverman, Kaja. *The Threshold of the Visible World* (New York and London: Routledge, 1996)

Smith, Sidonie. *Subjectivity, Identity and the Body: Women's Autobiographical Practices in the Twentieth Century* (Bloomington: Indiana University Press, 1993)

—— and Julia Watson eds. *Women, Autobiography, Theory: A Reader* (Madison: University of Wisconsin Press, 1998)

Snaith, Anna. *Virginia Woolf: Public and Private Negotiations* (Basingstoke: Palgrave, 2000)

Spence, Donald P. *Narrative Truth And Historical Truth: Meaning and Interpretation in Psychoanalysis* (New York: W.W. Norton, 1982)

Spielgelman, Art. *Maus II* (Harmondsworth: Penguin, 1991 [1986])

Stansky, Peter and William Abrahams. *Julian Bell and John Cornford: Their Lives and the 1930s* (London: Constable, 1966)

Steiner, George. *Extra-territorial: Papers on Literature and the Language Revolution* (London: Faber, 1972)

Stephen, Leslie. *Some Early Impressions* (London: Hogarth, 1924 [1903])

Stern-Gillet, 'Eva Hoffman's *Lost in Translation*', *New Comparison* 16 (1993) 130–8

Stone, Martin. 'Shell-shock and the Psychologists', in W. F. Bynum, Roy Porter and Michael Shepherd eds. *The Anatomy of Madness: Essays in the History of Psychiatry Volume II Institutions and Society* (London: Tavistock, 1985) pp. 242–71

Stonebridge, Lyndsey. 'Bombs and Roses: The Writing of Anxiety in Henry Green's *Caught*', in Rod Mengham and N.H. Reeve eds. *The Fiction of the 1940s: Stories of Survival* (Basingstoke: Palgrave, 2001) pp. 46–69

Swanson, Gillian. 'Memory, Subjectivity and Intimacy: the Historical Formation of the Modern Self and the Writing of Female Autobiography', in Susannah Radstone ed. *Memory and Methodology* (Oxford and New York: Berg, 2000) pp. 111–133.

Tal, Kali, *Worlds of Hurt: Reading the Literature of Trauma* (Cambridge: Cambridge University Press, 1996)

Tate, Trudi. *Modernism, History and the First World War* (Manchester: Manchester University Press, 1998)

Thatcher, Nicole. 'Charlotte Delbo's Voice: The Conscious and Unconscious Determinants of a Woman Writer', *L'Esprit Créateur* XL.2 (Summer 2000) 41–51

——. *A Literary Analysis of Charlotte Delbo's Concentration Camp Re-presentation* (Lewiston: Edwin Mellen Press, 2000)

——. 'La Mémoire de la Deuxième Guerre mondiale en France et la voix contestataire de Charlotte Delbo', *French Forum* 26.2 (2001) 91–110

Todorov, Tzvetan. 'Bilingualism, Dialogism and Schizophrenia', *New Formations* 17 (1992) 16–25

Tylee, Claire. *The Great War and Women's Consciousness: Images of Militarism and Womanhood in Women's Writings, 1914–64* (London: Macmillan, 1990)

Van Alphen, Ernst. *Caught By History: Holocaust Effects in Contemporary Art, Literature and Theory* (Stanford: Stanford University Press, 1997)

Van der Kolk, Bessel and van der Hart, Onno. 'The Intrusive Past: The Flexibility of Memory and the Engraving of Trauma', in Cathy Caruth ed. *Trauma: Explorations in Memory* (Baltimore and London: Johns Hopkins University Press, 1995) pp. 158–82

Velmans, Edith. *Edith's Book* (Harmondsworth: Penguin, 1999)

Vidler, Anthony. *The Architectural Uncanny: Essays in the Modern Unhomely* (Cambridge: MIT Press, 1992)

Viner, Katherine. 'Dear Diary', *Guardian*, 21 January 1997

Waaldijk, Berteke. 'Reading Anne Frank as a Woman', in Hyman Aaron Enzer and Sandra Solotaroff Enzer eds. *Anne Frank: Reflections on Her Life and Legacy* (Urbana and Chicago: University of Illinois Press, 2000) pp. 110–20

Wallace, Diana. *Sisters and Rivals in British Women's Fiction 1914–39* (London: Macmillan, 2000)

Walter, Natasha. 'Why Anne is Still Hidden from Us', *Guardian*, 23 January 1997

Wardi, Dina. *Memorial Candles: Children of the Holocaust* trans. Naomi Goldblum (London: Routledge, 1992)

Wayland-Smith, Ellen. ' *"En mémoire d'une Site"*: Freud, Mallarmé, and the Space of the Uncanny', *French Forum* 23.2 (1998) 179–96

West, Rebecca. *The Return of the Soldier* (London: Virago, 1980 [1918])

Whitehead, Anne. 'A Still, Small Voice: Letter-writing, Testimony and the Project of Address in Etty Hillesum's *Letters from Westerbork*', *Cultural Values* 5.1 (2001) 79–96

Wiedmer, Caroline. *The Claims of Memory: Representations of the Holocaust in Contemporary Germany and France* (Ithaca and London: Cornell University Press, 1999)

Williams, Linda Ruth. *Critical Desires: Psychoanalysis and the Literary Subject* (London: Edward Arnold, 1995)

Winter, Jay. *Sites of Memory, Sites of Mourning: The Great War in European History* (Cambridge: Cambridge University Press, 1998)

—— and Emmanuel Sivan eds. *War and Remembrance in the Twentieth Century* (Cambridge: Cambridge University Press, 1999)

Woolf, Leonard ed. *The Intelligent Man's Way to Prevent War* (London: Victor Gollancz, 1933)

——. *The War for Peace* (London: Routledge, 1940)

Woolf, Virginia. 'The Art of Biography' (1939) in *The Crowded Dance of Modern Life: Selected Essays Volume II* ed. Rachel Bowlby (Harmondsworth: Penguin, 1993) pp. 144–51

——. *Between the Acts* (London: Hogarth Press, 1941)

——. *The Complete Shorter Fiction of Virginia Woolf* ed. Susan Dick (London: Hogarth Press, 1985)

——. *The Diary of Virginia Woolf Volume I: 1915–1919* ed. Anne Olivier Bell (London: Hogarth Press, 1977)

——. *The Diary of Virginia Woolf Volume IV: 1931–1935* eds Anne Olivier Bell and Andrew McNeillie (London: Hogarth Press, 1982)

——. *The Diary of Virginia Woolf Volume V: 1936–1941* eds Anne Olivier Bell and Andrew McNeillie (London: Hogarth Press, 1984)

——. *Jacob's Room* (London: Hogarth Press, 1922)

——. *Leave the Letters Till We're Dead: The Letters of Virginia Woolf Volume VI: 1936–1941* eds Nigel Nicholson and Joanna Trautmann (London: Hogarth Press, 1980)

——. *Moments of Being: Unpublished Autobiographical Writings* ed. Jeanne Schulkind (London: Sussex University Press, 1976)

——. *Mrs Dalloway* (London: Hogarth Press, 1976 [1925])

——. *Orlando* (London: Hogarth Press, 1977 [1931])

——. *The Pargiters: The Novel-Essay Portion of The Years* ed. Mitchell A. Leaska (London: Hogarth Press, 1978)

——. *The Question of Things Happening: The Letters of Virginia Woolf Volume II: 1912–1922* eds Nigel Nicholson and Joanna Trautmann (London: Hogarth Press, 1976)

——. *Roger Fry: A Biography* (London: Hogarth Press, 1940)

——. *A Room of One's Own* (London: Hogarth Press, 1974 [1929])

——. *The Sickle Side of the Moon: The Letters of Virginia Woolf Volume V: 1932–1935* eds Nigel Nicholson and Joanna Trautmann (London: Hogarth Press, 1979)

——. 'Thoughts on Peace in an Air Raid' (1940) in *The Crowded Dance of Modern Life: Selected Essays Volume II* ed. Rachel Bowlby (Harmondsworth: Penguin, 1993) pp. 168–72

——. *Three Guineas* (London: Hogarth Press, 1977 [1938])

——. *To the Lighthouse* (London: Hogarth Press, 1967 [1927])

——. 'Virginia Woolf and Julian Bell', in Quentin Bell, *Virginia Woolf: A Biography Volume II: Mrs Woolf* (London: Hogarth Press, 1972) pp. 255–9

——. *The Voyage Out* (London: Hogarth Press, 1957 [1915])

Young, James E. *The Texture of Memory* (New Haven: Yale University Press, 1993)

Zaborowska, Magdalena J. *How We Found America: Reading Gender Through East European Immigrant Narratives* (Chapel Hill: University of North Carolina Press, 1995)

Zwerdling, Alex. *Virginia Woolf and the Real World* (Berkley: University of California Press, 1986)

Unpublished Source

Woolf, Virginia. 'A Memoir of Julian Bell', MH/A8, Monks House Papers, University of Sussex.

Index